MW01087205

Tom + ur

Under the Country Sky

Grace S. Richmond

ISBN: 1986726843

ISBN-13: 978-1986726849

Table of Contents

CHAPTER I

HEART BURNINGS

She did not want to hate the girls; indeed, since she loved them all, it would go particularly hard with her if she had to hate them; love turned to hate is such a virulent product! But, certainly, she had never found it so hard to be patient with them.

They were all five her college classmates, of only last year's class, and it was dear and kind of them to drive out here into the country to see her, coming in Phyllis Porter's great family limousine, the prettiest, jolliest little "crowd" imaginable. They had been thoughtful enough to warn her that they were coming, too, so that she could set the old manse living-room in its pleasantest order, build a crackling apple-wood fire in the fireplace, and get out her best thin china and silver with which to serve afternoon tea—she made it chocolate, with vivid recollection of their tastes; and added deliciously substantial though delicate sandwiches, with plenty of the fruitiest and nuttiest kinds of little cakes. She had donned the one real afternoon frock she possessed, a clever make-over out of nothing in particular. Altogether, when she greeted her guests, as they ran, fur-clad and silk-stockinged after the manner of their kind, into her welcoming arms, she had seemed to them absolutely the old Georgiana.

They had brought her a wonderful box of red roses—and Phyllis had caught her kissing one of the great, silky buds as she put it with the rest in a bowl. "I don't believe she's seen a hothouse rose since she left college," thought Phyllis, with a stab of pity at her tender heart. But for the first hour of their stay Georgiana had been her gay and brilliant self, flinging quips and jests broadcast, asking impertinent questions, making saucy comments, quite as of old. It was only when Dot Manning, toward the end of the visit, began a sober tale of the misfortunes which had come thronging into the life of one of their classmates, that Georgiana's face, sobering into sympathetic gravity, betrayed to her companions a curious change which had come upon it since they saw it last.

Meanwhile, in answer to her questioning, they had told her all about themselves. Phyllis Porter and Celia Winters were having a glorious season in society. Theo Crossman was deep in settlement work—"crazy over it" was, of course, the phrase. Dot Manning was going abroad next week for a year of travel in all sorts of beguiling, out-of-the-way places. As for Madge Sylvester, who was getting ready to be married after Easter, the first of the class, she sat mostly in a dreamy, smiling silence, looking into the fire while the others talked.

No, Georgiana did not want to hate the girls, but before their stay was over she found herself coming dangerously near it—temporarily, at least. They were dears, of course, but they were so content with themselves and so pitiful of her. Not, of course, that they meant to let her see this, but it showed in spite of them. They wanted to know what she did with herself, whether there were any young people, and any good times going on—Georgiana led them to the window, just at this point, and pointed out to them a vigorous young man striding by in ulster and soft hat, who looked up and waved as he passed, showing one of those fine and manly young faces, glowing with health and hopefulness, which always challenge interest from girlhood.

"Oh, have you many like that?" Celia had asked, and when Georgiana had owned that James Stuart was the only one precisely "like that," Dot had inquired if Mr. Stuart belonged to Georgiana, and, being answered in the negative, shook her head and sighed: "One swallow *may* make a summer, Jan, but I doubt it!"

Theodora Crossman, the settlement worker, inquired particularly whether Georgiana were doing anything worth while, using that pregnant modern phrase which has been decidedly overworked, yet which hardly can be spared from the present-day vocabulary.

"Worth while!" cried Georgiana, flashing into flame in an instant in the way they knew so well. "Worth while—yes! You haven't seen my father, have you, ever? It's a pity this happens to be one of his bad, spine-achey days, for he'd be a good and sufficient answer to that question. Father Davy is one of the Lord's own saints on earth, and he possesses a magnificent sense of humour, which not all saints do, you know. To love him is a liberal education, and to take care of him is better 'worth while' than to have any number of fingers in other people's pies."

"Of course, dear," Theo had answered soothingly. "We know there's nothing in the world so well worth while as looking after one's father and mother. Your mother died long ago, didn't she, dear? And your father would be dreadfully lonely without you. At the same time, it doesn't seem as if he could absorb all your energies. You remember the splendid things Professor Nichols used to say about the duty of the college girl, after college, particularly in a small town? I suppose you have no foreigners here, but I thought perhaps you might find quite a wonderful field for your endeavour in stimulating the women of the place into clubs for study and work. It's——"

A curious exclamation from her hostess caused Miss Crossman to pause. In fact, they all stared wonderingly at Georgiana. She stood upon the hearthrug, her colour, usually ready to glow in her dusky face, now receding suggestively, her dark eyes sparkling dangerously. "The only trouble with that sort of thing," she answered with suspicious quietness, "or rather the two troubles with it are these: In the first place, the women have pretty nearly a club apiece already, which suits them much better than anything I could 'stimulate' them to; and, in the second place, I have 'quite a wonderful field for my endeavour,' as you call it, Theo—did you crib that phrase?—in the upper regions of my own home. I—in fact, I may be said to belong to the I. W. W.; I'm one of the industrial workers of the world!"

"Jan, you haven't gone into anything crazy——" Dot was beginning, when Georgiana, obeying an impulse, walked away from her hearthrug toward the door, beckoning her guests to follow.

"Come on," she invited. "Since you have so poor an opinion of the possibilities for serious labour in a world of woe offered by my residence in a small country village, you may come and see for yourselves."

They came after her, with a rustle and flutter of frocks and a patter of smartly shod feet, up the old spindle-railed staircase, through a chilly and unfurnished upper hall, and up a still chillier narrow second staircase, into an attic region which could hardly be properly characterized as chilly, for the reason that the atmosphere there was frankly freezing.

As near as possible to the gable window stood a monster structure the nature of which the beholders did not instantly recognize. Phyllis was the first to cry out: "A loom! It must be a very old one, too. Oh, how fascinating! What do you make, Jan—fabrics?"

"Rugs," explained Georgiana, pulling at a pile upon the floor. "Such rugs as these. Good looking? Yes, dear classmates?"

"Stunning!" cried Madge Sylvester, with a smothered shiver at the penetrating cold of the place.

"Simply wonderful!" "Too clever for anything!" and, "Oh, Jan, do you make them to sell?" "Can I buy this one?" "I'm wild over this dull blue and Indian red!" came tumbling from the mouths of the eager girls, as in the fading light from the attic window they examined the hand-woven rugs. There was sincerity in their voices; Georgiana had known there would be; she was sure of the art and skill plainly to be found in her product.

5

"I'm afraid not, Phyl. These are all orders, and I'm weeks behind. They go to certain exclusive city shops, and I have all I can do."

"You must have struck a gold mine. I'm so glad!" congratulated warm-hearted Phyllis.

"Well, not exactly. It's rather slow work, when you do housework, too," acknowledged Georgiana. "However, it does very well; it keeps us in firewood—and oysters—for the winter."

She instantly regretted this speech, for it led, presently, as she might have known it would, to delicately worded expressions of hope that she would in the future give her friends the pleasure of purchasing her wares.

Down by the fireplace again Georgiana turned upon them in her old jesting way, which yet had in it, as they all felt, a quality which was new. "Stop it, girls. No, I'll not sell one of you a rug of any size, shape, or colour. I'm far behind, as I told you. But—I'll send Madge a gorgeous one for a wedding present, if she'll tell me her preferences, and I'll do the same for each of you, when you meet your fates. Now stop talking about it. I only showed you to demonstrate that this is a busy world for me as well as for you, and that I'm very content in it. Dot, don't you want just one more of these fruitkins? By the way, since you like them so much, I'll give you the recipe. I made it up—wasn't it clever of me?"

"You're much the cleverest of us all, anyway," murmured Dot meekly, nibbling at the delicious morsel, while her hostess rapidly wrote out a little formula and gave it to her with a smile.

They were soon off after that, for the early winter twilight was upon them, and the lights in the waiting car outside suddenly came on with a suggestive completeness. Georgiana assisted her guests into luxurious coats and capes made of or lined with chinchilla, with otter, with sable; handed gloves and muffs; and listened to all manner of affectionate parting speeches, every one of which contained pressing invitations for visits, short or long. Each girl made promises of future calls, and professed herself eager to come and stay with Georgiana at any time. Then the whole group went away on a little warm breeze of good-fellowship and human kindness.

"They are dears," admitted Georgiana, as she waved her arm at the departing car; "but, oh!—*oh!* I can't stand having them sorry for me! The old manse *is* shabby, and every girl of them knew how many times this frock has been made over—I saw Celia recognize it even through its dye. No wonder, when it's been at every college tea she ever gave. But I won't—*I won't*—be pitied!"

The door opened, and a slender figure in an old-fashioned dressing-gown came slowly into the firelit room.

Georgiana turned quickly. "Father Davy! Do you feel better? If I'd known it, I'd have brought you in to meet the girls. They would have enjoyed you so."

"I'm not quite up to meeting the girls perhaps, daughter, but decidedly better and correspondingly cheerful. Have you had a good time?"

He placed himself as carefully as possible upon the couch by the fire, and his daughter tucked him up in an old plaid shawl which had lain folded upon it. She dropped upon the hearthrug and sat looking into the fire, while her father regarded the picture she made in the dyed frock, now a soft Indian red, a hue which pleased his eye and brought out all her gypsy colouring.

The head upon the couch pillow was topped with a soft mass of curly gray hair, the face below was thin and pale, but the eyes which rested upon the girl were the clearest, youngest blue-gray eyes that ever spoke mutely of the spirit's triumph over the body. One had but to glance at David Warne to understand that here was a man who was no less a

6

man because he had to spend many hours of every day upon his tortured back. It was three years since he had been forced to lay aside the care of the village-and-country parish of which he had been minister, but he had given up not a whit of his interest in his fellowmen, and now that he could seldom go to them he had taught them to come to him, so that the old manse was almost as much a centre of the village's interest and affection as it had been when its master went freely in and out. A new manse had been built nearer the church, for the new man, and the old house left to Mr. Warne's undisputed possession—proof positive of his place in the hearts of the community.

"A good time?" murmured Georgiana, in answer to the question. "No, a hateful, envious, black-browed time, disguised as much as might be under a frivolous manner. The girls were lovely—and I was a perfect fiend!"

Mr. Warne did not seem in the least disconcerted by this startling statement. "The sounds I heard did not strike me as indicating the presence of any fiend," he suggested.

"Probably not. I managed to avoid giving in to the temptation to snatch Phyl's sumptuous chinchilla coat, Madge's perfectly adorable hat, Theo's bronze shoes, Dot's embroidered silk handbag, and Bess's hand-wrought collar and cuffs."

"It was a matter of clothes, then? How much heart-burning men escape!" mused Mr. Warne. "Now, I can never recall hearing any man, young or old, express a longing to denude other men of their apparel."

Georgiana shot him a look. "No, men merely envy other men their acres, their horses, their motors—and their books. Own up, now, Father Davy, have you never coveted any man's library?"

The blue-gray eyes sent her back a humorous glance. "Now you have me," he owned. "But tell me, daughter—it was not only their clothes which stirred the fiend within you? Confess!"

She looked round at him. "I don't need to," she said. "You know the whole of it—what I want for you and me—what they have—*life*! And lots of it. You need it just as badly as I do—you, a suffering saint at fifty-five when other men are playing golf! And I—simply bursting with longing to take you and go somewhere—anywhere with you—and see things—and do things—and *live* things! And we as poor as poverty, after all you've done for the Lord. Oh, I——"

She brought her strong young fist down on the nearly threadbare rug with a thump that reddened the fine flesh, and thumped again and yet again, while her father lay and silently watched her, with a look in his eyes less of pain than of utter comprehension. He said not a word, while she bit her lip and stared again into the fire, clenching the fist that had spoken for her bitterly aching heart. After a time the tense fingers relaxed, and she held up the hand and looked at it.

"I'm a brute!" she said presently. "An abominable little brute. How do you stand me? How do you *endure* me, Father Davy! I just bind the load on your poor back and pull the knots tight, every time I let myself break out like this. If you were any minister-father but yourself, you'd either preach or pray at me. How can you keep from it?"

He smiled. "I never liked to be preached or prayed at myself, dear," he said. "I have not forgotten. And the Lord Himself doesn't expect a young caged lioness to act like a caged canary. He doesn't want it to. And some day—He will let it out of the cage!"

She shook her head, and got up. She kissed the gray curls and patted the thin cheek, said cheerfully: "I'm going to get your supper now," and went away out of the room.

In the square old kitchen she flung open an outer door and stood staring up at the starry winter sky.

7

"Oh, if anything, anything, *anything* would happen!" she breathed, stretching out both arms toward the snowy shrubbery-broken expanse behind the house which in summer was her garden. "If something would just keep this evening from being like all the other evenings! I can't sit and read aloud—*to-night*. I can't—I *can't*! And the only interesting thing on earth that can happen is that Jimps Stuart may come over—and he probably won't, because he was over last evening and the evening before that, and he knows he can't be allowed to come all the time. He——"

It was at this point that the old brass knocker on the front door sounded—and something happened.

CHAPTER II

SOMETHING REALLY HAPPENS

It might have been any of the village people, as Georgiana expected it would be when she closed the kitchen door with a bang and went reluctantly to answer the knock. Since it was almost suppertime it was probably Mrs. Shear, who seldom made a call at any other hour, knowing she would as surely be asked to stay as it was sure that David Warne's heart would respond to the wanness and unhappiness always written on Mrs. Shear's homely middle-aged face. As she went to the door, Georgiana felt an intensely wicked desire to hit Mrs. Shear a blow with her own capable fist, which should send her backward into the snow. Georgiana did not believe that the lady was as unhappy as she looked. It seemed to be a day for expression by the use of fists!

But when the door was opened and the light from the bracket lamp in the manse hall shone out on the figure standing upon the porch, all desire to hit anything more with her fist vanished from the girl's heart. For with the first look into the face of the man outside her instant wish was to have him come in—and stay. Somebody so evidently from the great world which seemed so far away from the old village manse—somebody who looked as if he could bring with him into this dull life of theirs all manner of interest—it was small wonder that in her present mood the girl should feel like this. And it must by no means be supposed that Georgiana was in the habit of experiencing this sort of wish every time she set eyes upon a personable man. Personable men had been many in her acquaintance during the four years of her college life, and more than one of them had followed her back to the old manse to urge his claim upon her attention.

"Is the Reverend Mr. Warne at home?" asked the stranger in a low and pleasant voice. "I have a letter of introduction to him."

"Please come in," answered Georgiana, and led him straight into the living-room and her father's presence. Then, though consumed with curiosity, she retired—as far as the door of the dining-room, where she remained, ready to listen in a most reprehensible manner to the conversation which should follow.

There was an exchange of greetings, then evidently Mr. Warne was reading the letter of introduction. Presently he spoke:

"This is quite sufficient," he said, "to make you welcome under this roof. My old friend Davidson has my affection and confidence always. Please tell me what I can do for you, Mr. Jefferson."

"I should like," replied the stranger's voice, "to have a room with you, and possibly board, if that might be. If not, perhaps I could find that elsewhere; but if I might at least have the room I should be very glad. I am hard at work upon a book, and I have come

8

away from my home and other work to find a place where I can live quietly, write steadily, and be outdoors every day for long walks in the country. Doctor Davidson suggested this place, and thought you might take me in—for an indefinite period of time, possibly some months."

"That sounds very pleasant to me," Georgiana heard her father reply. "We have never had a boarder, my daughter and I, but, if she has no objection, I should enjoy having such a man as you look to be, in the house. Your letter, you see, is not your only introduction. You carry with you in your face a passport to other men's favour."

"That is good of you," answered Mr. Jefferson—and Georgiana liked the frank tone of his voice. It was an educated voice, it spoke for itself of the personality behind it.

"I will go and talk with my daughter," she heard her father say, after the two men had had some little conversation concerning a book or two lying on the table by Mr. Warne's couch.

Georgiana fled into the kitchen, where her father found her. When he appeared, closing the door behind him, she was ready for him before he spoke.

"If he were the angel Gabriel or old Pluto himself I'd welcome him," she said under her breath, her eyes dancing. "To have somebody in the house for you to talk with besides your everlasting old parishioners—why, it would be worth a world of trouble! And it won't be any trouble at all. Go tell him your daughter reluctantly consents."

"You heard, then?" queried Mr. Warne, a quizzical smile on his gentle lips.

"Of course I heard! I was listening hard! I was all ears—regular donkey ears. He's a godsend. His board will pay for sirloin instead of round. We'll have roast duck on Sunday—twice a winter. He can have the big front room; I'll have it ready by to-morrow night."

"Come in and arrange details," urged Mr. Warne.

Georgiana stayed behind a minute to compose her face and manner, then went in, the demurest of young housewives. Not for nothing had been her years of college life, which had made, when occasion demanded, a quietly poised woman out of a girl who had been, according to village standards, a somewhat hoydenish young person.

As she faced the stranger in the full light of the fire-and-lamp-lit room, she saw in detail that of which she had had a swift earlier impression. Mr. Jefferson was a man in, she thought, the early thirties, with a strongly modelled, shaven face, keen brown eyes behind eyeglasses, a mouth which could be grave one moment and humorous the next, and the air of a man who was accustomed to think for himself and expect others to do so. He was well built though not tall, well dressed though not dapper, and he looked less like a writer of books than a participant in action of some kind or other. His dark hair showed a thread or two of gray at the temples, but this suggestion of age did not seem at all to age him.

The stranger, on his part, saw a rather more than commonly charming Georgiana, on account of the Indian-red silk frock.

"It's not fair to him," thought Georgiana, "to show him a landlady who looks so festive and fine. I can't afford to wear this often, even for his benefit." But to him she said: "I know it will give my father much pleasure to have some one in the house besides his daughter. And I am quite willing to have you at our table. I must warn you that we live very simply, as you must guess."

"I live very simply myself," Mr. Jefferson assured her. "There are few things I do not like. My one serious antipathy is Brussels sprouts," he added, smiling. "With that confession the coast is clear. And—you would not mind my smoking in my room?"

Georgiana glanced at her father with a suddenly mischievous expression. He was studying the prospective boarder with interested eyes.

"I think," confessed Mr. Warne, "that merely to catch a whiff now and then of a fragrance which is singularly pleasant to me, but which I am denied producing for myself, would add to the things that give me comfort. If you wouldn't mind smoking in the hall now and then, or, better yet, by my fireside, I should be grateful."

Mr. Jefferson nodded. "Thank you, sir. And now—when may I come? I have a room at the hotel, so don't let me in until you are quite ready."

"You may come to-morrow night for supper," promised Georgiana. "But you haven't seen the room." She rose.

"It will be in the upper right front?" hazarded Mr. Jefferson. "And it will have the customary furnishings and some means of heating?"

"I should prefer to have you see it," she insisted, and lighted a candle in an ancient pewter candlestick with an extinguisher at the side.

So the stranger, following her upstairs, surveyed his room and professed himself entirely satisfied. It looked bare enough to Georgiana as she showed it to him, but she told herself that there were possibilities in the matter of certain belongings of her own room which could be transferred to give an air of homelikeness to this.

"It is large, and I can have plenty of light and air," commented the prospective boarder. "If I might have some sort of good-sized table by that south window, for my work, I should consider myself provided for."

"You will find one when you come," promised the girl.

"Thank you. Now, I will take myself off at once. Then you may have a chance to discuss with your father the probabilities in favour of your not regretting your quick decision," he said as he descended the stairs.

"Father and I always make quick decisions," Georgiana remarked.

"Good! So do I. Do you hold to them as well?"

"Always. That's part of father's creed."

"That's very good; that speaks for itself. Well, I promise you I shall be busy enough not to bother this household overmuch. By the way"—he turned suddenly—"that table you spoke of putting in my room—if it is large, it must be heavy. Your father cannot help you lift it, and you should not lift it alone. Don't put it in place until I come—please?"

She smiled. "That's very thoughtful of you. But I am quite equal to moving it alone."

"Then let me help you now, won't you?" he offered.

She shook her head. "It's really not ready to be moved. Don't think of it again, please."

He bade them good-night and went away, with no lingering speeches on the road to the door. He had the air of a man accustomed to measure his time and to waste none of it. When he had gone Georgiana went back to her father. He looked up at her with a twinkle in his still boyish eyes.

"Well, daughter, it looks to me as if this had happened just in time to prevent a bad explosion from too high pressure of accumulated energy. You can now lower the position of the indicator on the steam gauge to the safety point by spending the whole day to-morrow in sweeping and dusting and baking. If there are any spare moments you can employ them in making over your clothes."

"Father Davy! Where did you get such a perfectly uncanny understanding?"

"From observation—purely from observation. And I myself confess to feeling considerably excited and elated. It is not every day that a gentleman of this sort knocks at the door of a village manse and asks to come in and write a book. If it had not been that my old friend Davidson is always bringing people together who need each other, I should think it the strangest thing in the world that this should happen. Davidson is the minister of a great New York church where this Mr. Jefferson attends; and Davidson has never forgotten me, though he took the high road and I the low so soon after he left the seminary. Well, it will give us a fresh interest, my dear, for as long as it lasts."

Georgiana thought it would. She was up betimes next morning, to begin the sweeping and dusting and general turning upside down of the long-unused upper front room. In the course of her window washing, her shoulders enveloped in an old red shawl, she was vigorously hailed from below.

"Ship ahoy! Your name, cargo, and destination?"

Without turning she called merrily back: "The Jefferson, with a cargo of books, bound for the public!"

"What's that? I don't get you."

"Never mind. I'm too busy to be spoken by every passing ship."

"I'll be up," called the voice, and footsteps sounded upon the porch. The front door banged, the same ringing male voice was heard shouting a "Good-morning, sir!" and the owner of the voice came leaping up the stairs and burst into the room without ceremony. He advanced till he was close to the open window, and nodded through the glass at the window-washer, who sat on the sill with her upper body outside.

He was a fine specimen of youth and brawn and energy, the young man whom Georgiana had pointed out to her friends as one of her resources when it came to the good times they were so anxious to know of. His name was James Stuart, and he was a near neighbour of the manse. He was a college graduate of three years' longer standing than Georgiana, and he, like her, had returned to the country home and his father's farm because his aging parents could not spare him, and he was the only son whose lack of other ties left him free to care for them. He and this girl had been schoolmates and long-time friends—with interesting intervals of enmity during the earlier years—and were now sworn comrades, though they still quarrelled at times. It looked, after a minute, as if this would be one of those times.

"I didn't just get you," complained James Stuart through the window.

"Wait till I come in. I can't tell all the neighbours."

Georgiana polished off her last pane, pushed up the window and slipped into the room, quite unnecessarily assisted by Stuart.

"I can't understand," began the young man, eying with approval her blooming face, frost-stung and smooth in texture as the petals of a rose, "why you're washing the windows of a room that's always shut up."

"Jimps, if you were Mrs. Perkins next door I'd understand your consuming curiosity. As it is——"

"Going to have company?"

She shook her head.

"Then—what in thunder——"

"We're going to have a boarder, if you must know." Georgiana began to attack the inside of the window.

"A boarder! What sort?"

"A very good sort. He's a literary person with a book to write."

"Suffering cats! Not the man at the hotel?"

"I believe he was to exist at the hotel—if he could—for twenty-four hours," admitted Georgiana.

"But that man," objected Mr. James Stuart, "is a—why, he's—he doesn't look like that sort at all."

"What sort, if you please?"

"The literary. He looks like a—well, I took him for a professional man of some kind."

Georgiana laughed derisively. "Jimps! Isn't authorship a profession?"

"Well, I mean, you know, he doesn't look like an ink-slinger; he looks like some sort of a doer. He hasn't that dreamy expression. He sees with both eyes at once. In other words, he seems to be all there."

"Your idea of literary men is a disgrace to your education, Jimps. Think of the author-soldiers and author-engineers—and author-Presidents of the United States," she ended triumphantly.

"It doesn't matter," admitted Stuart. "The thing that does is that he's coming here. I can't say that appeals to me. How in time did he come to apply?" Georgiana told him briefly. Stuart looked gloomy. "That's all right," he said, "as long as he confines himself to being company for your father. But if he takes to being company for you—lookout!"

"Absurd! He's years older than I, and he said he would be working very hard. I shall see nothing of him except at the table. Heavens! don't grudge us anything that promises to relieve the monotony of our lives even a little bit."

Stuart whistled. "Monotony, eh? In spite of all my visits? All right. But I'd be just as well pleased if he wore skirts. And mind you—your Uncle Jimps is coming over evenings just as often as and a little oftener than if you didn't have this literary light burning on your hearthstone. See?"

He went away, his thick fair hair, uncapped, shining in the morning sunlight, his arm waving a friendly farewell back at the window, where a white cloth flapped in reply.

"Dear old boy!" thought the young woman affectionately; "what should I do without him?"

That afternoon, just before the supper hour, the boarder's trunk arrived. It was borne upstairs by the village baggageman, complaining bitterly of its weight. It was an aristocratic-looking trunk, and it bore labels which indicated that it was a traveled trunk. Shortly afterward the boarder himself appeared and was allowed to betake himself at once to his room, from which he emerged at the call of the bell, and came promptly down. Meeting Mr. Warne limping slowly through the hall, he offered his arm, and in the dining-room placed his host in his chair with the gentle deference so welcome from a younger man to an older.

Georgiana, as she served one of the undeniably simple but toothsome meals for the cooking of which she was equipped by many years' apprenticeship, noted how bright grew Father Davy's face as the supper progressed, and how delightfully the newcomer talked—and listened—for if he was an interesting talker he proved to be a still more accomplished listener. When the supper was over Mr. Jefferson lingered a few minutes by the fire, then went up to his room, explaining that he must unpack his books and make ready for an early attack in the morning upon his work.

In her own room, that night, Georgiana lay awake for a long time. Just before she went to sleep she addressed herself sternly:

"My child, I shouldn't wonder if you've jumped out of the frying pan of monotony into the fire of unrest. It certainly means trouble for you when you can't get a perfect stranger's face out of your mind for an hour. Now, there's just one thing about it: you've always despised girls who let themselves leap into liking any man and are so upset by it that everybody sees it. This one is undoubtedly either married or engaged to be, and even if he's the freest old bachelor alive you are to behave as if he were the tightest tied. You are to go straight ahead with your work and to remember every minute that you are a poor minister's daughter with only a college training for an asset. He's very clearly a man of importance somewhere; he couldn't look like that and be anything else. He will never think twice of you. Whatever attention he gives you will be purely because he is a gentleman and he can't ignore his host's daughter—nonsense, his landlady—I might as well face it. He's a boarder and I'm his landlady. Gentlemen don't take much interest in landladies. So now, Georgiana Warne, landlady—keeper of a boarding-house, be sensible and go to sleep."

But before she went to sleep her mind, in spite of her, had imaged for her again the interesting, clever-looking face of the stranger under the roof, with his clear, straightforward glance that seemed to see so much, his smile which disclosed splendid teeth, his strongly moulded chin. And she had owned, frankly, driven to the confession just to see if it wouldn't relieve her:

"It's just such a face as I've seen and liked—in crowds sometimes—but I never knew the owner of one. It's such a face as a woman would remember to her grave, if its owner had just belonged to her one—hour! Oh, dear God, I've prayed you to let something happen—anything! And now I'm—afraid!"

But, in the morning, when pulses beat strongly and courage is bright, Georgiana had another tone to take with herself. She faced her image in the glass, which looked straight back at her with unflinching dark eyes.

"I'm ashamed of you! To moon and croon like that! Now, brace up, Miss Warne, and be yourself. You've never lacked spirit; you're not going to lack it now. You're going to be strong and sane about this thing. You're going to be the sort of girl whose mind no man can guess at. You're going to weave rugs for your life, and enjoy Jimps Stuart as you always have, and there's not going to be a whimper out of you from this hour, no matter what happens—or doesn't happen. Do you hear? Well, then—attention! Head up, shoulders back, heart steady; forward, *march*!"

Two hours later, when, in the absence of the new inmate, Georgiana went into his room to put it in order for the day, she found it impossible not to note the character of his belongings. They were few and simple enough, but in every detail they betrayed a fastidious taste. And among the articles in ebony and leather which lay upon the linen cover of the old bureau stood one which held her fascinated attention. It was a framed photograph of a young and very lovely woman in evening dress, and the face which smiled over the perfect shoulder was looking straight out at her.

Georgiana stared back. "Who are you?" she whispered. "I might have known you would be here!"

"And who, please, are you?" the picture seemed to query lightly, smiling in return for the other's frown. "As for me, don't you see plainly? I belong to him. Else why should he have me here? You see I'm the only one he cared to bring. Doesn't that speak for itself?"

"Of course it does," agreed Georgiana; then stoutly: "And why should I care? Of course I don't care. To care would be—absurd!"

CHAPTER III

A SEMI-ANNUAL OCCURRENCE

"Father Davy, the 'Semi-Annual' has come!" Georgiana, tugging with both strong young arms, hauled the big express package into the living-room of the old manse, and shut the door with a bang. Breathing rapidly from her exertions, her cheeks warmly flushed, her dark eyes glowing, she stood over the package, looking at her father with a curious sort of smile not wholly compounded of joy and satisfaction.

"That is very good," said Father Davy in his pleasant voice; "and very opportune. It was but yesterday, it seems to me, that I heard daughter declaring that she was 'Oh, so shabby!'"

"Yes, yes—but what do you wager there is there?" questioned Georgiana. "I can tell you before I take the cover off. Three evening gowns, frivolous and impossible for a little town like this; one draggled lingerie frock, two evening coats, and possibly—just possibly—a last year's tailored suit, with a tear in the front of the skirt and not a scrap of goods to make a fold to cover it. Why, oh, why, do they never have any pieces?"

"The reason seems obvious enough," Mr. Warne suggested, as the girl stooped and began to wrestle with the cords which tied the big package. His glance fell musingly on the down-bent head with its masses of dark-brown hair, upon the white and shapely arms from which the sleeves were rolled back,—Georgiana had been busy in the kitchen when the expressman came,—upon the whole comely young figure in its blue-print morning dress. "They never have need of the pieces, I should judge," said he.

"But I have. Jeannette might think of me when she orders her clothes, not just when her maid is packing the box with a lot of castaways. Well, here's hoping there's just one thing I can use," and she lifted the cover of the box and looked within, it cannot be denied, with eager curiosity.

"There are always many things you can use," her father gently reminded her; "you, who are so ingenious."

"Here's the evening frock!" cried his daughter, lifting out the top garment and holding it up before them both. "Oh, what a dress to send a poor country cousin! Fluff and flimsy, trimmed with sparklers; cut frightfully low, no sleeves, and a draggly train. Doesn't it look suitable for me?" She flung it aside with a gesture of scorn. "Ah, here's something a shade better! A little dancing frock of rose-coloured chiffon—and her clumsy partner stepped on the hem of it. The maid in the dressing-room sewed it up for her to have her last dance in, and then she came home and threw it into the box for me. Well, I can get a gorgeous motor veil out of it—I who have so many drives in the cars of the rich!"

"The—the under part looks available to me," suggested Mr. Warne, striving to be of comfort.

Georgiana shrugged her blue-clad shoulders. "Oh, yes, if I could dress in slitted silk petticoats and you could wear them for dressing-gowns, we'd have plenty. Well, look at *this*! Here's a velvet—cerise! What a glorious, impossible colour! And here's the lingerie frock; that's not so bad; I really think it will stand a couple of launderings before it falls to pieces in my hands. And here's the evening coat—pale gray with fox trimmings—and she's fallen foul of some ink or something, and the cleaner couldn't get it all out. Father Davy, look!"

"It seems to me," said Mr. Warne in his gentle tones, which were yet not without more firmness than one might expect from so frail a person, "that I have heard somewhere a homely proverb to the effect that it is not quite in good taste to——"

"'*Look a gift horse in the mouth*,'" finished Georgiana. Her eyes were rebellious. "And there's another: '*Beggars mustn't be choosers*.' Yes, I know. Only, semi-annually I certainly do experience a burning wish that my dear rich relations were persons with a trifle keener sense of discernment as to which of their old clothes would be most appreciated by their poor cousins. They must now and then, Father Davy, wear something

14

sensible. They must have morning clothes and street clothes—adorable ones. Why do they send only the worldly clothes to the manse? And why—*why* do they never put in so much as one of Uncle Thomas's discarded cravats for the Little Minister himself?"

"Your Uncle Thomas and I may possibly have different tastes in the matter of neckwear," replied Mr. Warne with such gravity of manner but such a sparkle of humour in his blue-gray eyes that his daughter laughed in spite of herself. "Come, come, dear, is there nothing you can approve among all those rich materials? You might make me innumerable cravats, and I am such a fop I could wear a fresh one each day—to please you."

"Father Davy!" Georgiana sat back on her heels. She had slipped her bared arms into the armholes of the sleeveless white "fluff-and-flimsy" evening frock, and the "sparklers" of the low-cut bodice now framed her blue-print clad shoulders with an astonishing effect of incongruity. "I have a wonderful inspiration. Let's ask Jeannette out here for a visit— an object-lesson as to the state of life whereunto the country cousins have been called. She hasn't seen me in ten years, and all I remember of her is a fluffy, yellow-haired girl with a sniffly cold in her head. What do you say, Father Davy? Shall we ask her?"

Her father's gaze, quiet, comprehending, more than a little amused, met Georgiana's, audacious, defiant, mischievous, yet reasonable. The two looked at each other for a full minute.

"Do you think she would come?" Mr. Warne inquired doubtfully.

"Why shouldn't she come? She's had a gay winter so far, but not a happy one. She's no debutante any more, you know; she's an 'old girl' in her fifth season. That's what the society girls get by coming out at eighteen. Now I, who am only a year out of college and who never 'came out' in my life, am as keen at the game of being grown up as if I were just putting up my hair for the first time. Well, Jeannette's been keeping up the pace all winter, is thoroughly worn out and unhappy, and doesn't know what to do with herself. It's March—and Lent—the time of year when the society folks betake themselves to spring resorts to recover their shattered nerves. Don't you think she'd jump at the chance to come to the little country town and try what our air and our cookery would do for her?"

"You seem to know all about her in spite of not having seen or known her—except through these boxes of clothes—since she was a little girl."

"Ah, that's just it—through her boxes—that's how I know her!" Triumphantly Georgiana held up the cerise velvet gown. "Don't I know a girl who would wear that? Wild for excitement—that's why she chose the colour. But she didn't get the fun she expected; he didn't like it—or somebody said she looked too pale in it—and she fired it at me before she had done more than take the freshness off. *I* can wear it—see here!"

She got to her feet, untied the little black silk tie which held the low-rolling collar of her working dress at the throat, unfastened a row of hooks, and let the blue print slip to her feet. Over the glory of her white shoulders and gleaming arms she flung the cerise velvet—gorgeous, glowing, wonderful colour, as trying to the ordinary complexion as colour can well be. But as the gown fell into place, and Georgiana, backing up to her father, was fastened somewhat tentatively into it, it would have been plain to any beholder that if the rich girl could not wear the queenly, daring robe the poor girl could— as she had said.

She swept up and down the room, her head held high. She played the part of a lady of fashion and held an imaginary reception, carrying on a stream of "society" talk with a manner which made the pale man on the couch laugh like a boy. Holding a dialogue with a hypothetical male guest, she led him out into the hall, still within sight of Mr. Warne's couch, and was in the midst of a scene as inspiredly clever as anything she had ever done

15

at college, where she had been the pride of a dramatic club whose fame had waxed greater than that of any similar organization for many years, when the front door of the house suddenly opened, and a gust of chilly March air rushed in with the person entering.

Georgiana wheeled—to find herself confronting the amused gaze of her boarder, Mr. E. C. Jefferson, as read the address upon his mail.

Mr. Jefferson was by this time, after a month under the roof of the old manse, well established as a member of the household, though after the somewhat remote fashion to be expected of a man whose absorbing work filled most of his waking hours. He closed the door quickly as he caught sight of Georgiana in her masquerade, removed his hat, and bent his head before the cerise velvet.

Georgiana, blushing as vividly as if it were the first time mortal man had ever beheld her pretty shoulders, threw him a laughing look, murmured: "Dress parade in borrowed finery, Mr. Jefferson; don't let the blaze of colour put your eyes out!" and retreated toward the living-room where her father sat, much amused by the situation.

She was followed by her boarder's reply: "I find myself still happily retaining the use of my eyes, Miss Warne. You need not be too much in haste; it is very dull outside, I assure you."

He went on up the stairs, but she had caught his smile, momentarily illumining a face which was ordinarily rather grave. Georgiana closed the living-room door upon the sight of the lithe figure rapidly ascending the staircase without a glance behind. As she faced her father she assumed the expression of a merry child caught in mischief.

"Our new lodger has certainly come upon me in all sorts of situations, not to mention disguises," she remarked, "but this is the first time he has met me in the role of leading lady on the melodramatic stage. Please unhook me, Father Davy; the play is over, and it's time to get the pot-roast simmering. And what do you say to inviting lovely Jeannette Crofton to visit us? Would it be too hard on you?"

"Not at all, my dear. I should be glad to see your Uncle Thomas's daughter. Invite her, by all means. You have far too little young companionship; it will do you good to have a girl of your own age in the house."

"I wonder how we shall get on," mused Georgiana. "Anyhow she'll see what a market this is for evening frocks cut on her lines!"

CHAPTER IV

A LITERARY LIGHT

Many hours afterward, the labours of the day over, Georgiana bent her dark head above an old-fashioned writing-desk in a corner of the living-room, and dashed off the contemplated letter to her almost unknown cousin. How the invitation would be received she had little idea, but since a letter of thanks was undeniably due in response to the "Semi-Annual" box, it was certainly a simple and natural matter enough to offer in return for it a possible pleasure and a certain benefit.

"I'll run straight down to the post-office and mail it," declared Georgiana, sealing and stamping her letter after having read it aloud to her father. "A run in this March wind will be good for me after baking and brewing all day."

"Do, daughter; and take a tumbler or two of jelly to Mrs. Ames, by the way. And pick a spray or two of the scarlet geranium to go with it." Mr. Warne spoke from the depths of an old armchair by the living-room fire, where, with a lamp at his elbow, he was not too deep in a speech of the elder Pitt on "Quartering Soldiers in Boston," to take thought for an invalid whom he considered far less fortunate than himself.

"I will—poor, disagreeable old lady. She doesn't admit that anything tastes as it should, but I observe our jelly is never long in disappearing."

Georgiana, now wearing in honour of the close of day a simple frock of dark-blue wool with a dash of scarlet at throat and wrists, donned a big military cape of blue, scarlet lined, and twisted about her neck a scarf of scarlet silk (dyed from a Semi-Annual petticoat!), which served less as a protection than as the finishing touch to her gay winter's night costume. She was likely to meet few people on her way, but there were always plenty of loungers in the small village post-office, and not even a college graduate could be altogether disdainful of the masculine admiration sure to be found there, though she might ignore it.

As she closed the house door, lifting her face to a cold, starlit sky from which the clouds of the day had broken away at sundown, another door a few rods down the quiet street banged loudly, and the sharp creak of rapid footsteps was immediately to be heard upon the frozen gravel. Georgiana smiled in the darkness at the coincidence of that banging door.

"Well met!" called a ringing voice. "Curious that I should break out of Mrs. Perkins's just as you came along!"

"Very curious, Jimps. How do you manage it? I stole out like a cat just to avoid such a possibility. I knew you were there."

"Did you, indeed?" inquired the owner of the voice, coming up and standing still to look at what he could see of the military-caped form. His own strongly built figure took up its position beside hers as if by right. His hand slipped lightly under her arm, and he turned her gently to face the direction in which he himself had set out. "That's like your impertinence. To pay you for it you shall come this way," he insisted. "It's only a step farther, it's not quite so hackneyed, and it will bring us out where we want to be. Look at the stars!"

"They're wonderful!"

"Carrying something under that cape? Give it to me, chum."

"It's only a bit of a basket, Jimps; never mind, you might spill it."

"You can't carry a bit of a basket when I'm around! Spill nothing! Hand it over."

"Terribly dictatorial to-night, aren't you?"

"Possibly. I've been bossing a lot of new hands to-day, who didn't know a pick from a gang-plough."

"But you've been outdoors every minute!" Her tone was envious.

"Every blessed minute. And you've been in, puttering over a lot of house jobs? See here, you need a run. Let's take the time to go up Harmon Hill and run down it—eh? There'll not be a soul to see."

She laughed doubtfully. "I'd love to, but—the jelly?"

"That's easy." He dropped her arm, turned aside to a clump of trees at the corner of an overgrown old place which they were passing, and deposited the little basket in the shadow. He came back and caught her arm again.

"Easy, now, up the hill. I wish the snow wasn't all gone, we'd have a farewell coast at the end of the season. But there'll undoubtedly be more. Honestly, now, George, hasn't the coasting and tramping helped you through this first winter?"

"Jimps, I don't know what I should have done without it—or you."

"Thanks; I think so myself. The first winter back in the little old town, after the years away at school and college—well—— Anyhow, I pride myself the partnership has worked pretty well. We've been about as good chums as you could ask, haven't we now?"

"About as good."

"All right." His tone had a decided ring of satisfaction in it, but he did not pursue the subject further. Instead he changed it abruptly: "How does the new boarder come on?"

"Very well. We really don't mind having him at all, he's so quiet, and Father enjoys his table talk."

"Father does, but daughter doesn't?"

"Oh, yes, I do—only he doesn't talk much to me. I sit and listen to their discussions— and jump up to wait on them so often that I sometimes lose the thread."

"The duffer! Why doesn't he get up and wait on you?"

Georgiana laughed. "Jimps, we're going to have another guest."

"Another man?" The question came quickly.

"Not at all. A girl—my cousin, Jeannette Crofton. At least I'm writing to ask her for the fortnight before Easter."

"Those rich Crofton relations of yours who hold their heads so high for no particular reason except that it helps them to forget their feet are on the earth?"

"James Stuart, what have I ever said of them to make you speak like that?"

"Never mind; go on. Is it the girl whose picture gets into the Sunday papers—entirely against her will, of course—as the daughter of Thomas Crofton? She's reported engaged, from time to time, and then the report is denied. She's——"

"I shall tell you no more about her," said Georgiana Warne, with her head held quite as high as if she belonged to that branch of the family to whom James Stuart had so irreverently alluded.

"All right. I'm not interested in her anyhow, and you'll want your breath for the run down. Come on, George; one more spurt and we're up.... All ready. Take hold of my hand. Come on!"

In the March starlight the two ran hand in hand down the long, steep Harmon Hill which led from the east into the little town. Stuart's grip was tight, or more than once Georgiana would have slipped on the rough iciness of the descent. But she did not falter at the rush of it, and she was not panting, only breathing quickly, when they came to a standstill upon the level.

"Good lungs, those of yours, George," commented Stuart, in the frank manner in which he might have said it to a younger brother. "You haven't played basket ball and rowed in your 'Varsity boat for nothing. Sure you're not letting up a bit on all that training, now that you're back, baking beans for boarders?"

"And sweeping their rooms, and carrying up wood for their fires, and——"

"What? Do you mean to say that literary light allows you to tote wood for him?" They were walking on rapidly now. "I'll be over in the morning and take up a pile that'll leave no room for him to put his feet. What's he thinking of?"

"Jimps, boy, how absurd you are! How should he know who puts the wood in his room? I don't go up with armfuls of it when he's there."

"If you did, he'd merely open the door for you and say: 'Thank you very much, my good girl.' I don't like this boarder business, I can tell you that. Do you let him smoke in his room?"

"Why not, you unreasonable mortal? He smokes a beautiful briarwood, and such delicious tobacco that I find myself sniffing the air when I go through the hall in the evening, hoping I may get a whiff."

"Does, eh? When I bring up the wood I'll smoke up your hall so you won't have to sniff the air to know you're enjoying the fragrance of Araby."

In this light and airy mood the pair went on their way, enjoying each other's company as might any boy and girl, though each had left the irresponsible years behind and had settled down to the sober work of manhood and womanhood. To Georgiana Warne, whose necessary presence at home, instead of out in the great world of activity where she longed to be, Stuart's society, as he had intimated, had been a strong support during this first year and a half since her return. The singularly similar circumstances which had shaped the plans of these two young people had been the means of inspiring much comprehending sympathy between them. An almost lifelong previous acquaintance had put them on a footing of brotherly and sisterly intimacy, now powerfully enhanced by the sense of need each felt for the other. It was small wonder that their fellow-townsmen were accustomed to couple their names as they would those of a pair long betrothed, and that, as the two came together into the village post-office, where as usual a group of citizens lounged and lingered on one pretext or another, the appearance of "Jim Stuart and Georgie Warne" should cause no comment whatever. To-night more than one idler noted, as often before, the fashion in which the two were outwardly suited to each other. Both were the possessors of the superb health which is such a desirable ally to true vigour of mind, and since both were understood to be, in the village usage, "highly educated," their attraction for each other was considered a natural sequence—as it undoubtedly was.

The mail procured, the letter posted, and the small basket delivered to a querulously grateful old woman, the young people set out for home. They had somehow fallen into a more serious mood, and, walking more slowly than before, discussed soberly enough certain problems of Stuart's connected with the commercial side of market gardening. He spoke precisely as he would have spoken to a man, with the possible difference that he made his explanations of business conditions a trifle fuller than he might have done to any man. But his confidence in his friend's ability to grasp the situation was shown by the way in which, ending his statement of the case, he asked her advice.

"Now, given just this crisis, what would you do, George?" he said.

She considered in silence for some paces. Then she asked a question or two more, put with a clearness which showed that she understood precisely the points to be taken into consideration. He answered concisely, and she then, after a minute's further communion with herself, suggested what seemed to her a feasible course.

Stuart demurred, thought it over, argued the thing for a little with her, and came round to her point of view. He threw back his head with a relieved laugh. "I admit it—it's a mighty good suggestion; it may be the way out. Anyhow, it's well worth trying. George, you're a peach! There isn't one girl in a hundred who would have listened with intelligence enough to make her opinion worth a picayune."

"I'm not a girl, Jimps. I don't want to be a girl—at twenty-four. I can't; I haven't time."

"That's a safe enough statement," replied James Stuart, looking down at the dark head beside him under the March starlight, "as long as you continue to act enough like a normal girl to run down the hills with me after dark. Well, here we are, worse luck! I suppose you're not going to ask me in?" There was a touch of appeal in the lightly spoken question.

"Not to-night, Jimps; I'm sorry. Father Davy overdid to-day, in spite of all my efforts, and I must see him to bed early and read him to sleep."

19

"After he's gone the literary light won't come down and smoke his spices-of-Araby mixture by your fire, instead of his own, while you entertain him, will he?"

Her low laugh rang out. "You ridiculous person, what a vivid imagination you have! Every evening at about this time the literary light goes off for a long tramp by himself, and often doesn't come back till all our lights are out, except the one we leave burning for him. He is absolutely absorbed in his work. We really see nothing at all of him except at the table."

"Just the same, the time will come," predicted James Stuart. "Some night he'll take his regular place at your fireside, as he does at your table. I know your father's soft heart. Yours may not be quite so vulnerable, but if the boarder should happen to look low in his mind after a telegram from anywhere, or should get his precious feet wet——"

"Jimps, go home and be sensible. When Jeannette comes—if she does come, which I doubt more and more—you may be asked over quite a number of times during her visit."

"I presume so. And that's the time you'll have Jefferson down, and you'll pair off with him, while I do my prettiest not to look like an awkward countryman before the lady who has her picture in the Sunday papers."

"Good-night, James Stuart—good-night."

"Good-night, Georgiana—dear," Stuart responded cheerfully. But the last word was under his breath.

CHAPTER V

SHABBINESS

"I positively didn't know how shabby the house was till I'd read Jeannette's letter of acceptance!"

She did not say it to her father—not Georgiana Warne. She said it not to James Stuart, nor to Mr. E. C. Jefferson. Being Georgiana, she said it to no one but her slightly daunted self. She was standing in the hall as she spoke, the wide, plain hall which ran straight through the middle of the wide, plain house, with its square rooms on either side and its winding, old-fashioned staircase at the back. Of the house itself, Georgiana was not in the least ashamed. She knew that it possessed a certain charm of aspect, from the fanlight over the entrance door to the big quaint kitchen with its uneven floor dark with time. It was when one came to details that the charm sordidly vanished—at least to the critical vision of the young housewife. Like the worn white paint upon its exterior, the walls and floors within called loudly for a restoring hand. As for the furnishings, Georgiana looked about her with an appraising eye which took in all their dinginess. The old rugs and carpets were so nearly threadbare; the furniture was so worn; the very muslin curtains at the windows, though white as hands could make them, had been so many times repaired that even artful draping could not wholly conceal their deficiencies.

In other ways the household's lack of means made itself plainly apparent to the daughter of the house, as she went from room to room. The linen press, for instance— how pitifully low its piles of sheets and towels had grown! Hardly a sheet but had a patch upon it, hardly a towel but had been cut down and rehemmed, that it might last as long as possible. There was, to be sure, one small tier of towels, handed down from Georgiana's grandmother and carefully preserved against much using, of which any mistress of a linen press might be proud. There were also two pairs of fine hand-made linen sheets with borders exquisitely drawn; two pairs of pillow cases to match, and a quite wonderful old bedspread of knitted lace.

"I can keep washing out the best towels for her," Georgiana reflected resignedly as she counted her resources.

In the china cupboard there was left quite a stock of rare old plates and dishes which could be used as occasion demanded. The blue-and-white crockery which must serve a part of the time was pretty meagre, the supply of antique silver good as far as it went; it did not go very far.

But—"After all," said Georgiana to herself determinedly, "we can give her good things to eat, and served as attractively as need be—why should I mind about the rest? Father in his armchair is a benediction to any meal, and Mr. Jefferson can talk as few guests can who sit at the Crofton table, I'll wager. I'll not be apologetic, even in my mind, no matter how much I feel like it. I've asked her and she's coming. She wouldn't be coming if she wasn't in a way willing to take what she finds. We'll have a good time out of it."

Whereupon she betook herself to the room which was to be given to her cousin, and fell to work with a will, for this was the last thing to be done before the arrival of the guest.

When it was in order she looked about it, not ill content. It would be an exacting guest, surely, who could not be comfortable here—and there are many guest-rooms of elaborate appointments where guests are not wholly comfortable. This room was large and square and airy, with its four windows facing east and south, and the view from the eastern ones was far-reaching, with a glimpse of blue mountain ranges in the distance. If the matting upon the floor had been many times turned and refitted, its worn places were now all cunningly hidden and it was as fresh as the newly scrubbed paint on the woodwork. There was a luxuriously cushioned, high-backed chair—would Jeannette, by any possibility, recognize the blue silk of those cushion covers? Georgiana wondered. Jeannette, who never wore a frock long enough really to become familiar with its pattern, would only know that the cushions were soft to her comfort-accustomed body. The woven rag rugs of blue and white upon the floor were of Georgiana's own making. An ancient desk, which had belonged to Mr. Warne's mother, was carefully fitted with all the small articles one could desire in reason, taken from Georgiana's cherished college equipment. The washstand in the corner, behind a home-made screen of clever design, was furnished with two beautiful old blue-and-white ewers—the pride of Georgiana's heart, for they had come over from England with her great grandmother; and the rack was hung as full with towels as fastidious bather could desire. There were two or three interesting old prints upon the walls. Altogether, with its small bedroom fireplace laid ready for a fire, and a blue denim-covered woodbox filled to overflowing with more wood——

She had forgotten to fill the woodbox, as yet. It was nearly time to dress for Jeannette's coming. Georgiana ran hurriedly downstairs and through the kitchen, warm and fragrant with the baking of the day in preparation for the coming supper, and in that pleasant order which the kitchen of the good housewife shows at four in the afternoon. In the woodshed beyond she gathered a great armful of wood, not to bother with the basket, which would not hold so much—and hurried back again, making toward the front stairs this time, because the back stairs were narrow and steep, and one could not rush up them at great speed with one's arms full of wood.

"Wait a minute, please, Miss Warne!"

The front door of the house shut with a bang, and hasty footsteps caught up with Georgiana at the foot of the stairs, just as one big stick tumbled loose from her hold and went crashing down behind her.

"Oh, never mind," she panted. The load was much heavier than she had realized, but she had not meant to be caught upon the front stairs with it—not even if it had been James Stuart who came to her rescue.

It was not Stuart, but evidently one quite of Stuart's mind, for Georgiana now found her arms unburdened of their heavy incumbrance without further parley, and herself put where she belonged by this cool command:

"Never carry a load like this when you have a man in the house."

"But—but we haven't!" objected Georgiana, her voice a trifle breathless. She followed Mr. Jefferson, as he strode up the stairs with the wood. She opened the door of the guest-room and lifted the cover of the woodbox.

"Haven't?" he questioned, dumping the wood into the box, and then stooping to rearrange it. "Would you object to telling me what you consider me, then?"

It was on the tip of her tongue to tell him that he was supposed to be a literary light, but she restrained the too-familiar speech.

"You are, of course, a boarder—a 'paying guest,' as we should say, if we were some people," she observed with gravity. "You are expected to complain of whatever service you receive, not to offer any under any circumstances."

"I see. Were you intending to fill this box?"

He stood upright, and his glance wandered from the box in question around the pleasant room in its fresh and expectant order. But it came discreetly back to Georgiana's face.

"Not at all," she denied. "There's quite enough there for to-night."

He nodded, and went toward the door. "The woodshed is, I suppose, beyond the kitchen, after the fashion of woodsheds, and the kitchen is beyond the dining-room?"

"Please don't bother!"

Of course it was useless to protest—and she followed him down the stairs, through dining-room and kitchen to the woodshed. As he passed through the kitchen he stopped and stood still in the middle of it.

"May I look for a minute?" he asked. "It takes me back to my boyhood. My mother used just such a kitchen as this. I thought it the best room in the house."

His lips took on a smile as he looked. Georgiana, with her own hands, had scoured every inch of that kitchen, had made to shine brilliantly every utensil which had in it possibilities of shining. It was impossible not to feel a housewifely pride in the appearance of the place, and to exult in the spicy odours which told of the morning's bakings.

Mr. Jefferson, going on into the woodshed and returning with a well-balanced load of wood which put Georgiana's late attempt to the blush, assured her that he felt personally competent to attend to the woodbox without further aid from her, and marched away as if he were quite accustomed to such tasks.

It may be here stated that next day, when in his absence she looked into his room to see if the woodbox there were quite empty, she found it quite full, though she could not possibly remember when he had discovered the opportunity to do the deed without her knowledge. And from this time forth, during the remainder of his stay, she was obliged to resign herself to the fact that the "man in the house," though he might be a boarder, would permit no interference with this self-assumed task.

Jeannette had written that she would arrive on a certain Thursday afternoon between four and five, being conveyed by motor from the large city, sixty miles away, which was her home. Georgiana, therefore, with memories of college days again strong upon her, made ready to serve afternoon tea beside the living-room fire.

22

"Be prepared to have this function every day while the guest is here, Father Davy," said she. "Jeannette's undoubtedly accustomed to it and would miss it more than she could miss any other one thing. But she's to have only the plainest of thin bread and butter with it, since our six-o'clock village supper comes so soon after. We mustn't pamper her, must we?"

Mr. Warne, in his armchair by the fireside, ready to welcome the guest, looked up at his daughter with bright eyes. "Pampering," said he, "is the atmosphere of this house. Jeannette cannot escape it. I am pampered beyond belief every day of my life. At this very moment my eyes are feasting upon the sight of my child in what must be an absolutely new old dress!"

A peculiar expression crossed Georgiana's face as she glanced down at the soft gray-blue of the afternoon frock she had donned for the occasion.

"I'm wondering if she will recognize it," she murmured. "It was one of the white evening gowns in that last 'Semi-Annual.' I coloured it myself—as usual. It really came out pretty well, but it gives me a queer, conscious feeling to be wearing it when I meet her. Do you suppose she'll know it, Father Davy?"

"And if she does?" The tone was that of a tender irony.

"I suppose I'm an idiot to care! I don't care—*but I do*!" Georgiana flung a look at the slim man in the big chair, which said that she was confident of his understanding her, no matter what she said.

"No false pride, daughter," he warned her. "You can tell the big man from the little one by the character of the things he is willing to accept. There was never any stigma attached to wearing the discarded garments of another, provided they were come by honestly. And when one has coloured them, into the bargain—and looks like the 'Portrait of a Lady' in them——"

"Father Davy, you're the most comforting creature!" And Georgiana dropped a kiss upon the top of the head which rested against the back of the worn old armchair.

If she had not been watching from the window she would not have known when the Crofton car drew up at the door, so quietly did the great, shining motor roll down the macadamized road which ran through the main street of the little town. She was out and down the manse path in hospitable alacrity, yet not without the dignity of which she was mistress.

So this was the guest whom she had ventured to ask down to the hospitality of the shabby old village manse! If she had been a princess, Miss Jeannette Crofton could not more thoroughly have looked the part. Georgiana had known many rich men's daughters at college and had found close friends among them, but no one of them had ever suggested such a background of luxury as did this slim and graceful girl, as she set her pretty foot upon the old box-bordered gravel path. She was rather small of stature, her fair-haired beauty was of a strikingly attractive type, and every detail of her attire and belongings breathed of wealth and fashion. Georgiana felt herself instantly a buxom milkmaid beside her.

CHAPTER VI

WHEN ROYALTY COMES

"It was so good of you to ask me," said Jeannette in a voice of much sweetness, as she put out her hand to her cousin. Then she turned to the man in livery who stood at attention by the door of the car. "You may take this coat back with you, Dennis," she said; and she let him remove from her shoulders the long, fur-lined cloak she had worn for the March drive. He gathered together her belongings, as she walked up the path with Georgiana, and he afterward went back for a long motor trunk which had been brought upon the back of the car. Besides this was a larger receptacle of black leather which he brought and deposited in the hall.

"Dennis can take all these to my room for me," said Jeannette, with more appreciation of the situation than Georgiana had expected. Dennis did not look altogether pleased with this task, but he performed it and was rewarded by a smile from his young mistress, which promised to soothe his injured dignity at some future time.

Mr. Warne, rising slowly from the armchair as Jeannette was brought into his presence, looked keenly into the face of his sister's daughter. Her fine clothing was nothing to him; he could not have told what she wore; but he was interested in learning what she might be, herself. It was something of a test for any stranger, the meeting of that clear look of his, kindly though it was sure to be. With all his appearance of frailty and exhaustion, one felt instinctively that whatever had happened to the body, the mind was intact and resolute with energy, the judgment swift and accurate.

As they all took tea together Georgiana could feel their guest striving to adjust herself to her entertainers. Her manner was very charming, though a little languid, a little weary, as if she were tired with her long drive—and with other things besides. But there was that about her which proclaimed her unmistakably the gentlewoman, and this was good to know. She got on well with her newly discovered uncle, and he with her. Indeed, the simplicity and straight-forwardness of Father Davy's manner with every one, his keen observation, his ready imagination, would have put him instantly on an equal footing with the most exalted of his fellow-creatures. It could do no less with his niece, no matter how new to her his type of man might be, nor how new to him the fashion of her speech and smile.

This was a pleasant beginning. But if Georgiana, before her guest arrived, had thought the old house shabby, she felt it now to be positively shambling. She struggled mightily against this attitude of mind, knowing that it was unworthy of her, but, as she led this wonderful, winsome creature, whom she knew to be accustomed only to the softnesses of life, up over the worn stair carpeting to the room she had prepared for her, she was wondering how she herself had ever conceived the preposterous idea of inviting her cousin to visit her; the task of making this daughter of luxury comfortable, even for a fortnight, seemed suddenly so impossible.

"Oh, how very attractive!" exclaimed Jeannette, as she was taken into the room over which Georgiana had spent so much thought. "I shall love it here!"

That was to be her attitude, thought Georgiana. Being exceedingly well-bred, the guest was prepared to like everything that was done for her. Though this was precisely what was to be expected and desired, Georgiana found herself already irritated by it—most unreasonably, it must be admitted.

"I'm a jealous goose!" said she sternly to herself, and fell to helping her cousin. There was something appealing about the girl's helplessness, because she evidently tried hard not to show it. As the two lifted the garments from the carefully packed trunk trays it was Georgiana who found the right places for them in clothespress and bureau drawers. She had seldom seen, never handled, such exquisite apparel, from the piles of sheer, convent-embroidered linen to the frocks and wraps and négligés which went into retirement on the padded hangers she had provided. She realized, too, that elaborate as seemed to her the array of clothing Jeannette had thought it necessary to bring for her visit, it was probable that the girl herself had felt that she was having packed only the simplest of her wardrobe and the least that a civilized being could do with.

It was when Jeannette herself spread forth upon the little dressing-table—cleverly contrived out of an old washstand, a long and narrow mirror, and some odds and ends of muslin and lace—the articles she was accustomed to use every day of her life, but which might have been matched only in the homes of princes, that the young hostess found it hardest to control the pang of envy which smote her. Such silver, such crystal, such genuine ivory—and such sheer beauty of design and finish! Yet Jeannette was almost awkward in her disposal of the imposing array, saying with a laugh that she really couldn't remember how the things went at home, but that it didn't matter in the least.

She set about removing her traveling clothes as if she never had been waited upon in her life. It was only when she failed to discover how she was put together that Georgiana had to come to the rescue.

"It's dreadfully stupid of me," protested Jeannette, her delicate cheeks flushing, "but I simply can't find that absurd hook."

It was then that Georgiana frankly took the situation by its horns and did away with all embarrassment.

"You must let me help you, Jean," she said, finishing the unhooking with ease, "whenever you need it. I shall love to do it, for you might have rather a bad time trying to do everything for yourself. There you are—and please call me when you are ready to be fastened into your other frock. I'm just around the corner, and there's nobody else at home now."

Before supper was served, Georgiana prepared her cousin to meet "the boarder." Not on any account would she have let his presence be accounted for on the score of his being a guest in the house; not even would she call him a "paying guest."

"Mr. Jefferson came to us through a letter from a friend. He said he wanted a quiet place to work in, away from all interruptions by friends or claims of any sort. He is writing a book, and we see as little of him as if he were not in the house—except at the table. I think you will like him. It's so long since we have had a man in the house we're not yet used to it, but on the whole it's rather comforting."

"How interesting—to have a book being written in the house! Is it fact or fiction, do you know?"

"I don't imagine it's fiction. He has piles of reference books, and a great deal of mail, and—somehow—he doesn't look as if he wrote fiction."

Yet, as Mr. Jefferson came into the dining-room that night, Georgiana found herself wondering why she should think he did not look as if he would write fiction—not foolish fiction, certainly, but sensible fiction, made possible by keen observation and set off by a capacity for quiet—possibly even biting—humour. He looked at least as if he might write essays, thoughtful, clever essays, full of searching analyses of his fellow human creatures, of their oddities, their hopes, their aspirations, their sins, and their virtues. Or—was he, after all, writing on scientific matters—facts, pure and simple; inferences, deductions, conclusions from facts? She wondered, more than she had yet done, as to the nature of his work.

"I think Mr. Jefferson is delightful," said Jeannette cordially, beside the living-room fire, when supper was over, and the boarder, after lingering in the living-room doorway for a minute, but declining on the score of work Mr. Warne's invitation to enter, had gone his way upstairs. On this first night Georgiana had let the disordered dining table wait, and had accompanied the others to the fireside as if she had a dozen servants to attend to her household affairs. "After this, she won't notice so much," she had argued with herself.

"I don't want to have her offering to help. I don't mean to do a thing differently on her account, but I can't help—well, *shying* at the dishes the very first minute after supper!"

"A man of fine intellect," Father Davy responded to his niece's observation, "and accustomed to think worthy thoughts. One can see that at once. It is a real pleasure to have him here. It is good for us, too. Georgiana and I were growing narrow before he came. He has broadened us; we get his point of view on subjects that we thought had been disposed of for all time—and find them not disposed of at all."

Before the moment arrived when, in Georgiana's mind, the waiting work in the kitchen must be done without further postponement, the front door was besieged by James Stuart. A basket of late winter apples in hand, he came in, looking the image of vigorous youth, his well-set-up figure showing its best in the irreproachable clothes he always wore when his day's work was over, his manner, as usual, that of the friend of the house. He had not received Georgiana's permission to come in upon this first evening of Miss Crofton's visit, but he had taken his welcome for granted and was not disappointed in receiving it. It was impossible not to be glad to see his smiling face, for his good looks were backed by a capacity for adapting himself to whatever company he might find himself in, though it should be of the most distinguished.

Presenting Stuart to her cousin, it occurred to Georgiana to wonder as to the impression each must make upon the other. Jeannette was wearing a frock of a peculiar shade of blue which the firelight and lamplight, instead of dulling, seemed to make almost to glow. It was the sort of apparently simple attire which is the product of high art, and in it, sitting just where all lights seemed to play together upon hair and cheek and perfect throat, the visitor was, as Georgiana owned to herself, certainly worth looking at.

She left them together presently and went off to the kitchen. Here she covered from view with a big pinafore her own undeniably attractive figure and fell upon her task, proceeding to dispatch it with all the speed compatible with quiet. She had cleared the table, and, having arranged her dishes in orderly piles, was just filling her dishpan with the steaming water which made suds as it fell upon the soap, when a familiar footstep was heard upon the bare kitchen floor.

Georgiana looked over her shoulder, words of reproof upon her lips: "Well—having come without an invitation, the least you can do is to stay where you belong and entertain the guest."

"There's a characteristic welcome for you!" The intruder seemed in no wise daunted by his reception, but picked up a dish towel and stood at ease, waiting the placing of the first tumbler in the rinsing pan. "And where should I belong, if not standing by a chum in distress?"

"I'm not in distress, if you please."

"Don't mind washing dishes while the guest sits by the fire?"

"Not a bit—more than usual," Georgiana amended honestly.

"Why don't you pile 'em up and let 'em wait till morning?"

"I shouldn't sleep for thinking of them."

"My word, but you're a hustler! I don't know whether I can keep up."

"Don't try. Go back to the other room, please, Jimps. You can be of real use there."

"Well, I like that!"

As he wiped away assiduously, Stuart surveyed his companion's face in profile. It belied the dictatorial words, for Georgiana was smiling. Her cheeks were of a splendid colour, her dark hair drooped over the prettiest white forehead in the world, and the whole outline of her face was distracting. Here was a lamplight effect which rivalled the one in the living-room, though it was thrown from a common kitchen lamp, unshaded, and fell upon a figure in a red-and-white checked apron. Georgiana glanced at her self-appointed assistant and encountered the flash of an eye which told her that, however Stuart objected to her words, he liked the look of what he saw.

"Isn't Jeannette a beauty?" she inquired hastily, and plunged her hands into her pan with such energy that she sent a splash of hot, soapy water upon Stuart's cheek. He surreptitiously wiped it off with a corner of his dish towel.

"She sure is," he assented cordially. "I wasn't prepared for quite such a looker. She doesn't seem to have brought with her that proud and haughty expression she had in the Sunday papers."

"She's a dear, and not in the least proud and haughty. I'm going to enjoy her visit, I know. If I can only make her enjoy it!"

"I'll be glad to help," Stuart offered. "This isn't a very promising time of year for the country, but if you think she'd like any of the good times we can give her here, I'll get them up."

"Our sort of good times is just what I do want to give her. She's had enough of her own kind and needs the diversion. What would you get up, for instance?"

"I'll take overnight to think it out, but I can promise you it'll be an outdoor affair. Would she be up to any kind of a tramp, do you think?"

"Oh, no, Jimps! Not yet, at any rate."

"All right. I'll harness up my best team and carry her most of the way. We must have another man, I suppose. Shall we ask the literary light, just for a lark? It would give tone to the company to have him along, eh?"

"He probably wouldn't go."

"Don't you fool yourself. A fellow who covers as many miles a day as he does will jump at it, no matter how important his next chapter is. Do you know, I'll have to admit I rather like him since I tramped a couple of miles in his company the other day. There are a lot of interesting ideas in his head, and I got him to give me the benefit of a few of them. Drew him out, you know. Though to be strictly honest"—with a laugh—"when I thought it over afterward I wasn't exactly sure that he hadn't drawn me out rather more than I drew him. Anyhow, the interest seemed to be mutual, and that flattered me a bit. It's perfectly evident that he's a great student of affairs."

They finished the work at a gallop. Georgiana slipped off her pinafore, and Stuart, who had insisted on waiting for her, hung it upon its accustomed nail.

"Do you suppose pretty cousin ever wore one?" he queried.

CHAPTER VII

SNOWBALLS

Mr. E. C. Jefferson laid down his pen, ran his hand through his heavy brown hair, rumpling it still more than it had been rumpled before—which is saying considerable—and stretched his legs under the table upon which he had been writing steadily since half-past one o'clock. He heaved a mighty breath, stretched his arms to match his legs, looked round at his windows, which faced the west, and so had kept him supplied with strong light longer than windows on any other side of the house would have done, and took out his watch.

27

Nearly half-past four. Time, and more than time, for his late afternoon tramp. He set the piles of sheets before him in order, sheathed his pen and put it in his pocket, and rose from his place, the light of achievement in his eye, but crampiness and fatigue in all his limbs.

As he approached his windows to ascertain what kind of weather was to be found outside, he became aware of sounds which would indicate that some event of activity and hilarity was going on below. He realized now that he had been hearing these sounds—quite without hearing them, after the fashion of the absorbed workman—for the last half-hour. Looking out, he beheld an interesting affair in full swing.

At each end of the side yard the heavy snow which a late March storm had brought overnight had been shovelled and manipulated into the semblance of a fort such as lads are wont to make. Between these two entrenchments a battle was raging. But it was no lads who held the places of the combatants. Instead, as he looked, Mr. Jefferson saw rising warily from behind the fort nearest him, a girlish figure in a scarlet blanket suit, its dark head half shielded by a scarlet toboggan cap very much awry. A mittened hand flung a snowball with strength and precision straight into the opposite fort, and the assailant immediately dodged down behind the embankment.

From the opposing stronghold then cautiously appeared a head snugly bound in a blue scarf, from which locks of fair hair escaped at divers points. A second snowball, accompanied by a loose flutter of snow, wended its way uncertainly through the air, and fell a foot short of the fort behind which crouched the scarlet figure. The figure immediately rose and fired an answering volley. Peals of laughter and gay shouts rang through the air.

At this very moment a third person ran into the yard from the street, calling: "For shame, George! I'm going to take sides with the enemy, and we'll have you out in no time!"

Jefferson saw this third figure, in sweater and cap, dash across the open, narrowly escaping a vigorous shower of missiles from the near fort, and disappear behind the farther one.

The battle was now on in earnest. Let Scarlet Toboggan fire as fast and as furiously as she might, a merciless bombardment of her protecting walls had begun. The girl in the blue scarf—and priceless furs—had sunk laughing upon the floor of her refuge, while her new ally, bringing to bear the full strength and skill of his sex, battered at the entrenchments across the yard, and began to make havoc thereon.

Georgiana was a brave foe, but though she fought with surprising endurance she was beginning to be seriously worsted, several feet of her snow rampart having been shot away, when a voice behind her cried out a command, and an arm, more sinewy than hers, sent a hard shot whizzing past her head into the opposite fort with that directness of aim and effectiveness of delivery which only the male arm can accomplish.

"Duck down and make snowballs while I fire!" the voice ordered, and Georgiana, breathless but still undaunted, obeyed.

"Keep behind me, and pile the balls at the right," directed Jefferson. His voice was eager as a boy's. He also had pulled on sweater and cap, and as he and James Stuart faced each other across the twenty yards which separated them, they might have been a couple of school-fellows wrestling for supremacy.

"Keep 'em coming—faster—faster!" Stuart urged Jeannette, the lust of battle upon him. "Stop laughing and work! George is a"—he stooped to make a ball for himself—"fiend at making 'em; you've got to learn! Keep 'em coming."

The wet snow was precisely in the right state for quick packing, and Georgiana was indeed an expert at the business. Jefferson found her hard, round balls splendid missiles,

28

and he used them with all the energy of an arm which welcomed the change from the labours of the past hours to those of the present.

"Ha! there goes that left corner!" he exulted with his comrade-at-arms, as the last of a series of well-directed shots reduced a part of the enemies' defences to a gratifying slump. "And here comes a bit of ours," he added, as a ball of Stuart's ploughed through a weakened upper portion of their own rampart.

"He'll be game to the last," panted Georgiana, working furiously.

"So will we! We'll fight to a finish, if we go without our suppers."

The battle raged on. The combatants took no heed of passing time, until Jeannette, growing reckless with excitement, lifted an incautious head and received a spent ball full upon her chin. No harm was done, as she protested, but Stuart raised a flag of truce and Mr. Jefferson ran across the lines to apologize.

"It didn't hurt a bit," Jeannette reaffirmed, showing a very pink chin.

"It's lucky it didn't. I wasn't properly protecting you," Stuart declared warmly.

"Both sides come in to supper!" commanded Georgiana. "Please stay, Jimps; it's the only amends we can make you, and you must be as hungry as a bear."

"Thanks; I'd like to, but I'm not properly dressed, I'm afraid."

"Jean and I won't make a change, and you can take us coasting this evening, if you will. Do you suppose Mr. Jefferson would dream of staving off his dignity a bit longer and going, too?"

They all looked at the person mentioned and their glances were all gayly audacious.

"Is that an invitation or a challenge?" He put it to Georgiana.

"Whichever you choose to take it."

"I'll take it as I choose, then, and accept. The spirit of sport is upon me; I couldn't work this evening if I tried."

"Good for you! 'All work and no play,' you know," quoted Stuart, as they went in together, a moist and merry company.

Upstairs, while Jeannette dried her hair, she reflected that she didn't know when she had had so gay a time. She ran in to say this to Georgiana, but found that that young woman had already put her hair in order without drying it, as its damply curling locks above her forehead testified, and was rushing away downstairs to the kitchen.

"Won't you take cold?" suggested Jeannette, struggling with her own wet braids, and very naturally wishing for her maid to dry and put them in order.

"Mercy, no; not over the kitchen stove. They'll be dry soon enough," was the reply; and Georgiana vanished, the supper on her mind.

When Jeannette came down, half an hour later, and appeared in the kitchen doorway, she saw that the speed of her young hostess's labours and the warmth of the kitchen were quite likely to prevent all chance of undried locks.

There was system about Georgiana's work, fast as was its pace. Each trip across the floor, from pantry to dining-room and back again, demonstrated housewifely efficiency. Both hands were always full and she seemed never to forget what she meant to do. If she passed the stove on her way somewhere she stopped to stir something or to glance into the oven, and when she went to the storeroom for cream she brought away bread and butter as well.

Jeannette commented admiringly. "Don't you ever forget and have to run back for something?" she inquired.

"Goodness, yes! But when you've been over certain ground several million times, it's a pity if you can't make your head save your heels as a rule. Excuse me, dear; but if you wouldn't mind standing just a foot or two to the left——"

Jeannette turned. "I see; I'm in the way when I'd like so much to help. Isn't there anything I could do?"

"All done, thank you—except—would you just arrange that boxful of scarlet geraniums Jimps brought over, for the table? That would help very much. Take any bowl or glass from the dining-room cupboard that looks appropriate to you."

"I'd love to." And Jeannette fell to work—if it could be called work. Never in her life had she arranged scarlet geraniums as a table decoration, or, for that matter, seen them so used. But as she placed the splendid, thrifty blooms, each with its accompanying rich green leaves, in the plain brown bowl which she felt best matched their undistinguished beauty, she discovered for the first time that other blossoms besides roses and orchids, chrysanthemums, and the rest of the ordinary florists' products, may charm the eye from the centre of a snowy cloth.

"That's gorgeous! Thank you so much! Aren't they the jolliest flowers in the world for a winter night? Jimps's greenhouses certainly are doing well. Don't you want a bit of a blossom in your hair? Their grower would feel tremendously complimented."

"Red's not my colour, but it is yours. Let me tuck this little sprig in these braids, and I'll risk the grower's being better pleased than if I wore them."

Georgiana submitted, and promptly forgot all about the scarlet decoration. But the others did not—found forgetting it, indeed, quite impossible. As they gathered about the table, it caught the eye of each in turn. Georgiana's cheeks, from the vigorous exercise in the frosty air, were glowing brilliantly; her eyes were wonderful to look at; her dark cloth dress had upon it no relief of colour; so the scarlet geranium in her hair was the touch of the artist which drew the eye and held it. She had placed upon the table, instead of the customary lamp, one of the few treasures of the house, a fine old candelabrum, with pendent crystals, and the burning candles threw their mellow light directly into her face.

She looked up suddenly, after having served each one from the dish before her, and found them all looking at her. James Stuart's fork was suspended above his plate, but the others had not yet taken theirs. She gazed at them in amazement.

"Why, what is the matter?" she cried. "Do I—is something queer about me? Have I missed a point somebody has made?"

They all turned then, laughing, to their plates, and nobody would tell her what was wrong. Stuart seemed to think it a great joke—her mystification. When she removed the plates for the second course—there were but two in the simple, hearty little supper—she glanced into the small kitchen mirror. Her eye caught the scarlet geranium.

"I suppose I look ridiculously sentimental with that flower just there," she thought. "But I won't take it out after Jean put it there. No wonder they laughed."

An hour afterward they were all out upon the hill nearby. Stuart possessed a splendid pair of "bobs," and they were soon dashing down the hill at a pace which, while it made Jeannette hold her breath with mingled fear and joy, made Georgiana cry out, "Oh! is there anything so glorious?" and made Mr. Jefferson, just behind her, watching over her shoulder, respond with heartiness: "The snow fight took five years off my age, and now here goes another five. I must be almost as young as you are now, Miss Warne."

"Oh, no; I'm only ten myself to-night," she answered. "Coasting was one of my earliest joys. I was so proud when I could steer Jimps Stuart's first pair of bobs—small and primitive ones compared with these."

She found Mr. Jefferson beside her when it came to the walk back up the hill. A new side of him was visible to-night. He was not the quiet student and writer, the man who discussed with her father and herself the course of the world's events or the problems of social service, but a light-hearted boy, much like Stuart, and ready to abet all the other man's efforts for the amusement of the party.

The fun went on for an hour; then Jeannette, unaccustomed to so much vigorous exercise, began quite against her will to show evidences of fatigue, and after one particularly long, swift flight the party went back to the house. There followed another gay hour before the fire, while Stuart roasted chestnuts, and Georgiana, sitting on the floor against her father's knee, told stones of madcap pranks at college, illustrating them by such changes of facial expression and such significant gestures that her hearers spent themselves with their laughter.

Jeannette, lying back in a shabby but comfortable old armchair, looked and listened with the absorbed interest of one to whom such simple pleasures as these had the flavour of absolute novelty. Her eyes wandered from Georgiana's vivid face to her father's delicate one; to James Stuart's comely features glowing ruddily in the firelight as he tended his chestnuts, showing splendid white teeth as he roared at Georgiana's clever mimicry or turned to laugh into Jeannette's eyes as he offered her a particularly plump and succulently bursting specimen of his labours; to Mr. Jefferson's maturer personality, his brown eyes keenly intent, his face lighted with enjoyment, his occasional comments on Georgiana's adventures flashing with a dry humour which matched hers and sometimes quite outdid it. To Jeannette they were all an engrossing study. As for herself——

"She's the loveliest thing I ever saw," thought Georgiana from time to time as she glanced up at her cousin, whose fair hair against the dark cushion of the old chair caught and held the charm of the fire's own warmth in its gleaming strands. Jeannette's eyes were matchless by lamplight; her cheeks and lips were glowing from the outdoor life of the day and evening; her smile was a thing to imprison hearts and hold them fast. If she spoke little no one thought of her as silent, and the charm of her low laughter at the sallies of the others was the sheerest flattery, it was so evidently born of genuine delight in the cleverness she did not attempt to emulate.

"I'm a clown beside her," said Georgiana to herself. "Who cares how a woman talks when she looks like that? Every line of her is absolute grace and beauty, every turn of her head is fascination itself. I never saw such eyes. That little twist in the corner of her lip when she smiles is the most delicious thing I ever saw. Jimps looks at it forty times in every five minutes and I can't blame him. Mr. Jefferson keeps his chair facing that way so he can have her all the time in focus, though he doesn't eat her up as Jimps does. I can't blame either of them. And I shall go on being a clown, because that's what I can do and it amuses them. If I should lie back in a chair like that and just smile without saying anything, Father Davy would say, 'Daughter, don't you feel quite well?' and Jimps would propose getting me a cup of tea. Oh, well—how absurd of me to mind because another girl looks like a picture by a wonderful painter while I look like—a lurid lithograph by nobody at all!"

Whereupon she set her strong, white teeth into a hot, roasted chestnut, cracked it, and, regarding the halves, said: "This reminds me of the night Prexy lost his head"—and brought down the house with the merriest tale of all. It was so irresistibly absurd that Jeannette, helpless with her mirth, buried her face in her cobweb handkerchief, Stuart rocked upon his knees and made the welkin ring, and Mr. Jefferson laughed in a growling bass that gathered volume as the preposterousness of the situation grew upon him with consideration of it. Even Mr. Warne, whose expressions of amusement were usually noiseless, gave way to soft little chuckles of appreciation, and wiped his tear-filled eyes.

31

Georgiana, finishing her chestnut, looked upon them all and told them they were the most gratifying audience she had ever addressed, but that she feared it was not good for them to give way to their emotions so unrestrainedly, and that she should therefore not open her lips again that night. As they found it impossible to break down this resolution, even with entreaties backed by offerings of worldly goods, the party broke up. Georgiana carried off her guest to put her to bed with her own hands, while Mr. Jefferson and James Stuart smoked a bedtime pipe together in the boarder's room; after which Stuart let himself quietly out of a door that was never locked, to reflect, as he tramped homeward over the snow, on what an inordinately jolly evening it had been.

CHAPTER VIII

SOAPSUDS

"Will you think I'm dreadful, Georgiana dear," asked Jeannette, lying luxuriously back upon her pillow while her cousin sat braiding her own thick locks by the little bedroom fireplace in which the last remnants of the fire were smouldering, "if I say I shouldn't have believed I could possibly have such a good time in such a way? I never did anything the least bit like it."

"Never coasted?"

"Never."

"Never threw snowballs?"

"Not that I can remember."

"Nor roasted chestnuts?"

"I never tasted one before—except perhaps in the stuffing of a fowl."

"Poor child! But at least you've sat by the fire with other girls and men and told stories, little Jean?"

The guest considered. "Of course—at house parties. Yet I can't seem to recall any such scene as the one we just left, down by your fire. I certainly never sat on the floor with my arm on my father's knee, with a group of people around, while somebody told stories— sure not such stories as you told. Oh, you're the cleverest girl I ever knew, to tell such things in such a way! It was perfectly splendid! How those two men did enjoy it! I don't know when I've heard men laugh in just that way."

"Just what way? Please tell me how they laughed differently from other men. To be sure, Jimps just lets go when he's amused and raises the rafters with his howls of glee; but so do other young men of his age. And certainly Mr. Jefferson laughed decorously enough."

"Yes, but it was so whole-souled with both of them; and yet there wasn't a thing in your stories but—oh, I can't tell you just what I mean, if you don't know. But somehow it all struck me so differently from the way any girl-and-man evening ever struck me before. There—there seems a different air to breathe here—if that expresses it—from any I've ever been in."

The two regarded each other, Jeannette from between half-closed, deeply fringed eyelids as she lay back upon her pillows, one arm, half veiled with the finest of linen and lace, outstretched upon the treasured old-time counterpane, the other beneath her neck; Georgiana sitting up straight, with two long, dark braids hanging over her shoulders, her dusky eyes wide open, her cheeks still bright with colour balanced by the scarlet hue of the loose garment she had put on.

"I've no doubt there is," agreed Georgiana thoughtfully. "Still, though you live a very different life from any I've ever known, I didn't suppose your education in the matter of roast chestnuts—and the things that go with them—had been quite so badly neglected. To think of never having had them except so disguised by the manipulations of a French *chef* that you couldn't recognize them! And to have gone to balls and horse shows and polo games—and never to have built a snow fort! Dear, dear, what we have to teach you! Life hasn't been really fair to you, has it, my dear?"

This was sheer audacity, from a poor girl to a rich one, but it was charming audacity none the less and by no means wholly ironic. To Jeannette, studying her cousin with eyes which were envious of the physical superiority for lack of which no training in the social arts or mere ability to purchase the aid of dressmaker and milliner could possibly atone, conscious that Georgiana possessed a mind far keener and better trained than her own, the question called for a serious answer. She half sat up and pushed her pillow into a soft mountain behind her as she spoke:

"No, it hasn't! I thought so before I came here and now I'm sure of it. I feel a weak and helpless creature beside you—helpless in every way. I can't do anything you can. If my father should lose his money and I should be thrown upon my own resources, I shouldn't be able to make so much as a—snowball for myself!"

Both laughed in spite of Jeannette's earnestness, for the words brought back vivid memories of the wild sport of the afternoon. Then Georgiana's ready brain leaped to the inevitable corollary:

"Ah, but there'd be sure to be a man ready to dash into your fort and make your snowballs for you!"

"I'm not so sure."

"I am."

"Of course the men I know don't seem to mind whether a girl is helpless or not, if she can look and act the way they want her to. But—I'm discovering that there are other kinds of men, and somehow I like this new kind. And I imagine this kind wouldn't care for helpless girls. You made snowballs for your man to throw, and they were good hard ones, as my chin can still testify."

"You can learn to make hard snowballs," said Georgiana, smiling.

Jeannette held up one beautifully modelled but undeniably slender arm and clasped it with her hand. "Soft as——" She paused for a simile.

"Sponge cake," supplied Georgiana, coming over to feel critically of the extended arm. "It *is* pretty spongy. It needs exercise with a punchball or"—she flashed a mischievous glance at the languid form beside her—"a batch of bread dough."

"Bread dough! Would that help it?"

"Rather! So would sweeping, and scrubbing, and moving furniture about. But you're born to a life of ease, my dear, so those things are out of the question for you. But fencing lessons would be good for you—and fashionable, too, which would double their value, of course."

"Georgiana!" Jeannette sat straight up and laid two coaxing arms about her cousin's firmly moulded neck. "Teach me to make bread, will you, while I'm here?"

"Oh, good gracious!" Georgiana threw back her head to laugh. "Hear the child! What good would that do, if you learned? You wouldn't do it when you went back."

"I would!—Well, of course, I might have difficulty in—but mother wants me to be strong; she's always fussing about it because I can't endure the round of society things she says any girl ought to—and enjoy. If you thought bread-making would really help——"

"It would be a drop in the bucket of exercise you ought to take."

"Nevertheless, I want to learn," persisted Jeannette as Georgiana moved away, evidently with the intention of leaving her for the night. "I'd like to feel I knew how. And your bread is the most delicious I ever tasted. Please!"

"Oh, very well; I'll teach you with pleasure. I shall be setting bread sponge at six to-morrow morning. Will you be down?" Georgiana's smile was distinctly wicked.

"Six o'clock!" There was a look of mingled incredulity and horror in the lovely face on the pillow. "But—does bread—does bread have to be made so early?"

"Absolutely. After the morning dew is off the grass, bread becomes heavy."

Jeannette stared into the mocking eyes of her cousin; then she laughed. "Oh, I see. You're testing me. Well,"—with a stifled sigh—"I'll get up if you'll call me. I'm afraid I should never wake myself—especially after all that snowballing——"

"Exactly. And I'll not call you. So lie still in your nest, ladybird, and don't bother your pretty head about bread sponges. What's the use? You'll never need to know, and you'll soon forget having had even a faint desire toward knowledge. Good-night—and sleep sweetly."

"Oh, but wait! I'm really serious. Please call me!"

"Never!"

With one laughing backward look and with a kiss waved toward the slender figure now sitting up in bed, Georgiana opened the door and fled. That she did not want to teach her cousin an earthly thing, even if she could have believed Jeannette serious in her request, was momentarily growing more evident to her own consciousness. Just why, she might have been unwilling to explain.

Next morning, however, she found herself destined to carry out the plan Jeannette had so impulsively proposed. She crept downstairs as quietly as the creaking boards under the worn stair carpet would permit, and began her work in a whirl of haste. But she had not more than assembled her ingredients on the scrupulously scoured top of the old pine table when she heard the kitchen door softly open. Wheeling, she beheld a vision which brought a boyish whistle to her lips.

Jeannette, enveloped in a long silken garment evidently thrown on over her night attire, a little cap of lace and ribbon confining her hair, the most impractical of slippers on her feet, stood smiling at her cousin, sleep still clinging to her eyelids.

"I'm down," she announced in triumph.

"So I see. But you're not up," replied Georgiana, regarding the vision with critical eyes.

Jeannette's gaze left the trim morning garb of the young cook, her perfectly arranged hair, her whole aspect of efficiency, and dropped to her own highly inappropriate attire, and she flushed a little. But she held her ground.

"You didn't call me, and when I woke it was so near six I didn't dare wait to dress. Can't I learn unless I'm dressed like you?"

"If a French doll had come to life and offered to help me in the kitchen I couldn't feel more stunned. What will happen to all those floating ends of lace and ribbon, when they get mixed with flour and yeast? Be sensible, child, and go back to bed."

"I'll pin everything out of the way, and perhaps you'll lend me an apron. I really don't want to bother you, Georgiana, but I do want to learn."

Georgiana relented. "Very well. Come here, and I'll cover you up as best I can. Or I'll wait while you run up and dress—if you've anything to put on that's fit for bread-making."

"Nothing much fitter than this, I'm afraid," admitted Jeannette reluctantly.

"Poor little girl!" Georgiana's momentary irritation was gone, as it usually was, in no time at all. "Well, here go the frills under a nice big gingham all-over; and now you look like a combination of Sleeping Beauty and Mother Bunch! All right; here we go into business. Do you know how to scald that cupful of milk you see before you?"

"Scald it?" repeated Jeannette doubtfully—and so the lesson began.

Absolute ignorance on the part of the pupil, assured knowledge on that of the teacher—the lesson was a very kindergarten in methods. There were times when Georgiana had much difficulty in restraining her inward mirth, but she soon saw that this must be done, though Jeannette herself laughed at her own clumsiness, and evidently was determined to let nothing escape her.

"Kneading looks so easy when you do it," she lamented; "but I can't seem to help getting stuck."

"That will come with practice—if you ever try another batch, which I doubt. And it's the kneading that is so good for your arms."

"Yours are beautiful—and so strong, it must be fun to own them."

"There are times when a bit of muscle is of use in a hustling world," admitted her cousin. "There, I think that dough will do very well. Turn it over and lay it smoothly in the bowl—so. Cover it with its white blanket—so; and leave it right here, where it will have a good warm temperature to rise in. Now, run up and snatch another nap; you'll have plenty of time."

"You're not going back to bed?"

"Rather not!" Georgiana's smile strove to be tolerant. "There are just a few things to be done about the house, and they are best done before breakfast. Off with you, lady cousin!"

"Do you always get up so early?" Jeannette persisted.

"I have an extraordinary fondness for early rising," Georgiana explained. "It's foolish, of course, but it's an old habit. Good-bye, my dear; my next errand is down cellar," and she vanished from the sight of her guest, quite unable to keep herself longer in hand before the amazing point of view of this daughter of luxury.

The "next errand" was the washing of the handful of fine towels with which the painstaking hostess was keeping the guest-room supplied, unwilling to furnish the aristocratic young person upstairs with the coarser articles used by herself and the others. Jeannette, all unaware that the snowy linen with which her room was kept plentifully supplied was constantly relaundered in secret by Georgiana's own hands, was as lavish in her use of it as she was accustomed to be at home, and the result was a quite unbelievable amount of extra work for her cousin.

Mr. Warne, coming upon his daughter by chance in this very early morning flurry of laundering, expressed himself upon the subject in the gentle but positive way which was his.

"Why do it, my dear?" he questioned. "Are the sheets and towels we use not quite good enough for others?"

"Not half good enough for Lady Jean," responded the laundress, rubbing energetically away—yet carefully, too, for the old linen was not so stout as it once had been.

"You are intentionally deceiving her, aren't you, daughter? Why do that?—since it is not necessary for her comfort."

"But it is. She would shudder at the touch of a cotton sheet. As for a common huck towel——"

Mr. Warne shook his head. "I can't agree with you. So that the sheets and towels are spotless—as your sheets and towels are—the mere degree of fineness is not essential. And if she knew how much labour it costs you, I am very certain she would infinitely prefer to be less of a spendthrift in the matter of quantity."

"I've no doubt she would. But I'd rather wash my fingers off than not give her the fresh towel for her perfect face each time she uses one. I'd like it myself. I'd like a million towels, all as fine as silk. I'd like——" She stopped abruptly, seeing the look upon her father's face. "Oh, I'm sorry!" she flashed at him repentantly. "I truly don't mind being poor in most ways. It's the lack of certain things that go with nicety of living that grinds me most. I shouldn't mind wearing gingham outside, if I could have all the fine linen I want underneath. It's—it's—oh, well, you know! And I'm an idiot to talk about it when the thing we really need is books—books for your starving mind. If I could get you all you want of those——" Her voice broke upon the wish, always strong with her.

"My dear, my mind will never starve while it has the old books to feed upon. Listen, on what a pertinent thought did I come this morning. I was delving in good old Thomas Fuller, of those fine seventeenth-century writers whose works still glow with fire: *'Though my guest was never so high, yet, by the laws of hospitality, I was above him whilst under my roof.'*"

The girl laughed, dashing away a hot tear with the back of a soapy hand. "Trust you to find a classic to turn a tragedy into a comedy," she said. "Go away now, Father Davy, and I'll soon be through. It's a poor washerwoman I am to be thinning my suds with brine!"

CHAPTER IX

A REASONABLE PROPOSITION

"You'll come, too, Georgiana dear?" Jeannette, furrily clad for a walk with James Stuart, stood in the doorway looking back. "Please do."

"Come, George;—you need a good tramp," Stuart urged at Jeannette's elbow.

He looked the picture of anticipation. He had undertaken getting the visitor into training by increasingly long daily walks, and the result was proving eminently satisfactory. At the end of the first half of the visit Jeannette was looking wonderfully well and happy—hardly the same girl who had come to the little village to try if she could endure such life as was likely to be offered her there.

"Thank you, my dears, nothing could persuade me. Run along and leave me to diversions of my own," answered Georgiana gayly.

So they had gone, Jeannette wafting back a kiss, Stuart waving an enthusiastic arm. Georgiana had smiled at them, had closed the door softly behind them—and had immediately banged to another conveniently near at hand, one opening into a small clothespress under the stair landing.

"Diversions of my own!" she repeated with emphasis. "Happy phrase! I wonder what they think my diversions are—with this family to look after. Well, you got yourself into it, George Warne. You can stick it out if it kills you."

36

She deliberately thumped one door after another all the way along her progress through the empty rooms and up the stairs to the second floor. Her father was away for the afternoon on a rare visit to a neighbour who had sent for him, an old parishioner, who, falling ill, longed for the gentle offices of his friend and long-time minister. As for Mr. Jefferson, this was the time of day when he was always away on his usual long walk. It was a comfort to be alone in the quiet house—and to bang and thump.

In her room Georgiana arrayed herself in a heavy red sweater, then ascended to the attic and stood eying the great hand loom of antique pattern, a relic of an earlier century. It was equipped with a black warp, upon which a few rows of parti-coloured woof had been woven.

"Diversions!" she repeated, and shook her round fist at the lumbering object.

Then she sat down on the old weaver's bench and began to weave with heavy, jarring thuds which shook the floor, as with strong arms she pulled and pushed and sent her clumsy shuttle flying back and forth. The attic was very cold; but she was soon warm with the violent exercise and presently had discarded the sweater and was working away with might and main.

"Go at it—go at it!" she was saying to herself. "Jealous idiot that you are! Jealous of Jeannette, of her clothes, her money, her beauty, her power to attract—jealous because Jimps likes her so well—because Father Davy looks at her with the eyes of an appreciative uncle—because Mr. E. C. Jefferson talks to her as if he enjoyed it. Pound—pound—pound away at the old loom till your arms ache, and see if you can get the nonsense out of you!"

"I beg your pardon," said a deep voice at the top of the narrow stairs not far away.

The loom stopped with a jerk as the weaver flashed round upon the head and shoulders protruding above the rafters. "Oh! I'm sorry! Did I disturb you?" cried Georgiana, fire in her voice. She did not look in the least sorry. "I thought you were out, too. And I'm just over your head. Of course you came up to——"

"No, I didn't," replied Mr. Jefferson. He ascended two steps more, looking curiously at the loom "I came up because I thought something extraordinary had happened up here and I ought to find out about it."

"Nothing extraordinary, merely something very ordinary. I do this whenever I have time and the coast is clear. You usually go out at this hour," she said accusingly.

"So I do. I came back just now, when I saw Miss Crofton and Mr. Stuart starting off alone, in hopes that you might consent to go with me. It's a great day. Won't you?"

"Thank you, no," the girl replied. "I'm behind with my work. These rugs are orders very much overdue. I've been rather delayed lately, since my machine is so noisy I can't work when anybody is on the second floor."

"Please never mind me," urged her visitor. "I can time my work to fit in with yours, if you need to make haste. But that must be a rather strenuous business. It's a very old affair, isn't it? Do you mind if I look at it? I never saw one of just that pattern."

"I mind very much," replied Georgiana crisply, moving off the bench and standing on the floor. "But that's no reason why you shouldn't examine the Monster if you like. That's what I call it. I'll run down and be back when you are through."

And this she would have done, but that he barred her way.

"But I won't," he said gravely, "if you prefer that I should not. Come back, please! I'm intruding, and I'll apologize and go."

The light from a dusty attic window fell full on her face as she stood, and he saw that in it which made him look again.

"Miss Warne," he said gently, "something is wrong, I'm afraid. Can't I be of use to you in some way? The reason I wanted to look at this loom was that I saw your last two strokes with the bar as I came up, and I recognized what a tremendous push you had to give. I'm something of a mechanic and I wondered if I couldn't do a bit of oiling, perhaps, to make it easier. I'm afraid it's tiring you unduly."

"I need to be tired," she said, low but vehemently. "I'm in a black mood, and the more I tire myself the quicker I shall get the better of it. Now you know. I suppose you never have black moods."

"Do I not? So black that I could grind myself under my own heel. Do you have them, too? I might have known by the look of you."

"You don't look as if you ever had them," she said rather curiously, her eyes on his quiet face.

"Ah, you can't always tell—luckily. It's pretty cold up here. Are you sure you wouldn't do better to take a run in the wind with me? You know somehow heavy tasks look lighter after a breath of outdoor air."

"So you know what heavy tasks are?" For the life of her she could not resist the question.

He looked steadily back at her, smiling a little. His eyes were very clear in their quiet scrutiny. She felt as if he saw much that she would prefer to conceal. "I have known a few that seemed to me fairly heavy at the time," he said. "Afterward, I was thankful to have had them—to prepare me for heavier ones."

"Oh—but they weren't the same dismal round——"

"Weren't they? Most tasks are. But I never had one quite like this. I am concerned for you, lest this prove too heavy. Now that I am here—do you really mind so very much if I look the machine over?"

She permitted it, and she did not run away as she had meant to do. Presently he asked for a screw-driver and a can of oil, and when she had procured them he did a number of things to the cumbersome loom, the result of which, when she attacked it once more, proved that he had relieved to a certain extent the hardest of her efforts.

"But it is still much too severe for any woman," he said seriously, standing, oil can in hand, a little lock of hair, shaken down by his labours, straying across his forehead. "Please tell me, and don't think me merely curious—is there no way in which you can add to your resources except this? You have a college training——"

"And no way whatever to make use of it," she exclaimed with some bitterness. "But I can weave, and I have a feeling for colour and form and can work out effects which find a market. Hand-woven rugs bring their price these days. Really, Mr. Jefferson, I am no subject for pity and——"

"You don't want it. Let me assure you that I don't feel a particle. To be young and strong and fit for hard work is no cause for pity. But—I have reason for persisting in my inquiry. You see, I happen to know of some one in need of such training as you undoubtedly have. Would you consider giving a few hours daily to one who needs a copyist and critic?"

Georgiana scanned his face with intent, incredulous eyes. Then, "Do you mean yourself?" she questioned.

"I mean myself. I hesitate to mention that I am the candidate, knowing that that admission must instantly create a prejudice against me." He was smiling a little. "But I state an actual fact. I have reached a point in my labours where I need a copyist. Do you think it possible that I may secure one without sending away for her?"

"I must suspect you," she said slowly and with rising colour, "of manufacturing a need. It is very, very kind of you, Mr. Jefferson—but I think I must continue to weave my rugs."

"But I am not manufacturing a need," he insisted. "I declare to you that I have been on the point of consulting you for some time. If it had not been that your days seemed very full with your guest and your housewifery, I should have put it to you before now. I am in earnest, Miss Warne. Won't you, as a matter of everyday business, lend me your eyes and your hand—and your critical judgment? If you can't do it while Miss Crofton is here, may I engage your spare time after she goes? Please don't deny me." He began to descend the stairs. "I won't stay for an answer," he said. "Think it over, will you? And please don't refuse until you have consulted your father."

"Why do you ask that?"

"Because I know he will look at it as any man would, without unreasonable prejudice against accepting a business proposition simply because it happens to come from a temporary member of the household. It takes a woman to bother about that."

With this straight shot he left her, laughing back at her as he descended in a way that went far toward disarming her, though she would not at once admit it. Instead, she went back to her loom, putting into the next section of weaving a quite unnecessary amount of force purely from tension of mind over the possibilities opened up by this most unexpected offer. There was no denying that it was precisely the sort of thing which she had often longed to do, and for which, she knew, as he had suggested, she was more than ordinarily well fitted. It was impossible, as she had said, not to suspect the lodger of creating a want to fit her need of earning money, yet there could be no doubt of the fact that any writer of books who draws upon all manner of collected notes and reference books for his material must be able to make valuable use of an assistant in a variety of ways.

Why should she not take him at his word? Well, she would think of it. And meanwhile—suddenly—the black mood was gone!

CHAPTER X

STUART OBJECTS

That night, after Mr. Jefferson's unexpected proposal that she should assist him in his literary work, Georgiana, running out upon an errand in the business part of the village, encountered James Stuart. This had been a not infrequent happening in days past, but since Jeannette's arrival it had not once occurred. Stuart was much at the house, but not for a fortnight had Georgiana had ten minutes alone with him.

That he welcomed the chance as well as she was evident from his first word: "Great luck! At last I get you to myself for half a wink without a soul around. Where are you going? Wherever it is, you don't go back to the house till you've given me what I want."

"And what's that?" queried Georgiana.

Her tone was cool in spite of herself. She had missed the almost daily walks and talks with Stuart, glad as she had been to have him do his effectual part in helping her entertain her guests. And there had been, as she was obliged to confess to herself, a sense that if he had been very anxious not to lose altogether her society he would have managed, in spite of lack of ordinary opportunity, to bring about such meetings. How much she could feel the absence of his companionship she had not dreamed until she had been tried.

After the friendly village fashion of intimate acquaintance he lightly grasped her arm in its covering of the scarlet-lined military cape she always wore on such walks, and turned her from her course toward a side street leading away, instead of toward, the centre she had been approaching. She protested, but he was laughingly determined and she yielded. It was good, undeniably good, to have Jimps by her side again, and hear his voice in his old eagerly devoted tones in her ear. That he was really overjoyed at coming upon her in a free hour it was impossible to doubt.

"My word! George, but you've kept me on short rations lately," he began accusingly. "One would think you had suddenly put me on a diet list. Nothing but sweets, contrary to the usual prohibitions of the medical men for the husky male! Do you think I have no appetite for the good substantial food? Parties and drives and candy-pulls, always with the lovely guest, and never an old-time hobnob with my chum! What's the matter with you, George? What have I done?"

"But such sweets! And so soon they will be gone, and nothing for the hungry youth but plain bread and butter. How absurd of you to complain!"

"Bread and butter! Beefsteak and mushrooms, you mean; roast turkey and cranberry sauce! A fellow can live on them. But not on eternal honey and fudge—with my apologies to the lady."

"I should say so, Jimps. You're outrageous, and you don't mean it. I wouldn't walk another step with you if you did."

"She's undoubtedly the sweetest thing on earth," admitted Stuart. "There are times when I think I'd like to ask her to marry me on the spot—if she'd have me, which she wouldn't—me, a farmer! She dazzles me, bewitches me, makes me all but lose my head. And then I look at my chum, the girl I've known all my life, and I think—well, sugar is all right, but you can't get on without salt—and pepper—and ginger—and——"

"Jimps!" In spite of herself Georgiana was laughing infectiously, and Stuart joined her. "How absolutely ridiculous! I sound like a whole spice box, and nothing but the 'bitey' spices at that."

"That's what you are," declared James Stuart contentedly. "And when I'm with you I have no hankering after sugar. Mustard plasters for me; they're warming."

They walked on, the spirit of good fellowship keeping step with them. If Georgiana had allowed herself to believe that Stuart was completely absorbed with the enchantments of the beautiful guest, she now discovered that, quite as he had said, the enchantment was by no means complete and he had not lost appreciation of the old friendship and what it meant to him. This was good to feel. It was all she wanted. If she had been guilty of a creeping sense of jealousy as she watched Stuart and Jeannette together, so evidently enjoying each other's society to the full, it was because it made her suddenly and unpleasantly understand what it would be to her to live her days in this commonplace little village without Stuart at her right hand. But here he was, literally at her right hand, and he was making her walk with him, not a beggarly square or two out of her way, but a good three miles around a certain course which once entered upon could not be cut short by any crossroads. And all the way he was telling her, as he had always done, all manner of intimate things about his affairs, and asking her of hers.

Before the circuit had been made Georgiana had done that which an hour before she would have thought far from her intention, natural as such a procedure would have been a month ago, before Jeannette came—she had told Stuart of Mr. Jefferson's offer. If the truth must be confessed, after suffering the mood which had only lately been dissipated, she could not resist producing the effect she knew, if Jimps were still Jimps, was bound to be produced. Such is woman!

Quite as she had foreseen, he was aroused on the instant. The generous sharing of Georgiana Warne with other aspirants for her favour had never been one of James Stuart's characteristics, open-hearted though he was in every other way. He stopped short in the snowy path, regarding her sternly while she smiled in the darkness. This was balm for a heavy heart, indeed, this recognition she had of his disapproval even before he jerked out the quick words:

"Great Scott! You don't mean to tell me you'd do it! Spend hours every day working with E. C. Jefferson? Not a bit of it. Not so you'd notice it! Tell him to go to thunder!"

"James McKenzie Stuart! What a tone to take! Why on earth should you object?" Georgiana's tone was rich and sweet and astonished—it certainly sounded astonished.

"Because you're my chum, my partner; and I won't have you going into partnership with any other man—not much!"

"Partnership! Secretaries and stenographers aren't partners——"

"Aren't they, though! The most intimate sort. And a fellow like Jefferson, full of books and literary lore—he'd be breaking off work half his time to talk Montaigne and Samuel Johnson and—and Bernard Shaw with you. And you'd drink it all in with those eyes of yours and make him think——" Georgiana's uncontrollable laughter halted but did not stop him. "What's his work, anyhow? Writing a History of Art?" growled Stuart, marching on, with Georgiana beside him bursting into fresh mirth with every step. Her heart was quite light enough now; no danger that she had lost her friend!

"I've no idea what it is, but it's certainly not that. He seldom speaks of art in any form—except literary art, of course. I've an idea it's scientific research of some sort."

"Then why isn't he in a laboratory somewhere, boiling acids? Why isn't he digging in city libraries or hunting scientific stuff over in Vienna? Vienna's the place for him. I wish him there fast enough," irritably continued this asperser of other men's vocations.

"His research work has undoubtedly been done; he has pile upon pile of notebooks and papers on file. His handwriting is a fright; that's probably what he wants me for—to make it legible to the printer."

"Let him send for a typist then; that's what he needs if he writes an illegible fist. You can't typewrite."

"I could learn, if necessary. I've often wished I could."

"You could learn! Yes, you could learn to come when E. C. Jefferson whistled, I've no doubt! Oh, I beg your pardon, George—you needn't turn away. Nobody could ever fancy you coming at any man's whistle. I'm just seeing red, that's all, at the thought of your going into a thing like this, that's bound to throw you two into the closest sort of relations."

"That's all nonsense, Jimps. You're behaving like a little boy. And you know I can't afford to lose a chance like this. You know how slow the rug-weaving is——"

"You don't mean you're still at that?"

"Of course I am. The prices are very good now, and I'm——"

"Then you certainly can't lose them to go into copying manuscript by hand. Stick to the weaving; that's my advice."

"Mr. Jefferson saw the loom to-day. He thinks it too hard work for me," suggested Georgiana slyly.

This was a telling shot, for Stuart had often expressed himself in similar fashion in the past. As was to have been expected, her companion became instantly more nettled than ever.

"Oh, he does, does he?" he said hotly. "I'd like to know what affair it is of his. You know well enough I've protested scores of times against that weaving——"

"And now you tell me to stick to it!"

He wheeled upon her. His tone changed: "George, I know I'm absolutely unreasonable. Of course I don't want you pulling that back-breaking thing. I don't want you to have to hustle for money any sort of way; that's the truth. What I do want is—to keep you away from every other earthly beggar but myself!"

"O James Stuart, how absurd! That's not a brotherly attitude at all."

"The role of brother isn't always entirely satisfying," retorted Stuart under his breath. "You know well enough you've only to say the word and I——"

"Jimps dear"—Georgiana's voice was very gentle now—"remember we've left all that boy-and-girl sentimentalizing behind. It was quite settled long ago that you and I were to be brother and sister, 'world without end.' And I know you mean it as brotherly, all this fuss about my taking a bit of perfectly reasonable employment for just a little while."

"Little while? Do you know how long he expects to be at work on that confounded book?"

"No; do you?"

"He told me one night when we were smoking together that he had given himself a year to do this work in. He came in January; this is April. Do you wonder I'm a bit upset at the notion of my best friend's going into harness with him for a year?" Stuart's tone was grim.

Georgiana, now in wild spirits with the relief from her fears, and the suddenly opening prospect of a long period of such work as she dearly loved, had some ado to keep her state of mind from showing. "It doesn't follow," she said, outwardly sober, "that he intends to spend that whole year here."

"He will—if he gets you for a side partner. A man would be a fool not to."

"That's a great tribute—from a brother," admitted Georgiana, smiling to herself. "But as far as our lodger is concerned, you need have no fear of any but the most businesslike relations, even though I worked beside him—as is quite improbable—for a year. He's not that sort."

"Not what sort? Don't you fool yourself. He's human, if his mind is bent on writing a book. And you are—Georgiana!"

"Jimps, there's a path in your brain that's getting worn too deep to-night. Come—let's hurry home. Jeannette will wonder what's become of me."

"Let her wonder. George, are you going to do this thing?"

"Of course I am."

"No matter how I feel about it?"

"Why, Jimps—really, do you think you have any right——"

"Georgiana, I—love you!"

"No, Jimps, you don't. Not so much as all that. You have a brotherly affection——"

"Brotherly affection doesn't hurt; this does," was Stuart's declaration.

"No, it doesn't, my dear boy. You're just made with a queer sort of jealous element in your composition, and when something happens to call it out you think it's—something quite different," explained Georgiana rather lamely. "You know perfectly that you and I

42

fit best as good friends; we should be awfully unhappy tied up together in any way. Why, we settled that long ago, as I reminded you just now."

"It seems to have come unsettled," Stuart muttered.

"Then we must settle it again. Truly—you mean everything to me as a brother, friend, chum—whichever you like, and I—well, I should feel pretty badly to lose you. But——"

"I wish you'd leave it there. I don't fancy what you're going on to say."

"Then I'll not say it. Come, Jimps, give me your hand on the old compact."

"I will—on exactly one condition." Stuart stood still and faced her in a certain secluded spot just where the snowy path was on the point of turning into a wider, well-used thoroughfare.

"What is it? Make it a fair one."

"It is fair—the fairest between a man and a woman. It's this: leave the 'never-never' clause out. I'll agree to any terms of friendship you insist on if—well, just leave me a chance, will you—dear?"

There was a brief silence while Georgiana considered. She had not expected this, certainly not just now, when her long-time friend frankly admitted the drawing power of the winsome visitor. As she had implied, there had been between them, in the days of dawning maturity while they were yet in school together, certain youthfully tender vows which they had later exchanged for the more carefully considered terms of the warm but less sentimental friendship which had now existed for some years. That Stuart was really dearer to her, more a necessary part of her life than she had realized, had been made disconcertingly clear to her by the totally unexpected pangs she had suffered during the last fortnight, when it had seemed to her that she was likely to lose the fine fervor of his devotion. Now, however, that she was assured of his intense loyalty, she was the old Georgiana again, ready to stand beside her friend to the last ditch, if need be, but wholly unwilling to bind herself to his chariot wheels while no ditches threatened.

"'Never' is a big word," she said finally. "It isn't best to say 'never' about anything in this life."

"Then you won't ask me to say it?" His voice was eager.

"Not if you don't want to, Jimps."

"I don't. There was never anything surer than that. Give me your hand—chum."

She gave it. "All right—chum."

He had pulled off his own glove; he now gently drew off hers, and the two warm hands clasped. "Here's our everlasting friendship," he said, with a little thrill in his low voice. "Nothing shall come between us except—love."

"Jimps! That's not the old compact at all."

"It's the new one then. Isn't it sufficiently ambiguous to suit you?"

"It's much too ambiguous."

"I can make it plainer——"

"Perhaps you'd better leave it as it is," she admitted, recognizing danger.

"As you say."

He held her hand for a minute in such a close grasp that it hurt her, but she did not wince. Ah! if she might just have this pleasantly satisfying relation with the man whose presence in her life meant warmth and light and even happiness on the hard road of everyday routine, and then have somehow besides the contentment which comes of accomplishment along a line of chosen activity—and still remain free for whatever God in heaven might send her of real joy, she could ask no better.

"Jimps, I'm perfectly contented," she said radiantly, as they walked on.

"That's good. I wish I were."

"What would make you?"

"Your promise to earn your money making rugs—with me to help you."

"But you couldn't!"

"I could learn."

"Oh, how absurd! You haven't time, if there were no other reason."

He did not answer, and, since they were now back in the village and nearing the object of Georgiana's errand, no more was said until they were once again on their way homeward. They walked in silence until they reached the very doorstep of the manse. Then Stuart made one more protest.

"Not even to please me, George?" he asked, as she stood on the step above him, leading the way in to Jeannette and the warm fireside.

"Jimps, I'm sorry you feel that way about it. But I've talked with Father Davy and he agrees that it's a godsend. There's no reason in the world I could give Mr. Jefferson for refusing to help him when he needs it, and when I need it, too. Therefore—I'm sorry, Jimps, since you are so strange as to care—but I've made up my mind."

"You'll excuse me if I don't come in to-night," he said, and turned away.

She stood looking comprehendingly after him as he left her, then ran in and closed the door. The mood which held her now was so far from being black that it was rosy red.

CHAPTER XI

BORROWED PLUMES

"Uncle David, I was never so sorry to come to the end of any visit as I am this one," said Jeannette Crofton. She was holding Mr. Warne's frail hand in both her own, and looking straight into the young gray-blue eyes which looked affectionately back at her. She was dressed for her departure, and the great closed town car which had brought her was waiting at the door.

Near her stood Georgiana and James McKenzie Stuart. Mr. E.C. Jefferson had just appeared in the background, come to bid the guest farewell.

"You have given us much pleasure, my dear," responded Mr. Warne, "and if you have received it as well, the balance is pretty evenly struck."

"I might have stayed two days longer," declared Jeannette with evident longing, "if it hadn't been for that sister of mine. I'm sure she could have had a birthday dance without me—but no! How I wish I were taking you all with me—even you, Mr. Jefferson," she added with one of her adorable smiles, as she turned to him; "you, whom I can't possibly imagine caring to dance a step, not even with the prettiest girl I could find for you."

"You almost make me wish I knew how to dance a step," said Mr. Jefferson, advancing to take her hand. "As it is, I can at least wish that prettiest girl a partner worthy of her grace."

"While I am wishing," exclaimed Jeannette with characteristic impulsiveness, "why in the world don't I bring about my own wishes? Oh, where have my wits been! Georgiana, darling, run and dress and go with me! I'll send you back to-morrow in the car. And you, too, Mr. Stuart! Oh, come, both of you, and dance at Rosalie's birthday fête to-night!

44

Please—please do!" She turned to Mr. Warne. "Mayn't she, Uncle David? Couldn't you manage to spare her just for twenty-four hours?"

They looked at one another, smiling, hardly believing that the gay suggestion was a serious one.

But by Jeannette, accustomed to having her own way once a way had occurred to her, all objections were thrust aside. "Oh, but you must come!" she cried. "I'll not take no!"

"Come and talk it over a minute with me, crazy child," bade Georgiana; and she drew her cousin out of the room, where she could state the great difficulty which, being a woman, had instantly assailed her. "Jean, I hate to quash such a glorious idea, but—I shall have to be frank—clothes!"

"With loads of frocks hanging in my wardrobe at home? And half of them too trying for me to wear at all, while they would suit you perfectly. Nonsense! Oh, hurry and make ready. James Stuart will go if you will; I saw it in his eyes."

It could not be refused, this tempting invitation, with such a lovely tyrant to enforce her will. One word, however, did James Stuart and Georgiana Warne exchange in a corner before they capitulated.

"George, my evening togs—they've been put away for the four years since I left college. They must be about the most hopelessly ancient cut conceivable to eyes like hers. Shall I risk looking like a rustic in such a house as that?" But Stuart's eyes were eager as a boy's.

"I'll not go if you won't, Jimps. As for rusticity, I can keep you company. Can you bear to lose such a frolic? I can't."

"Neither can I, hang it! All right, I'll be a sport if you will," agreed Stuart with a laugh, and rushed away to pack a bag in short order, all the zest of irrepressible youth, in one who had been forced by circumstance to foreswear most of the joys of youth for stern labour, coming uppermost to bid him make merry once more at any cost of after fall of spirits.

"Thank goodness I've had the sense always to keep the latest of Jeannette's 'Semi-Annual' tailored suits pressed and trim," thought Georgiana as she dressed. "This is a year behind the extreme style, but I know perfectly well I look absolutely all right in it, and my hat, having once been hers, is mighty becoming and smart, if it is a make-over. It's lucky I can do those things; that's one benefit of going to college, anyhow."

A few other "make-overs" in the way of dress accessories, all of exquisite material, on account of their source, and daintily preserved because of their frailty after having served two owners, went into her traveling bag. For the dance itself, since there was no other way, she was not loath to accept Jeannette's generous offer, and, being a very human creature, could not help looking forward with delight to the prospect of finding herself arrayed in such apparel as would successfully sustain any scrutiny which might be brought to bear upon the country cousin. As for Stuart, she had no fears for him, for his years of college life had made him an acceptable figure upon any occasion, and she was confident his broad shoulders and fine carriage could atone for any slightly antique cut of lapel or coat-tail.

Altogether, it was a very happy young person who embraced Mr. David Warne, shook hands with Mr. Jefferson, and ran down the path to the great car in the wake of Jeannette, and followed by James Stuart looking extremely personable. Well-cut clothes were the one extravagance Stuart allowed himself now that he was immured for at least the early half of his life, as he expected, upon the farm of his inheritance.

"Well, well, I'm glad to have my little girl run away for a few hours," said Father Davy, from the window where, with Mr. Jefferson at his shoulder, he stood watching for the final wave of Georgiana's hand. "She has enjoyed her cousin's visit, but it has meant considerable extra labour for her. This seems a fitting return for Jeannette to make."

"One can hardly blame Miss Crofton for wanting to prolong her enjoyment of your daughter's society," observed Mr. Jefferson, his eyes watching closely the laughing faces behind the glass as the travelers settled themselves. "I can imagine one's feeling a very decided emptiness in a place which she had left."

"There, they're off!" announced Mr. Warne, waving his slender arm with eagerness, his delicate features alight with pleasure in this unexpected happening. "Emptiness, you say, Jefferson?" he added as the two turned away, with the car out of sight down the snowy road. "That quite expresses it. Even for a few hours I am conscious of a distinct sense of loneliness without Georgiana. Her personality is one which makes itself felt; it has individuality, audacity; even—I think—that curious quality which for want of a better name we call 'charm.' Am I too prejudiced?"

He placed himself upon his couch, plainly very weary with the flurry of the last hour. He lay looking up at Mr. Jefferson, who had lingered a little before going back to the work which loudly called to him. It was quite possible for the younger man to comprehend how desolate was the gentle invalid's feeling at being left, if only for a day and a night, in the care of the friendly neighbour who was to minister to his needs and who was already to be heard bustling about the dining-room, laying the table for the coming meal.

"You may be prejudiced," admitted his companion, "but it is a prejudice which can be readily forgiven—and even shared," he added, smiling.

"Her cousin," pursued Mr. Warne slowly, "would outshine her in beauty and in sweetness of disposition, perhaps, though I doubt if Jeannette has ever had a fraction of the tests of character and endurance my girl has had."

"She surely never has," agreed the other. "And as for mere sweetness of disposition, there are other qualities which make their own appeal."

A whimsical smile appeared upon the pale face resting against one of Georgiana's crimson couch pillows. "How she would make me signals of distress and warning," he mused, "if she could hear me carrying on an antiphonal service in her praise with our lodger, who, she would consider, knows her not at all. Well, well——

  "'Man, she is mine own,
 And I as rich in having such a jewel,
 As twenty seas, if all their sand were pearl,
 The water nectar, and the rocks pure gold.'
You'll forgive an old man's romanticism, Mr. Jefferson, I hope?"

"You are one of the youngest men I know. And if you may quote Shakespeare to your purpose, I may quote good old Doctor Holmes," said Mr. Jefferson, drawing the pillow into an easier position as he spoke:

  "'He doth not lack an almanac
 Whose youth is in his soul.'"

To Georgiana Warne, a year out of college, and during that year having sorely missed the many gayeties of the life she had known for four happy years, the present experience was delightful. She enjoyed every minute of the swift drive over the sixty miles to her cousin's home, enjoyed the arrival there, the meeting with the family and their house guests assembled for afternoon tea, the installment in a luxuriously furnished room where Jeannette presently brought her an armful of gowns to choose from for the evening. A small dinner was to precede the dance, and all sorts of scheming for Georgiana's pleasure had been fermenting in Jeannette's brain on the way home.

46

"I've arranged with Rosalie to put you next her special prize—the most wonderful man she knows. All her set are crazy over him, though he belongs in ours fast enough. It's Miles Channing, just home after a year's travel, and as good looking as any illustrator ever drew. You see you simply must be your most brilliant self. And here's the way to do it—wear this!"

She held up before Georgiana's disconcerted gaze such a marvel of colour and cunning as brought a gasp of astonishment and a quick denial: "Oh, my dear! Not that—for me. It's bad enough to wear your things at all, but don't give me something that will make everybody look at me, like that!"

"That's precisely what I want," laughed Jeannette. "And this is a thing I haven't ventured to wear and never shall, though I'm wild to do it. But I couldn't carry it off; you can. Those orange shades will be glorious with your eyes and hair. Besides, as for making you conspicuous above the rest, on account of any gorgeousness of colour or eccentricity of style, it simply can't be done these days. So put this on and see for yourself. You needn't wear it, of course, if you don't like it; but you will."

Reluctantly Georgiana allowed a slim French maid to slip the marvel of her country's art over the bared shoulders, and the next minute she was staring at herself in a long mirror, while Susette clasped her hands, and gay young Rosalie, passing the door at the moment and summoned to the private view, cried joyously:

"Oh, Georgiana, you're perfectly stunning! Of course you must wear it, and you'll be the star of the evening."

Rosalie rushed on, having settled the questions out of hand, after the manner of the youthful. Jeannette was laughing as she called her mother in to confirm the decision.

Mrs. Crofton, languidly interested, surveyed her niece with approval. She was an impressive lady, was Aunt Olivia, and was accustomed to have her opinion carry weight. "It suits you, my dear," was her verdict. "Those who can wear such daring effects should do it, for every scene needs points of light and intensity."

"And these other frocks," Jeannette declared, pointing to them where Susette had spread them out upon the bed, "are just colourless baby things that anybody can wear."

"They look exquisite to me," regretted Georgiana, eying them wistfully.

Somehow, now that she was here, she did not so much enjoy the thought of appearing in borrowed finery, and, since it must be done, would have preferred the simplest white frock in Jeannette's wardrobe. But this was not to be without displeasing her hostesses, and she reluctantly submitted. Susette begged leave to arrange her hair, Jeannette hunted out silk stockings and slippers to match the frock, and Rosalie contributed the long white gloves which completed the costuming.

When Georgiana was ready to descend she took one last look at the girl in the long mirror, and turned to Jeannette, herself a picture in the delicate colourings which she affected and which set off her golden beauty. "I feel like the old woman in the nursery song," she said, "doubtful of my identity."

"But you must admit you're simply glorious," cried Jeannette. "I knew you were a beauty, but I didn't know you were such a raving one as this."

"I'm no beauty," denied Georgiana with spirit. "It's just the clothes. But you—I never saw anything so enchanting as you to-night."

"Delightful! I'm so glad, for—there's somebody I want to enchant. Come on," and Jeannette led the way.

At the foot of the great staircase, about a wide fireplace, Georgiana saw James Stuart with a group of other young men, and noted swiftly that there was no too-striking contrast to be noted between her friend and his faultlessly attired companions, except that his face and hands wore a deeper coat of winter tan than theirs, and he looked stronger and more virile than any of them. And even in his outdoor colouring, there was among them one who rivalled him, the one who, as Georgiana instantly guessed, was the lately arrived traveler. A moment later she met Stuart's eyes and saw his look of astonishment as he gazed at her.

Presently, when those whom she had not already met had been made known to her, she found Stuart at her elbow. "Am I dreaming?" said his voice in her ear, "or is this my chum? I'm almost afraid to speak to you!"

"You look awfully nice, Jimps," she returned under her breath. "Yes, isn't it absurd for me to be peacocking like this? But they made me do it."

"You take my breath away."

"Look at Jean," she whispered. "Isn't she the loveliest thing you ever saw in your life?"

He looked. "You and she are a pair," he admitted.

Jeannette came up to them with the tall traveler, and Georgiana found herself looking up into a pair of dark eyes whose glance told her that their owner found her worth studying intently. Miles Channing was of the sort who waste no time in preliminaries. By the time she had sat out half the dinner by his side she felt as if she had been under fire for hours. All her youth and wit responded to his sallies, and she enjoyed the encounter as keenly as a girl might be expected to do, who for a year had seen no men but the slow village swains—always excepting James Stuart, who was her one reliance in time of famine.

Channing made no attempt to disguise his preoccupation with the most attractive of the few strangers in the set of young people whom he had known for years. Between the dinner and the dance, Jeannette, who had been observing without seeming to observe, dropped a word in Georgiana's ear:

"You've done it, dear. I never saw him lose his head so completely. You'll have to be careful or you'll have all the girls down on you. They're crazy over him, you know—including Rosalie."

"Absurd! I shall never see him again, so what does it matter?" retorted Georgiana.

"Don't be too sure of that. Nothing can stop him when he's interested. And you know you are a witch to-night; anybody would be caught in your snare. I didn't know you were such a clever thing at the game, though I might have guessed it."

"If I weren't, I might take lessons of you," Georgiana gave back. "You have Jimps slightly delirious, I can see. Is he the one you wanted to enchant? I'm sure you've done it."

"Isn't he splendid? He looks so much stronger and more interesting than half these boys I've known all my life. I do want him to have a good time."

"He's having it."

Georgiana was sure of this, but she was having so good a time herself she didn't mind. More than once she had caught Stuart's eyes across the table, and had noted how they were sparkling. The glance the two exchanged might have been interpreted to mean: "Fun, isn't it? You play up to your opportunities and so will I. This won't happen again in our lives, perhaps."

Presently the dancing began, in great rooms cleared for the purpose and decorated with every art of the florist. The music was all of a quality more perfect than any Georgiana had ever heard, and the strains which assailed her ears made her wild to dance to every note. She was besieged by invitations.

"But I haven't danced for more than a year, and I don't know one of the latest steps," she said regretfully.

48

"We'll soon remedy that," promised Chester Crofton, her cousin, who carried her off into an unoccupied room, where the music could yet be heard, and proceeded to teach her. She was easily taught, having all the foundations after four years of practice among college girls, and she was soon able to go upon the floor with young Crofton and the rest.

Miles Channing did not dance, but after watching for a time—while Georgiana was acutely conscious that his eyes constantly followed her—he claimed and bore her off before others could prevent. In a palm-shadowed corner well removed from observation he drew a long breath of content and settled down beside her.

"I hope you will not be too much bored at missing a round or two," he began in the slightly drawling speech which was somehow one of his charms, it was so curiously accompanied by his intent observation. "I haven't danced for so long I can't venture to attempt it, especially with you."

"I should be the most patient of partners, I'm so unaccomplished myself," declared Georgiana.

"Nevertheless I shouldn't want to try you. You dance like a sylph, I like an elephant."

"I don't believe it."

"You do grudge sitting out, then, do you?" he asked.

"Not a bit."

"It wouldn't really matter if you did, for I intend to hold my advantage now I have it. I care more to talk with you than for all the dances on the program. And the time is so short I must make the most of it. You go back to-morrow, I understand?"

"Yes, indeed."

"And you'll not be here soon again?"

"I don't expect to. I'm a very busy person at home and can seldom be spared."

"That means that whoever wants to know you must come to your home?"

Georgiana felt her pulse beats quickening. This was certainly losing no time. She assented to the interrogation, explaining that her father was an invalid and she was his housekeeper. She felt no temptation to represent things to Mr. Channing as other than they were. It was somehow an atonement for appearing in her borrowed attire that she should not allow appearances to deceive this new acquaintance into thinking her home the counterpart of her cousin's. The news did not appear in the least to disconcert him.

"I should like very much to meet your father," Channing said; and Georgiana liked him for taking the trouble to put it in that way. He instantly added: "And I should like still more to see you in your own home. May I have that pleasure?"

"We shall be very glad to see you," she promised, careful of her manner.

"No matter how soon I come?"

"I suppose you will allow me to reach home first?" she questioned gayly.

"Barely. This is Wednesday night. You go home to-morrow—Thursday. May I come Saturday?"

"You have been living on railway schedules so long you have acquired the habit," she gave back with slightly heightened colour. In the course of her experience she had seen more than one young man change his plans after encountering her, but she had never known one to form new ones as quickly as this.

"I have discovered that when one wants to reach a place very much, he can't start too soon," he said very low, with such obvious meaning that she had some difficulty in keeping her cool composure. It was not only his words, but his looks and manner which spoke. She had never dreamed that outside of stories men ever really did begin to fire on sight, like this.

49

The matter settled, Channing began to talk of other things, but through all his speech and acts ran the visible thread of his instant and powerful attraction to her, so that she was conscious of the colour of it. By the time two dances had gone by and she was sought and found by an eager claimant, the girl was quite ready to get away from this new and decidedly disturbing experience. And when, a little later, she allowed James Stuart to try one of the new steps with her, she had a comfortable sense of having got back upon known and solid ground, after having been swimming in a too-swift current.

CHAPTER XII

EARLY MORNING

"You've no idea, Jimpsy," Georgiana said, when she and James Stuart had assured themselves that they were able to suit their steps to each other and were moving smoothly down the floor, "how glad I am to be with some one I know, for a bit."

"Only some one? Not particularly me?"

"Yes, particularly you. My brain needs a little rest."

"There's a compliment for an old friend! But I didn't suppose dancing tired the brain. It's my feet that have bothered me. I've walked all over Jeannette's little toes, but she's perfectly game and won't admit it."

"I thought you and she were getting on beautifully together."

"So we were. I couldn't see how you and Channing got on together, because you went off and hid somewhere. That's not fair with a perfectly new acquaintance."

"Didn't you and Jeannette go off and hide somewhere?"

"We're not new acquaintances."

"Oh, indeed! How old ones are you?"

"A month is a long time compared with one short evening. I never knew, George, you were such a terrific charmer. You've had them all nailed to-night; and as for Channing— well—— Only I suppose he's a shark at the game himself. He shows it. Better look out."

"What an excellent opportunity a dance is for old friends to give each other good advice." Georgiana smiled up into his eyes.

He closed his own for an instant. "Don't do that; it dazzles me."

"Nonsense. You're learning the game yourself. Jeannette's been teaching you. We're all finding each other out to-night. I had no idea she could sparkle so."

"You're the sparkler. She simply glows with a steady light."

"Well, I like that!"

"You like everything to-night. You remind me of a peach—on fire."

"Jimps!" Georgiana's soft laughter assailed his ear. "I believe we're both a bit crazy with this sudden leap into dissipation—such dissipation! Just remember where we'll be to-morrow night."

"I don't want to—except that I'll be with you. We'll talk it all over by your fire, eh?"

"Of course. There'll be that much left, anyhow. Is this over? Thank you, Jimps, for the best dance I've had to-night."

"No use trying it on me," he murmured as he released her. "What's the use of capturing what you've already got?"

50

By and by it was all over and Georgiana was mounting the stairs with Jeannette, smiling back at certain faces in the disordered spaces below, where flowers lay about the floors and a group of young fellows, belonging to Rosalie's house party, were making merry before they broke ranks.

In Jeannette's room by a blazing fire the girls held brief session, sitting with unbound hair and swinging slippered feet, and cheeks still flushed with the night's gayety.

"Jimps and I were imagining ourselves sitting by the fire in our old living-room to-morrow night," said Georgiana softly, staring into the flame with eyes which reflected little points of light. "It will seem like a dream then, but we shall talk it all over, and remember what fun we had, and how lovely everybody was to us—and how beautiful you were in that blue-and-silver frock."

"You dear thing, you ought to have such times often and often!" cried Jeannette. "But—O Georgiana, you have times I envy you! While you are dreaming of our flowers and music I shall be dreaming of the dear old house, and the jolly evenings you gave me there, and envying you—oh, envying you——"

"Envying me! Are you crazy, child, or are you just——"

"Just speaking the truth. You can't think how many times I shall think of you sitting there with your three splendid men——"

"Jean! What are you talking about?"

"About Uncle David, and Jimps, and Mr. Jefferson——"

"But they're not mine," protested Georgiana, laughing. "Except Father Davy."

"Not—Jimps?"

"Oh, of course he's my friend, my very good friend. And Mr. Jefferson's only a 'boarder,'"—she made a little grimace at the word. "You speak as if I had them all about me all the time."

"But you do evenings, don't you?"

"They were there much more while you were visiting me than they will be now. Jimps has heaps of arrears to make up; he let lots of work go while you were there, you must know, my dear. As for Mr. Jefferson—he may never come down any more, now that Jimps won't be going up to beg him to make a fourth for your entertainment. So don't imagine me holding court with those three retainers. It will mostly be just Father Davy and I with a volume of Dumas or Kipling. Isn't it odd how my pale little father loves the red blood of literature?"

"Just the same——" but Jeannette did not finish that. She began afresh: "And oh! how I shall miss you, George—as Jimps calls you. Somehow I must have you before long for a real visit here, or wherever I may be for the summer."

"Thank you, Jean; but I can never get away."

"I'll arrange it somehow. That makes me think—Miles Channing was dreadfully disappointed that you were going in the morning. I've no doubt he will manage to see you off somehow. I think it's too bad of you to insist on going before luncheon. Think how little sleep you'll have."

She gave Georgiana a penetrating look as she said it, but saw only a pair of beautiful bare arms thrown up over a mass of dark locks, as her cousin, with a clever imitation of a half-smothered yawn, answered merrily: "Then we must go to bed this minute or I shall never have strength of mind to get up. And I can't leave Father Davy to the tender mercies of Mrs. Perkins longer than I can help. She'll give him everything that is bad for him, in spite of the best intentions."

It was a wide-awake Georgiana, nevertheless, who, fully dressed for the drive, leaned over Jeannette's bed at ten o'clock that morning and kissed a warm velvet cheek, murmuring: "Don't wake up, Jean. We're just off after breakfast. I'll write soon. You've been a perfect darling, and I'm more grateful than I can tell you."

"Oh, I'm dead to the world, I'm so tired!" moaned the girl in the bed. "I always have to pay up so for dancing all night. But you,"—she lifted languid eyelids to see her cousin's smiling freshness of face and air of vigour—"why, you look as though you had had twelve hours' sleep—and a cold plunge!"

"I've had the cold plunge," admitted Georgiana, laughing. "And I'm 'fit as a fiddle,' as Jimps says. He sent his good-bye to you and told me to tell you he'll never forget you—never!"

"Tell him I'll not let him forget me—or you, either. Oh, how I hate to have you go, both of you!"

Through a silent, sleeping house Georgiana and Stuart stole, the only member of the family up to see them off being Mr. Thomas Crofton himself, the oldest person under the great rooftree.

"My dear, you must come again, you must come often," he urged, holding Georgiana's hand and patting it with a paternal air. He was a handsome man in the early sixties, with graying hair and tired eyes. "You have done a great deal for our Jean; she looks much stronger than when she went to your home. But neither she nor Rosalie can enter the race with you for splendid health. That comes from your country life, I suppose. I envy you, I envy you, my dear."

"Come and see us, Uncle Thomas—do. Father Davy would be so happy; you know he's such an invalid. But his mind and heart are as young as ever."

"I will come; I will drive down some day, thank you, Georgiana. I should like to see David again. Mr. Stuart, come again, come again. Good-bye; sorry your aunt was too much done up to see you off this morning, my dear. Good-bye."

As the two emerged from the door a tall figure sprang up the steps. "What luck! I was passing and I suspected you were just getting off. Good morning! Can you possibly be the girl I saw dancing seven hours ago?"

"I don't wonder you ask, Mr. Channing," laughed Georgiana. "Evening frocks and traveling clothes are quite different affairs."

"Ah, but the traveling clothes are even the nicer of the two, when their wearer looks——" Channing glanced at Stuart standing by. "Confound you, sir!" said he, with a genial grin, shaking hands. "Since you're going to drive all the way home with Miss Warne can't you give me the chance to say something pleasant to her?"

"You can't make it too strong to suit me," observed Stuart—and remained within hearing.

"Saturday, then, if I may," said Channing, looking as far into Georgiana's eyes as he could see, which was not very far. She wore a close little veil, which interfered with her eyelashes, and clearly she could not lift her glance very high.

Then they were off, with Channing waving farewell, his hat high in air. A hand at another window also waved, and Georgiana knew Jeannette had seen this last encounter.

"Well, for sixteen hours' work," remarked James Stuart grimly, as the car gathered headway and the house was left behind, "I should say you had done some fairly deadly execution. Saturday, eh? Why does he delay so long? Isn't to-morrow Friday—and a day sooner?"

CHAPTER XIII

A COPYIST

The old study of David Warne was a square, austerely furnished room on the second floor of the manse, opposite the sleeping-room now occupied by Mr. Jefferson. It contained several plain bookcases, filled mostly with worn old volumes in dingy yellow calf or faded cloth. An ancient table served for a desk, with a splint-bottomed chair before it. On the walls hung several portrait engravings, that of Abraham Lincoln occupying the post of honour among them. The floor was covered with a rag carpet of pleasantly dimmed colours, and an old Franklin stove, with widely opening doors and a hearth with a brass rail, completed the furnishing of the room.

This was the place now swept and dusted and warmed for the joint labours of the writer of books and his new assistant. Mr. Jefferson had moved the materials of his craft to the new working quarters: he had brought up wood for the fire and had made that fire himself, according to the custom he had inaugurated soon after his arrival. The day and hour for the beginning of that which James Stuart insisted on designating as a partnership had arrived. At ten o'clock that April morning, when Georgiana's housework should have reached a stage when she could safely leave it for a more or less extended period, the study door was to close upon the two and shut them away undisturbed for the first details of their affair in common.

Georgiana had been up since before daybreak, planning and executing a system which should make all this possible. Now, at a quarter before ten, with all well in hand, she flew to her room for certain personal touches which should transform her from housewife to secretary. Two minutes before the clock struck she surveyed herself hurriedly in her small mirror.

"You really look very trim and demure," she remarked to her image. "Your colour is a bit high, but that's exercise, not excitement. Still, you are a little excited, you know, my dear, and you must be very careful not to show it. It's a calm, cool, business person the gentleman wants, George, not a blushing schoolgirl. It would spoil it at once if you should look conscious or coquettish. So now—remember. And forget—for the love of your new occupation—forget that Miles Channing is coming again to-night—again, after one short week! What does it matter if he is? Run along and be good!"

Half a minute left in which to run downstairs, kiss Father Davy on his white forehead, and receive his warm "Bless you, dear, and bless the new work. May you be very happy in it!" and to walk quietly upstairs again and knock at the door of the study. It opened under Mr. Jefferson's hand, and to the cheerful sound of snapping wood on the open hearth of the old Franklin stove he bade her enter.

His smile was very pleasant, his steady eyes seemed to take note of everything about her in one quick glance, as he said with a wave of his hand: "Welcome to my workshop! You see I've swept up all the chips, but we'll soon make more."

"You manage to keep your workshop remarkably free from chips," she commented. "You must have a great system of order."

"Pretty fair. I should be hopelessly lost if I let this mass of material become disordered. Will you take this chair? Must we begin at once or may we talk a little first?"

"I think we had better begin. You know there are just two free hours before I must be back downstairs, if you are to eat, this noon."

He laughed and she noted, as she had noted many times before, how young he looked at such moments, grave as his face could be when in repose.

"Very well," he agreed. "I have no doubt you will work at this task as you do at the loom, with all your might, and I shall have to lengthen my stride to keep up with you. But that promises well. One is likely to fall into habits of soldiering when one works alone. You have no idea how carefully I have to keep certain favourite books out of sight when I want to accomplish big stretches of work. And in this room—hard luck!—I see so many old treasures that I'm going to have a bit of trouble in resisting temptation."

His eyes led hers to the old bookcases. She nodded. "It's a shabby old collection, but it's very dear to father's heart."

"It well may be. Gibbon, Hume, Froude, Parton—Lamb, Johnson, Carlyle—Hugo, Thackeray, Reade, and Trollope—Keats, Shelley, and the rest. What matters the binding? Some time I must read you a passage in good old Christopher North that appeals to me tremendously. No, not now, Miss Warne; I see I must fall upon my task without delay or you will be slipping away on the plea of bad faith on my part. Well——"

He turned his chair toward the table and took up a notebook. His face settled instantly into an expression of serious interest.

"I am going to ask you first," said he, "to copy in order upon a fresh sheet each reference which you find marked with a red cross, so that the references may be all together. Be very exact, please, and very legible. German and French words are easily misread by the typist who will put this work finally into copy for the printer."

Georgiana, glancing at the first marked reference, found cause to credit this statement, for it read:

Cagnetto: Zur Frage der Anat. Beziehung zwischen Akromegalie u. Hypophysistumor, Virchow's Archiv., , clxxvi., . Neuer Beitrag. f. Studium der Akromegalie mit besonderer Berücksichtigung der Frage nach dem zusammenhang der Akromegalie mit Hypophysenganggeschwulste, Virchow's Archiv., , lxxxvi., .

"It would be best to print the words as clearly as I can, wouldn't it?" she suggested, suppressing her desire to laugh.

"That depends on your handwriting. Try a line and let me see, please."

When she had shown him a specimen of the peculiarly readable script which she had cultivated in college, he signified his approval with a hearty "Good! That's a splendid hand for work, the hand of a workman, in fact. I congratulate myself. Go ahead with the jaw-breakers, only verifying each reference before you leave it."

Thus the new task began, and thus it continued day after day—not always quite the same, for Georgiana soon recognized that her employer was diversifying her labours as much as he consistently could by changing the nature of the copying. Now and then he refreshed her endurance and rested her tired hand by asking her to read aloud to him several just finished pages of his own writing, walking the floor meanwhile or sitting tipped back in his chair with closed eyes while he listened with ears alert for error of statement or infelicity of phrase, and she wondered at the character of the words she read.

Of course she discovered at once what was the general subject of the book. No essay was this, no work of fiction, no "history of art," as Stuart had scornfully suggested. It could be only the sternest of research and experience which dictated such sentences as these:

The especial dangers to be contended with are that the ethmoid cells may be mistaken for the sphenoids; that we may go too low and enter the pons and medulla; that, laterally, we may enter the cavernous sinus, and above, that we may injure the optic nerve.

It was all more or less of a puzzle to her, but it was one which her taskmaster never explained further than the revelations of each day explained it. She understood that he was a scientist, that he undoubtedly had been an operator in some surgical field or was putting into shape the work of another in that field, but what he now was besides a writer of technical books she had no manner of idea.

"But I really enjoy it, Father Davy," she insisted, when she came down to him one day with hotly flushed cheeks and shaking hand after a particularly protracted siege of copying involved and incomprehensible material. "It's monotonous in a way, but it's intensely interesting, too. Mr. Jefferson is so absorbed in it, it's fun to watch him. To-day he was as happy as a boy over a letter he had just received from a Professor Somebody, a great authority in Vienna. It seemed it absolutely confirmed some statement he had made in a monograph he wrote last year which had been challenged by several scientists. The way he fell to writing his next paragraph after he had read that letter made one imagine he was writing it in his own heart's blood. He read it aloud to me." She laughed appreciatively at the recollection.

"Could you make anything of it?" inquired Mr. Warne with interest.

"Not very much. It was about the pituitary body;—oh, I've come to have a great awe of the pituitary body, it seems to be responsible for so many things. He chuckled over it like a boy, and said to me, 'Forgive these transports, Miss Warne, but this is food and drink to me. I wish I could explain it to you so that you might rejoice over it with me. Some day I will, when we are not so busy.' I hope he will. There's enough that I do understand to make me interested."

"I see you are—and rejoice, my Georgiana. Do you remember what Max Müller says, echoed by many another, *'Work is life to me; and when I am no longer able to work, life will be a heavy burden?'*"

He smiled as he said it, but his daughter read the seldom-expressed longing in the cheerful voice and laid her cheek for an instant against his. "He's quite right. And you have your work, Father Davy, and you're doing it all the time. I think you preach much more effectively now than you did in the pulpit, even when you don't open your mouth. And when you do open it angels couldn't compete with you!"

They laughed softly together, though Mr. Warne shook his head. "It's a curious thing," he mused, "that the weaker the body gets the harder does the mind have to strive to master it. But, thank God—*'so fight I, not as one that beateth the air.'*"

"'Not as one that beateth the air,'" murmured the girl. "I should say not, Father Davy. As one that delivereth hard blows on his own body, his poor, tired body. Oh, if I had one tenth the self-control——"

At which she ran away, as was quite like her, when emotion suddenly got the better of her. The darkest cloud on this girl's life was the frail tenure of her father's existence. The rest could be endured.

The work in the upstairs study went steadily on, in spite of the fact that James Stuart railed and that Miles Channing came at least once in seven days, driving the sixty miles in a long, swiftly speeding car which brought him to the door of the manse before the early May sunset, and which took him back when the shadows lay black upon the silent road. Two hours in the morning, three in the afternoon, Georgiana gave to the rigid performance of the tasks Mr. Jefferson set her, while outside below the windows at which she worked lay her garden, beloved of her affection, beseeching her not to neglect it.

It was hard sometimes not to betray how she longed to be outside, as she wrote on and on, copying the often difficult and uninteresting language of the more technical part of her employer's construction. And one afternoon, lifting her eyes to let them dwell on a great budding purple lilac tree, with the warm breath of the breeze which had drifted across the apple orchard fanning her cheek, and all the notes of rioting spring in her ears, she did draw in spite of herself one deep sigh of longing which she instantly suppressed—too late.

Her companion looked up quickly, noted the flush in the cheek and the hint of a weary shadow under the dark eyes, and suddenly pushed aside his paper. Then he drew it back, blotted it carefully, laid it with a pile of others, and capped his pen. He wheeled about in his chair to face his assistant.

"Put down your work, please," he commanded gently; "precisely where you are. Don't finish that sentence."

Georgiana looked up, astonished. "Not finish the sentence?"

"No. Did you never stop in the middle of a sentence?"

"I'm afraid I have. But I didn't suppose you ever did."

"I don't. But I want you to. Please. That's right. You will know where to start it again to-morrow."

"To-morrow?" In spite of herself her eyes had lighted as a child's might.

"Even so. To-day we are going for a drive in all this beauty—if I can find a horse and some kind of a vehicle, and you will go with me. It's only three o'clock. We can have a long drive between now and the hour when you invariably disappear to make magic for our appetites. How about it?"

"I can keep on perfectly well, you know," she said, with pen still poised above her paper.

"But I can't." He was smiling. "Now that the other plan has occurred to me, I can't keep on."

"Did you see inside my mind?" queried Georgiana, putting away her copying with rapid motions.

"Suddenly I did. I've been rather blind, a hard taskmaster. I've been conscious of what was going on outside when I went for my walks, but the work is absorbing to me and I have kept you too steadily at it. We both need a rest," he added as she shook her head.

CHAPTER XIV

OUT OF THE BLUE

Twenty minutes afterward he drove up to the door with the best that the village liveryman had to give for the highest price his customer could offer—a tall black horse of fair proportions, and a hurriedly washed buggy of the type in vogue in country districts. But as Georgiana went down the path she was conscious that the figure which stood hat and reins in hand awaiting her would lend dignity to any vehicle, short of a wheelbarrow, in which he might be seen to ride.

Then presently the pair were driving along country lanes in the very midst of all the burgeoning beauty of the season, and Georgiana was like a captive bird let loose. Her companion as well responded to the call of Nature at her loveliest, and the tireless worker of the study seemed changed at a word to a bright-eyed idler of the most carefree sort. The two gave themselves up without restraint to the enjoyment of the hour.

"I wonder how long it is," said Mr. Jefferson, letting the reins lie loose at a leafy curve of the road while the black horse willingly walked, "since I have had a drive like this. Not for ten years at least."

"You've lived always in a great city?"

"Since boyhood—in the heart of it."

"And have driven motors, not horses, for those ten years."

"Yes, like everybody else. But I spent all my summers as a boy on my grandfather's farm, and there I drove horses and rode them and did acrobatic feats on their bare backs. I was a wild Indian, a cowboy, and a captain of cavalry by turns. Those were happy days, and on a day like this they don't seem long ago."

"They can't be so dreadfully long ago," she dared, with a glance at the interesting profile beside her.

"Can't they? Don't I look pretty aged compared with your youth?"

"I'm not so remarkably young," she retorted.

"Aren't you? You are about ten years younger than I. That's a big leap and must make me seem a grandfather indeed."

"But you don't know how old I am."

"I could come pretty close to it," said he with a quick look.

"How could you know?"

"When you see a spray of apple blossoms like those"—he pointed toward a mass of pink and white at the stage of perfection beyond an old rail fence—"can't you tell at a glance whether they've been out a day or a week?"

"I should say that if things had happened to them to make them feel as if they'd been out a week when they had been out only two days——"

"A heavy rain, for instance? In that case we should be deceived—perhaps. But in the case of a human being those heavy rains sometimes only mature without fading—— Hello,——what's this?"

A small and very ragged boy had emerged suddenly from a meadow gateway, his face convulsed with pain and fright. He nursed one hand in the other and the colour had deserted his round cheek, leaving it pallid under its freckles. The only house nearby was an abandoned one and there were no others for some distance in either direction.

Mr. Jefferson stopped his horse. "Does it hurt badly, lad?" he asked in the friendliest of tones, which yet had a bracing quality. "Don't you want to let me see if I can help it?"

The boy stood still, tears silently making their way down his face. Giving the reins to Georgiana, Mr. Jefferson jumped out and gently examined the small hand, the middle finger of which, as the onlooker could plainly see, was badly distorted and somewhat swollen. The skin, however, did not seem to be broken.

"We can make that more comfortable right away," the man promised the little boy. "Sit down on the grass for a minute or two, laddie, while I find something I want."

He pulled out a handkerchief, as yet folded and fresh from its ironing, and handed it to Georgiana. "Will you tear that into strips an inch wide, please, while I take a look back here for a bit of wood?" and he disappeared down the road, while Georgiana with the aid of her strong white teeth tore the fine linen as he had bidden, and spoke comfortingly to the little fellow, who seemed glad enough to have fallen into friendly hands.

When he shortly returned Mr. Jefferson was rapidly cutting and whittling a stick into a little splint, which he then wound carefully with a strip of the handkerchief until it was covered from view. Then he took the injured hand in his own capable ones—his assistant had often noted those hands—and said quietly, "I'm going to hurt you just a minute, little man, but you'll be all right, so be game," and in two deft motions he had pulled and twisted the broken finger, and had set it straight as the others, with but one sharp outcry from the owner. In less time than it can be told in, the set finger was bound securely with its neighbouring finger to the padded splint, and the whole neatly bandaged with the torn linen, the entire procedure accomplished with the rapidity and skill of the practised hand. No amateur surgery this, as Georgiana understood well enough.

"There," said Mr. Jefferson, drawing forth another handkerchief as spotless as the first—she wondered if he went always thus provided against emergency—and improvising a little sling in which the bandaged hand swung comfortably, "I think you'll do. Rest a bit and then go home, and tell your mother not to touch that finger for three weeks. By that time it will be as good as new, only be careful with it when you first use it. Good-bye, laddie, and better luck next time."

Georgiana saw the uninjured hand of the boy close over something bright as the man's hand left it, and heard a low sound which might have been almost anything indicative of surprise and joy. Then the black horse was moving on, and Mr. Jefferson was saying: "Weren't we talking about apple blossoms?"

"We had finished with them, I think," Georgiana replied, wondering if he really were going to offer no explanation of the hint of mystery which had been about him ever since her work with him had begun.

But he did not offer any, only went on with the pleasant talk with which he had all along beguiled the way. Georgiana was recognizing this afternoon, more than she had yet done, what a well-stored mind was possessed by this unassuming man, whose manner and speech yet did not lack that quality of quiet assurance which is the product only of genuine knowledge and experience.

The black horse was within a mile of home, passing through the last stretch of woodland which would justify the walking pace, in which, greatly to his astonishment, he was being allowed to indulge at all such points, when a motor car, slowing down beside him, caused him to lay back his ears in displeasure.

Georgiana, turning, beheld the handsome, eager face of Miles Channing as he leaned toward her, his hand hushing his engine as he spoke.

"Miss Warne—Mr. Jefferson—forgive me for stopping you! I should have gone on and waited for you if I had been sure you were on your way home. But I'm a messenger from the Croftons; they beg you to let me bring you back with me to-night." His eyes rested on Georgiana.

"To-night? Is anybody ill?"

"Oh, no, no; nothing like that. It's for quite a different reason they want you; only I'm to ask you not to question me. You're to come on faith, if you will. And they'll agree to have you back in the morning by breakfast-time, if you insist."

Georgiana looked puzzled, but, being human, she was naturally interested and attracted by this mysterious plan. "It's very odd," she mused, "but if father can spare me——"

"I will undertake to see that your father is not lonely this evening," said Mr. Jefferson's quiet voice at her side. "And please don't bother about to-morrow morning or to-morrow at all, if you would like to be away."

"If Mr. Jefferson wouldn't object——" began Channing; but Mr. Jefferson anticipated him.

"Please don't hesitate to go on with Mr. Channing, if you would like to gain a little time," he suggested to his companion. "He will have you at home before I can reach the bend in the road."

Georgiana looked round at him. "I prefer to finish one ride before I begin another," she declared, smiling. "It's only a mile, Mr. Channing; we shall be there nearly as soon as you. Please go on."

It thus came about ten minutes later that James Stuart, walking up to his home from a field where he had been superintending an interesting new departure in cultivation, caught sight first of a now-familiar roadster of aristocratic lines whose appearance thereabouts had become most unwelcome, and shortly thereafter of a less pretentious vehicle, being rapidly drawn by a still more familiar black horse, and occupied by two people whom it gave Stuart no acute pleasure to see together.

"Well, I should say George was displaying her admirers in great shape this afternoon," he said gloomily to himself. "It's a wonder I'm not trailing on behind with a wheelbarrow. But I vow I'd like to know since when her contract with Jefferson has taken them out into the country—and in working hours, too!"

Afterward it was all rather a strange memory to Georgiana when she recalled it. She had flown about to prepare the appetizing early supper with which she was accustomed to serve her small family, and to which she now added a delicacy or two on account of its seeming the natural thing to ask Mr. Miles Channing to remain rather than to allow him to go to the small village hotel. Then she had cleared her table and left the after-work to the neighbour who was to come to the rescue as before. She had dressed with hurried fingers for the trip, and had driven away with a devoted escort who spared no pains to make her feel that he was exceedingly pleased at the success of his mission.

There was no place in her memory for something she did not see nor would have thought of imagining significant if she had seen it. When she left the house Mr. Jefferson was in his room, searching for a book from which to read aloud to his self-assumed charge of the evening. When he heard Georgiana's blithe cry of farewell to her father in the doorway below, he left the bookcase and went with a quick step to the window. He watched the car driven by Mr. Channing out of sight down the road; then he descended to the garden, pipe in hand. Before he returned to the house to take his place by the evening lamp and begin the reading to the gentle invalid stretched on the couch, he had covered many furlongs up and down the straggling pathways and had consumed much more than his usual quota of choice tobacco. And though all about him had been the May environment at its loveliest, through all his marching up and down he had never once looked up.

Miles away, and ever more miles away, Georgiana had flown like the wind in the swift car under its skilfully guiding hand. The drive was a blurred impression of slowly gathering rosy twilight, of the odour of the apple blossoms—somehow a different and more seductive fragrance than it had been in the sunlit afternoon—and always there was the sense of there being beside her a presence which disturbed. Channing's low laugh, his vibrant voice in her ear, the things he said, half serious, half earnest, always full of an only slightly veiled intent—the girl who had spent so many days of her life in hard study or harder housewifery could do no less than yield herself for the hour to the pulse-quickening charm of it and forget everything else.

Just as twilight settled into dusk and for the first time the headlights of the car came on with a long reach like a golden ribbon along the road, Channing, suddenly slowing down, a few miles out of the city, began a rapid speech on a subject so unexpected that it fairly took his hearer's breath away.

"It's not fair of me to tell you, but I've simply got to get in the first word. You must pretend you haven't heard it, but if there's any persuading to be done I want my share, and want it first. Your cousins are going to invite you to sail with them next week for a summer in England after a fortnight in Paris—Paris in June! You don't know what that means; you can't even imagine it. I can—I know it—don't I know it!" He laughed softly. "Since they're to be away and won't need her they'll send down their housekeeper—the most competent person in the world—to stay with your father and make him absolutely comfortable, so you don't have to hesitate on that score."

"It's perfectly wonderful, but"—Georgiana was staring at him through the dusk— "but—oh, I couldn't, Mr. Channing! how could I? Father is so feeble; something might happen."

"Not in summer. Things don't happen to elderly people in summer. It's in winter— pneumonia and things like that. And don't you know he'd be delighted to have you go? He wouldn't let you miss such a chance; I know him already well enough for that."

"But, you see, I'm engaged to work for Mr. Jefferson——"

"Well, he'll be all right; he's a traveled man himself; anybody can see that. He wouldn't stand in the way of your good, not for a moment; of course he wouldn't. He'd urge you to go. Why, there's nothing else for you to do. Think of the glorious summer we'll have— glorious! Why, I——"

"What do you mean? I don't understand." Georgiana felt her cheeks grow scarlet in the darkness.

"Mean? What could I mean? Why, I'm going, too, of course. Sailing when you do. Invited to spend a month in Devon with the Croftons—and you." His voice sank lower. "And that fortnight in Paris—oh, I'll be in Paris, too, no doubt of that! I'll show you what Paris is like on a June evening. Do you think I'd want to send you out of this country if I weren't going, too? Not I—Georgiana!"

CHAPTER XV

"GREAT LUCK!"

"Father Davy, are you sure, *sure*?" begged his daughter.

"Sure that I want you to go, daughter? Very sure. What sort of father should I be if I were willing to deny you this great pleasure merely to insure my own comfort? And I shall be comfortable. Why should I not be, with the good Mrs. Perkins to look after me, and our fine friend Mr. Jefferson to bear me company in the evenings, as often as he can? And with James Stuart, who is like a son—and with your letters arriving with every foreign mail? Dismiss these fears, my dear, and take your happy chance to see something of the Old World. Many a delightful evening will we have together next winter, you and I, over the photographs you will bring back, while you discourse to me of your adventures."

Thus Mr. David Warne in his most reassuring manner, while his daughter studied his delicate, pallid face, her heart smiting her for being willing to leave him to the loneliness she knew, in spite of all his protests, he would suffer in her absence. And yet opportunities like this one did not occur everyday, might not come again in her lifetime. And everybody was conspiring to make it possible for her.

"It goes without saying," Mr. Jefferson had told her at once, "that all other engagements should be cancelled in the face of such an invitation as this. We will all look after your father for you. And as far as your work with me is concerned, don't give it another thought. I shall make rather slower progress without you, of course, but when you return

60

we will take great strides and complete it well within the limit I have set. So go by all means, and good luck!"

As for James McKenzie Stuart, his words of persuasion seemed to be tempered by various other emotions than those of unselfish desire for Georgiana's pleasure.

"Of course it's great, and there's no doubt that you must go," he said. He was sitting upon the rear porch of the manse, looking off toward Georgiana's garden, on the second evening after her return from the hurried drive to the Croftons'. "I'll do all I can for your father, of course. But don't ask me to console the book-writer."

Georgiana laughed merrily. "He'll not need any consolation, Jimps. Nor you either. Jeannette told me to tell you that she'd write to you once a fortnight—if you'd answer."

"No! She didn't say that?"

"Yes, she did, and meant it. I'll write, too, of course. You'll be deluged with letters and picture post-cards. You ought to be satisfied with so much attention."

"Letters are all right—we won't say anything about the post-cards—and I hope you'll both keep your promises. But when I think of all these summer evenings without you——"

He heaved a gusty sigh which Georgiana had no reason to doubt was genuine. How much heavier would be his spirits, if he were told that Miles Channing was to be of the party, she had full consciousness. She was aware of the futility of attempting to keep this unwelcome news from him longer than the day of her departure, but she had not thus far ventured to mention it.

"I shall miss these evenings myself," she said soberly. "After all, Jimps, I expect there'll be nobody gladder to get back home than I. I shall see this old garden in my dreams." Then quickly, as another deep-drawn breath warned her that sentimental ground was dangerous, she cried: "Oh, but, Jimps! I haven't told you of the last and nicest thing that wonderful girl has done for me. She insisted on my bringing home the dearest little traveling suit of some kind of lovely summer serge that doesn't spot and doesn't muss and is altogether adorable. She insists it's not becoming to her, and it really isn't; but I almost know she planned not to have it becoming so she could give it away to me. And a perfect beauty of a little hat—and a big, loose coat, to wear on the steamer, that looks absolutely new, but she vows it isn't, and that she's tired of it. Was ever anybody so lucky as I?"

"It certainly does take clothes to stir up a girl," was Stuart's cynical comment. "Talk of separation and they pretend to be as sad over it as you are; but let 'em think about the clothes they're going to wear and their spirits leap up like soda water."

"Poor old Jimps! Doesn't he know the sustaining qualities of pretty clothes? Too bad! But really it's lucky I have something to sustain me, it's such a pull to make myself go. I didn't suppose I'd ever leave Father Davy this way while he is so feeble, but he's the most urgent of all to send me off, and I know I really can bring him back wonderful pleasure."

Thus the talks ran during the few days which elapsed before Georgiana's departure. Every spare hour was full with preparation, from the packing of the trim little steamer trunk which arrived by express, a gift from Uncle Thomas, to the careful mending and putting in perfect order of every article Father Davy would be likely to wear during the whole period of his daughter's absence. Georgiana's thoughts as she worked were a curious mixture of happy anticipation and actual dread.

"If only I could go as Jeannette is going," she said to herself, "without a care in the world except to plan how she will fill the summer, and to make sure her maid puts in plenty of silk stockings to last till she can buy some more in Paris. When I went to college it was with the fear that I ought not to accept father's sacrifice, even though Aunt Harriet was with him then, and he was far, far stronger than he is now. I've never done anything in my life without a guilty feeling that I ought not to be doing it. Why can't I do now as they all bid me—drop my cares and take my fun, like any other girl? I will—I must. It's only fair!"

The excitement of anticipation grew upon her as the busy hours slipped away; the regrets and anxieties diminished. With every day came fresh and delightfully interesting contributions to her outfitting from Jeannette or Aunt Olivia—a handsome little handbag of silk and silver to match the traveling suit; a snug toilet case of soft blue leather, holding everything mortal woman could want on train or ship; a great woolly steamer rug to use on shipboard. Georgiana could only catch her breath at such kindness, and dash off hasty notes of spirited thanks, and protests against any more of the same sort. But in spite of her pride it was impossible to resist accepting these and other gifts, they seemed prompted by such genuine affection.

The day came; the trunk was closed and strapped. Mr. Jefferson had done the strapping, coming upon the prospective traveler in the upper hall, where she was trying in vain to bring leather thong and buckle into the proper relations.

"Haven't I yet proved my right to the title of man in the house?" he inquired, as he did the trick with the masculine ease which is ever a source of envy to those whose hands are weaker.

"Indeed you have; but I shall never get over feeling that I have to do everything for myself."

"It will be some one's privilege to teach you better some time," was his rejoinder. "Meanwhile, those of us who are near at hand are only too happy to act as deputies."

Between her "three men," as Jeannette had called them, Georgiana was allowed to do little for herself at the last. She was to meet her cousins as the train went through their city, but Stuart had invited himself to accompany her to that point, thus giving himself a chance, as he said, to clinch that bargain with Jeannette concerning the promised letters and post-cards.

Therefore Georgiana's farewells were not to be all said at once, for which she was thankful. It was quite enough to take leave of Father Davy, who was looking, it seemed to his daughter's eyes, on that sultry June morning, a shade paler and weaker than usual.

"It's the sudden summer heat, dear," he said with the brightest of smiles, as with her arms about him she questioned him; "nothing more. There, there, my little girl; don't let your fancy get the better of you. I'm very well indeed, and shall soon be used to the summer weather. Go—and God be with you, dearest!"

"It doesn't matter about His going with me if He'll only stay with you," murmured Georgiana, vainly struggling with herself, that she might take a bright and tearless farewell of this dear being.

"He will go with you and He will stay with me," said Mr. Warne cheerfully, "so be at rest. Here—I've written you a steamer letter. Read it when the good ship sails, and think of me as rejoicing in your happiness."

It was over at last, and she was off. At the gate she had turned to Mr. Jefferson, who was carrying her handbag to the village stage, from which Stuart had leaped to run up to the porch and say a word of cheer to Mr. Warne, sitting in a big chair.

"I can't tell you what a comfort it is, Mr. Jefferson," she said as she gave him her hand, "to know that you are here. I haven't worked with you for six weeks not to understand that it is no mere author of a scientific treatise who is staying with my father."

"No?" He smiled into her lifted eyes, and his look was that of a friend whom one may trust. "Well, Miss Georgiana, if it is of any support to you to be told that whatever knowledge or skill I may have is all at the service of your father, then I am glad to assure you of that fact. I will do my best for him always. Good-bye, and may it be a happy time from first to last."

His hand held hers close as he said these words, and continued to hold it for a moment longer while he gave her a long and intent look. She felt a strange pang; it was almost as if she could think he was going to miss her. Yet she knew better. If he missed her it would be only because he had become accustomed to having her about. No sign of any more uncommon interest had he ever shown.

Then Stuart, farther down the path, was calling, "Come, George, we're all but late now"; and she was in the old stage and it was lumbering off down the road, while neighbours waved from their windows, and Georgiana strained her eyes to get a last look at the figure on the porch.

On the train she and Stuart somehow found little to say to each other in the ride of an hour and a half to the city station where the rest of the party came aboard. Stuart did not catch sight of Miles Channing until the last minute of the train's stop. He had filled the earlier period of the ten-minute detention in the station with a hurried talk with Jeannette, during which Georgiana noted that the two seemed thoroughly absorbed in each other. It was small wonder, for Jeannette had never been more radiantly lovely than in the distinguished plainness of her traveling costume. She seemed very happy as she presumably bargained with Stuart for letters, and Jimps himself had never looked more interested in any proposition than in that one.

Suddenly, however, the wait was over. Georgiana turned from greeting Channing, who had just come aboard followed by a porter with his luggage, when she heard Stuart's voice in her ear:

"George, is *he* going?"

"I believe he is," she admitted, trying not to let her colour rise beneath the accusing expression in his eyes.

"And you didn't mention it?"

"Didn't I? He's Jeannette's and Rosalie's friend, not mine."

"No; he's something more than a friend to you—or means to be. I might have known he'd work this scheme. It's good-bye to you in earnest then."

"Jimps! Please don't. It's nothing of the sort. I——"

The train began to move. But instead of a hasty leave-taking and a leap from the steps, James Stuart stood still. "I believe I'll go on for another hour," he said coolly, with a glance at his watch. "I can get off at the next stop. Meanwhile—Miss Jeannette, the observation platform seems to be nearly empty. Would you care to sit out there a while, since I've no chair in here now and the car is full?"

Georgiana, sitting facing Miles Channing—she wondered who was responsible for the fact that his chair proved to be next hers—saw his eyes, as he glanced toward the rear of the car, follow Stuart and Jeannette.

"He's a mighty nice fellow, isn't he?" he commented pleasantly. "Too bad he isn't coming along. Seems tremendously interested in Jeannette, and it's quite evident that she likes him—as much as is good for him. These partings—well, I'm sorry for him. But he means to make the most of this last hour. It would be unkind of us to follow them out there, wouldn't it?—though I was about to propose going out when he stole a march on me."

"It would be very unkind," agreed Georgiana gayly. "Yes, I wish he could have the whole journey; he deserves a rest and change. He's one of the finest men I know."

Now that Channing was beside her, with his handsome face and faultlessly dressed figure easily the most attractive man in the car, she could not begrudge Jeannette this final hour with Stuart, though her pride smarted a little under the change in his manner toward herself. She had read in her cousin's face, as Jeannette's eyes met Stuart's when she first caught sight of him, that she was much more than commonly glad to see him, and the observer had noted with what an air of joyous comradeship the two had hurried, laughing, down the aisle to the rear door after Stuart's proposal.

But the hour was soon over. It was not until the train stopped that Jeannette and Stuart returned to the others inside the car, and then the farewells were necessarily hurried. With a smiling face Stuart shook hands with them all, leaving his best friend to the last, according to the unwritten law of farewells.

When he came to her he looked very nearly straight into her eyes—not quite—it might have been her lower eyelashes upon which he brought his glance to bear.

"Great luck, Georgiana," he said distinctly, "and all kinds of a good time."

"Good-bye, Jimps, and thank you very, very much for coming," she responded.

It was hardly to be believed that James Stuart would not lower his voice and murmur some last word for her ear alone, for this had long been his custom. Instead, he gave her a brilliant smile—and turned again to Jeannette.

"Good-bye, once more," he said—and added something under his breath, in response to which Jeannette nodded, smiling, and went with him to the front end of the car, where she alone was the last to wave farewell as he looked back from the platform.

Georgiana caught a final glimpse of him as he ran along it with bared head, and the whole party waved hands and called parting salutes, in which she joined. Then Jeannette came back, and Georgiana looked searchingly at her, her own heart experiencing an uncomfortable sort of depression as she saw the exquisite flush on her cousin's cheek and the light in her eyes.

"'Dog in the manger!'" Georgiana sternly reproached herself in her own thoughts. "Isn't it enough for you to have one man looking devotion at you, but you must claim everybody in sight?" And she made a determined and partially successful effort not to mind that things had turned out as they had. Only—she and James Stuart had been friends a very long time, and she was sorry to have the parting from him tinged by a cloud of misunderstanding. It would have been much better, she admitted to herself now, to have told him frankly in the beginning that Miles Channing was to be of the party.

CHAPTER XVI

A LITTLE TRUNK

It was a journey of only a few hours to the dock where the party were to take ship, the sailing being set for early afternoon. Before it seemed possible they had left the train and were being conveyed by motor to the pier. It was at the first whiff of salt-water fragrance that Georgiana felt a sudden onset of dread of the sailing of the great ship. And when she caught sight of the four black funnels rising above the mass of smaller smokestacks and masts and spars which lifted beyond the dingy buildings of the pier, she experienced an unexpected and disconcerting longing to run away—back to her home.

Her father's face rose before her as she had seen it that morning, pale and worn, the inner brightness of the undaunted spirit shining through the thinnest of veils. What if anything should happen to that beloved face, so that she should never set eyes on it again? The thought shook her with a throb of pain.

They were on the pier, they were ascending the gangway, they were on one of the lower decks and entering the elevator which was to lift them past many intermediate decks to that one, next the highest of all, where their quarters lay. And when they came out upon that upper deck Georgiana was dimly conscious that they were a party to attract attention, even among many people evidently of the same class. Any party to which Aunt Olivia and Jeannette belonged, she felt, must necessarily expect to be noticed. Of her own contribution to the party's distinction she was entirely unaware.

But now that she was actually on shipboard, where during the last fortnight she had so many times imagined herself, Georgiana found to her distress that she could not for a moment banish the thought, the image itself, of that gentle, suffering face at home. Not that she wanted to forget it—not that; but she did want, now that her decision was made, to be able to appreciate what a happy occasion it was and how fortunate the circumstances which had brought about her presence here, the last place in the world she had expected ever to be in.

She entered the stateroom which she was to share with her cousins, and was amazed at the size and comfort of it. It was half filled with flowers and baskets of fruit and other offerings sent for the girls, with two boxes addressed to herself. Both Stuart and Mr. Jefferson had sent her flowers. As she examined them a hurried steward appeared with a third box, which proved to be also for her—a small box, which had come not from a city florist, like the others, but by mail.

It had been put up by unskilled hands, as its crushed shape and damp exterior clearly showed. She opened it, wondering, and found a little bunch of garden flowers, sadly wilted, their limp stems protruding from the moistened newspaper in which they were wrapped. She searched for a card, and found it. In a hand she knew well, a little cramped, a little wavering, but full of character, she read these words: "Blessing her, praying for her, loving her."

Georgiana's heart gave a great leap of fear. What were those lines, what the context? She knew them—knew them well. She had never heard her father quote them, and never read with him the lines from which they came. Did he know them, use them with intent, not imagining she would place them? As she well remembered, they were from "Enoch Arden," and she had spoken them herself, in a dramatized version of that pathetic poem, the last winter of her college life. And they ran thus:

> When you shall see her, tell her that I died
> Blessing her, praying for her, loving her.

At the moment she was alone in the stateroom, the two girls having been an instant before summoned by their brother to meet some friends who had come on board to see them off. She stood staring at the touching little bunch of faded bloom, knowing just how tender had been the thought of her which had prompted the effort. It had not occurred to Mr. Warne that there was any other way of sending flowers to ships than by mailing them from one's own garden. As for the words, she knew well enough that he had not dreamed of disturbing her content by quoting them, yet—she could but feel that the reason why they came to his mind when he was searching there for a bit of tender sentiment to send with his parting gift was the thought of his own possible end being not far away. And if he, too, were thinking of that——

With a fast-beating heart Georgiana stood staring out of the open porthole at the scene of activity outside. Far below her she could see the gangway over which she had come on board. In less than an hour—the party had arrived early—that gangway would be withdrawn, the water would slowly widen between pier and ship, and there would be no turning back. Could she go—could she bear to go—and take the chance? Were her fears only the natural forebodings of the unaccustomed traveler, or was there a real reason why she should never have allowed herself to be persuaded to leave one whose hold on life was so frail, the only being in the world to whom she was closely bound? She closed her eyes and tried to think....

Mrs. Thomas Crofton, turning from a group of friends at the touch of her niece's hand upon hers, would have drawn the girl into the circle and presented her with genuine pride in her, but the low voice in her ear deterred her:

"Aunt Olivia, please forgive me, but I must ask you to come away with me just for five minutes. Please——"

In a temporarily forsaken angle of the deck Georgiana laid her case before her aunt, speaking with rapid, shaken words, but none the less determinedly. Mrs. Crofton listened with an astonished face and with lips which protested even before they had the chance to speak.

"I know just how dreadful it will seem to you all—that I shouldn't have known my duty long ago. But I see it now—oh, so plainly! And it's not only my duty, it's my love that takes me back. I can't stop to tell you how I feel about leaving you all when you've been so kind, so wonderful to me. I can tell you that another time. But the thing now for me is to get off this ship before it sails. I must!"

"But, Georgiana, my dear child——"

"Oh, please don't try to keep me, Aunt Olivia! My mind is made up. I can't tell you how it hurts to do it, but I don't dare to leave my father. If anything happened to him I could never forgive myself—never. He isn't well. It would do no good to take me with you now. I should be so miserable I should spoil it all for you."

"Georgiana, listen." The calmly poised woman of the world held the clinging hand in a firm, warm grasp, the low voice spoke evenly. "Many people feel just as you do, dear, on the eve of sailing. Some are made actually ill, even quite old travelers. But they know that it is pure hysteria and they fight it off, and afterward they are able to laugh at their fears. My dear, you are quite mistaken about there being any danger threatening your father. He is in the best of hands, and he himself would be sadly disappointed——"

It was of no use. Mrs. Crofton took her niece to her stateroom, and, sending for Jeannette and Rosalie, even for Uncle Thomas, tried in vain to shake her.

Ten minutes before the hour of sailing, Rosalie, rushing about the deck in search of Miles Channing, finally discovered him and burst out under her breath with the appalling news:

"Georgiana's going back! She's got the idea somehow that her father mayn't live till she comes home. We can't do a thing with her. Oh, do come and see if you can't show her how absurd it is to do such a thing!"

"Going back!" Miles Channing seized Rosalie's arm. "Where is she? Why, she can't go back; the ship's all but casting off. What on earth is the matter with her? She's too sensible a girl to lose her head at the last minute. Good heavens! We won't let her go; we'll keep her in her stateroom till it's too late. Take me there—quick!"

They dashed along the narrow passageways, until, coming from the Croftons' suite, they encountered Georgiana pale but quiet, Jeannette flushed scarlet and in tears, and Mrs. Crofton evidently sorely exasperated, but keeping herself well in hand.

Channing walked straight up to Georgiana. "Will you give me five minutes?" he asked.

She shook her head with a faint smile. "It's no use, Mr. Channing. I shall not change my mind again. I should have known it in the first place, and there mayn't be five minutes to spare. I must be in sight of the gangway."

"I'll take you there," he said, and glanced at the others in a way which clearly said: "Give me my chance." They understood and let him lead Georgiana on ahead toward the place she sought.

He was a clever man and an experienced one in the ways of women, even though his years among them were not yet many. He realized that argument was of little use; there was only one weapon left with which to fight the girl's determination, and it was one he was not loath to use, though he had not meant to speak so plainly until quite different surroundings invited.

"This is a hard blow to my hopes," he said very low, as they stood where they could watch the manœuvres of the officers and men who were in charge of the embarkation of passengers. "I can't tell you what this voyage with you has meant to me; I don't know how to give it up. Now, please listen. Won't you do this? Come across with us, and then, when you are actually over—it's only a five-day crossing, you know—if you still feel you must go back, we'll not try to prevent you. You'll be away then only a fortnight, and nothing in the world can go wrong at your home in that little time. And meanwhile we shall have had this voyage together—Georgiana?"

His voice with its meaning inflections would have been very hard to resist, if the girl had not by now set her teeth upon her determination. Having suffered already so much humiliation for the sake of her sudden conviction, her pride would not have let her change again, though a voice from the skies had then and there assured her that all was and would be well with her father. So once more she shook her head and moved toward the gangway. Behind her, ready to follow her if must be, a deckhand waited with her luggage. The Croftons, their faces showing much concern, had remained in the background waiting for a signal from Channing that he had or had not prevailed.

"If you go ashore," threatened Channing, "I shall go with you. And the ship will sail without me."

This roused her to speech. "No, no; don't even say such a thing—just to frighten me. Good-bye, Mr. Channing, and—I'm truly very, very sorry."

"I mean it," he urged hotly. "The whole thing is nothing to me without you; you know that perfectly well."

"I should never forgive you," she said, turning to look once into his eyes, as if to convince him of the reality of her prohibition; and he saw there all the spirit he had reckoned with, and saw, too, such a world of possibilities for one who could arouse that intense and purposeful nature, that he was swept off his feet.

"But you will forgive me if I come back by the next ship," he said quickly.

"No. Not if you come a day sooner than you intended."

Once more their glances met, like blows; then Georgiana moved rapidly toward the gangway, where the sailor in charge was beckoning. The Croftons, one and all, hurried forward, and the retreating traveler suffered their embraces.

"My child, you are forcing us to leave you here alone to look after yourself, after our promising to take every care of you," mourned Mrs. Crofton. "I shall be most uneasy about you."

"No, no, dear Aunt Olivia, you mustn't be. I am a perfectly independent person, and I can take myself home without a particle of trouble. Good-bye—and please, please forgive me, all of you!"

She was off at last, with Jeannette's hot tears on her cheek, Rosalie's reproachful and all but angry final speech, "I didn't think you'd actually do it, Georgiana Warne!" ringing in her ears; and Chester's explosive, derisive prediction following her, "By thunder, but you'll be a sorry girl when it's too late. I can tell you that!"—to make her feel that nobody really understood or sympathized with her.

It was Uncle Thomas who applied the one touch of balm to his niece's sore heart:

"David Warne is a rich man, my dear girl, to have you," he said gently, as he kissed her. "Don't feel too badly over disappointing us; it's all right. Take good care of yourself going home, and give my love to your father."

She smiled bravely back at him as she ran down the gangway with half a score of belated visitors to the ship. In a moment she was only one of the crowd of people who were watching the huge bulk of the liner draw almost imperceptibly away from the pier. Through blurred vision she looked up to the spot where they were all waving at her and smiling—thank heaven, they were smiling, as it was obviously their duty to do, no matter what their feelings.

When their faces had become indistinguishable, and the great ship had backed far out into the waters, and was headed toward the Atlantic, Georgiana turned to a porter at her elbow. "No," she said, "I didn't sail. Yes, this trunk is mine; it's to go back."

Somehow, as she followed the man through the long, dingy building, the thing which drove home the ache in her heart was the sight of the little, aristocratic-looking, leather-covered steamer trunk, Uncle Thomas's gift, packed with so many high hopes, now riding alone on a great truck. Of all the baggage which that truck had borne to the lading of the ship, hers was the only little, lonely piece to come back!

CHAPTER XVII

REACTION

In the darkness of the summer midnight Georgiana descended from the "owl" train, the only passenger, as it happened, to alight at the small station. She had hoped to slip away unobserved for the half-mile walk home, but the station master was too quick for her. He was a young station master, and he had known Georgiana Warne all his life—from afar.

"Well, I certainly did think I'd seen a ghost," said he, confronting her. "I thought you'd gone to Europe. Get a message to come back? Your father ain't took sick, has he?"

"No, I hope not. I—something happened to make it best for me to come back."

"Well, that's too bad, sure," said he, curiously regarding her. "Say, wait five minutes and I'll walk down the road with you. It's pretty late for you to be out alone."

"Thank you, Mr. Parker; I don't mind a bit, and I'm anxious to get on. I've only this small bag to carry, and it's bright moonlight. No, truly, please don't come. Good-night, and thank you."

Could this really be herself, Georgiana Warne, she wondered, as she made her escape and walked rapidly away down the road under the high arches of the elms. How had it come about? Why was she here, she who had expected to be out on the first reaches of the great deep when midnight came this night? As she passed silent house after silent house, familiar and yet somehow strangely unfamiliar in the light of what might have been, it was hard enough to realize that she had had this wonderful chance to stay away for two happy months from the sober little old place, and had herself relinquished it.

Before she knew it she was nearing her home, the old white house standing square and stern in the moonlight—she had been seeing it all the way in the train. She loved it dearly, no doubt of that, but it had been no attack of homesickness which had brought her back to it.

As she came up the path she saw, past the sweeping branches of the great trees which surrounded the house, that Mr. Jefferson's windows were still alight. This was no surprise, for she knew he had often worked till late hours before she began to help him; and it looked as if, now that he had to continue alone, he meant to keep up the rate of advance by working overtime.

Georgiana stole upon the porch and tried the door. It was bolted as usual. She slipped around the house, and tried the side and rear doors in turn, to find them fast. She had had no plan as to how to make an undisturbing entrance at this hour, but had counted on being able to discover some unguarded point. She and her father had never been careful as to thorough locking of the house in a neighbourhood where thefts were almost unknown, but evidently their boarder, accustomed to city ways and chances of trouble, had taken pains to make all fast.

There seemed to be only one thing to do, and Georgiana did it. After all, it was probably better that somebody should know of her return, in case she had to go about the house and make any betraying sounds. She stooped to the gravel path, and scooping up a handful of pebbles flung them up at one of the lighted windows, where they rattled like small bird shot upon the wire netting of the screen.

It took a second fusillade before the absorbed worker within was attracted and appeared at the window, a black figure against the yellow radiance of the oil lamp.

"It's some one who belongs here," Georgiana called softly. "Please come down very quietly and let me in."

"Wait a minute," returned the voice above.

In less than that minute the door swung softly open, and the tall figure, clad in loose shirt and trousers, the former open at the neck and revealing a sturdy throat, stood before the applicant for admission. There was no light upon Georgiana, for the moonlit yard was behind her.

"What can I do for you?" Mr. Jefferson was beginning in a pleasant tone, as of one not at all disturbed by being summoned at this hour, when a voice he had heard many times before said, with an odd thrill in it, as if it struggled between tears and laughter:

"You can let me in and try not to consider me an idiot. I got my father on my mind and couldn't sail, so I came back. That's absolutely all there is of it."

"My dear girl!" Mr. Jefferson put forth a hand and took hers, as he came out upon the porch. "Of course, I beg your pardon," he added, releasing her hand after one strong pressure, "if you consider that my rather natural surprise isn't apology enough. But—you can't mean that the ship—and the party—have sailed without you?"

"Just that. Is—is my father as well as he was this morning?"

"He was quite as well, apparently, at bedtime. The heat has been trying, but he has borne it without complaint."

"I don't know what I expected," confessed Georgiana rather faintly; "but I don't think I expected that. I'm very thankful. I'll come in and slip upstairs. Thank you for coming down."

She would stay for no more; it seemed to her that she could bear no further explanations to-night. As if he understood her, Mr. Jefferson was silent as he followed her in, bolted the heavy door, and took from her the handbag she carried. He deposited this at the door of her room upstairs, and spoke under his breath in the darkness relieved only by the rays which shone from the open door of his own room at the front of the hall:

"Good-night—and welcome back!"

It was almost daylight when she fell asleep, and she wakened again at the first sound of Mrs. Perkins's footsteps in the kitchen below her. She dressed slowly, her heart heavy with the sense of having made a probably needless sacrifice. With the waking in the familiar old room, all the realization of that which she had lost had come heavily upon her. Why was not the sunlight pouring in through portholes, bearing the refreshing breezes from the sea, instead of beating in over the hot tin roof of the ell upon which her windows looked? Was it merely as Aunt Olivia had warned her, the hysteria of the inexperienced traveler? Why had she not at least accepted Miles Channing's eminently reasonable suggestion that she make the voyage, giving her emotions time to cool? At the longest, if she made an immediate return, she would have been absent but little more than a fortnight.

But she dressed with unusual care none the less, and when she descended the back stairs she was looking as fresh and trim as ever in her life. She encountered the good Mrs. Perkins in the kitchen and had it out with her, receiving the first encouragement she had felt that somebody would think her rational in her return.

"Well, I must say," declared that lady, standing still, as if she had been struck, in an attitude of astonishment, "while I'm more than sorry for you to lose your trip, Georgie, I shall feel safer now you're back. Your father cert'nly does look awful peaked to me and kind of weak-like, more so than I ever noticed before. Perhaps it's just because I felt the responsibility settlin' down on my shoulders the minute you was out of the house. And I guess he was goin' to miss you pretty awful much; though, of course, he wouldn't say so."

Georgiana took in her father's tray when it was ready, quite as usual, her heart beating fast as she entered and beheld the white face against the propped-up pillows. After the first gasp of surprise she saw the unwonted colour flow into the pale cheeks.

"My dear, dear child," he said, as she set down the tray and flew to clasp him in her arms, "this is—this is almost more than I can grasp. What has happened Is the sailing of your ship deferred?"

"My sailing on it is deferred," she told him. "I couldn't leave you, Father Davy; that's the simple truth. Your daughter is an infant-in-arms."

She did not try to make it clear to him; but let him guess the most of her reason for returning, and was rewarded by his fervent: "Well, dear, it was a very wonderful thing for you to do. But you should not have done it. You should have trusted the good Lord to take care of me, as I bade you. You must do it yet. We will arrange for you to follow your Uncle Thomas's party on the next boat. I cannot have you lose so much just for me."

"It's no use," she asserted, her eyes studying the blue veins so clearly outlined on the fair forehead. "I've made my decision; I ought to have made it that way in the beginning. So long as you need me I shall not leave you."

At the breakfast table she met Mr. Jefferson. It was only twenty-four hours since she and he had breakfasted together, but somehow it seemed to Georgiana as if at least a week had gone by. Mr. Warne was seldom present at the first meal of the day, and it had come to seem very natural to Georgiana to sit down with her boarder and pour his coffee and talk with him. This morning, however, there was a curious constraint in the girl's manner. After the first interchange of observations on the promise of even more extreme heat than on the preceding day and the possibilities of dress and diet to suit the trying conditions, the talk flagged.

"I am strongly tempted," said Mr. Jefferson, as he rose after making an unusually frugal meal of fruit and coffee, "to let up on work till there comes a change in the weather. I believe I shall try how it feels to idle a little. You surely will indorse that, Miss Warne, as far as you are concerned?"

"No," she said quickly, sure that this plan was the result of consideration for herself; "as far as I am concerned I should much prefer to work. I am sure you can give me something to do, even if you are not working yourself."

"Do you mean that? Then if you do, I shall be with you, though I think it would be good for you to rest. This last week has been pretty full for you, even though you haven't been with me on the book."

She shook her head. "I want to go on with it," she insisted; and he agreed.

News in a small village travels fast, and Georgiana was fully prepared to have James Stuart appear with the first fall of dusk. He came through the hedge at the foot of the garden, and found her on the seat under the old apple tree which was her favourite resort. His greeting was full of the astonishment which had been his all day.

"My word, George, but I never would have believed this! How on earth did you come to do it?"

"I had to," she said simply and rather wearily. She had explained to at least twenty persons that day, as well as she could explain. She was not willing to confide to any one the incident of the flowers and the card which had brought about the impulse to return that had hardened so quickly into action. She had listened to all kinds of comments on the situation, some few sympathetic, but most of them curious and critical. Many had said to her that they never would have believed Georgie Warne would ever change her mind about anything. Others had added that perhaps it was a good thing, since her father certainly was pretty feeble and nobody knew when he might take a turn for the worse. Altogether, it had not been a happy day for the object of the village interest.

Stuart sat down beside Georgiana on the old bench which bore his initials from one end to the other of it, the earliest ones hacked out during his small boyhood, the later more than once coupling Georgiana's with his own. His hand, as he settled into place, rested on one of these very monograms.

"It seems like the natural thing to say I'm glad to see you back," he said slowly, "but—there's a reason why I can't say it at all."

"Then don't dream of saying it." Georgiana leaned her head listlessly against the seamy old tree trunk behind her.

"It's not that I wanted you to go; you know I was altogether too selfish for that," he went on. "But—something happened at the last that made me entirely reconciled to having you go. Can you guess what it was?"

"Possibly."

"But you can't. Of course I was pretty well dashed at finding Channing booked for the trip. But—I got over that when—I made up my mind to come, too."

"To come, too!" The head resting against the tree trunk turned quickly. "What *do* you mean?"

"Jeannette suggested it," said he, with something in his voice which his listener could not quite analyze. "She put it up to me to come over while they should be staying in Devonshire, and join their house party. At first I said I couldn't, but the more I thought of it the more it seemed possible to get over there for a fortnight anyhow. The plan was not to tell you, and to surprise you by walking in on you."

Georgiana stared at him, as well as she could see him through the fervid twilight. "Jimps! Why, how could you get away?"

"There's never a time when it's easy to get away," he admitted; "but everything's in full sail now for the summer, and just lately I've succeeded in getting hold of an awfully competent man who could run things for the month well enough. Anyhow, of course I was dippy at the thought of going and—I promised her I would if I could manage it. I've never had the chance to travel much, and it suddenly struck me that I didn't have to deny myself every possible thing. But, of course, now that you're back——"

"But that makes no difference!" she cried quickly, "Why should it? Jeannette asked you because she wanted you. Of course you must go, if you really can get away."

"She never would have asked me if you hadn't been going. And it was only an afterthought then. If I hadn't gone on for that last hour it wouldn't have occurred to her."

"It occurred to her to wish it, because she said so more than once to me the day I was there. But she didn't dream you could do it. I don't know why we should all consider you a fixture, for your father is much stronger than mine and it couldn't harm him at all to spare you for a little. Of course, you must go, Jimps! When will you start?"

"Do you honestly want me to go, George?" He seemed to be scanning her face through the dimness.

"I should be a selfish thing enough if I didn't," she protested.

He was silent for a minute; then he said: "To be frank, I wrote last night for a berth on a ship that sails in two weeks. Jeannette warned me not to delay, the travel is so heavy this time of year. I talked it over with my father and he seemed pleased at the idea. You can imagine I felt a bit dizzy this morning when I heard you hadn't sailed. I didn't believe it at first."

"Never mind, you will go just the same—and all the more. It's a pity somebody shouldn't carry out the plan, and you've had less fun than I, for you've been at home longer since college. Go, Jimps, and take the goods the gods provide."

She maintained this spirit throughout the ensuing fortnight, in spite of his evident effort to make her acknowledge that she would feel her own disappointment the more for his going. When he came over to say good-bye he found her apparently in the gayest of spirits; and she gave him such a friendly send-off that he went away marvelling in his heart at the ways of young women, and the ways of Georgiana Warne in particular.

CHAPTER XVIII

"STEADY ON!"

On the day following the departure of James Stuart for England, while the two literary workmen were hard at it in the old manse study, the July weather having mercifully turned decidedly cooler for a space, the village telegraph messenger, a tall youth with a shambling gait, appeared with a message for Mr. Jefferson. Georgiana brought it to him, and waited to know whether there was a reply.

She saw the message—evidently a long one—twice read, and noticed a peculiar lighting of the grave face which had bent over it. Mr. Jefferson wrote an answer, briefer than the message received, and himself took it to the waiting boy. When he returned he sat down and began to put in order the papers on which he had been working.

"I have another trade, as you have guessed," he said to Georgiana. "It seems necessary for me to go away and work at it for a few days, perhaps a fortnight. It is fortunate for me that you are here, for I should not have felt that I ought to leave your father, and yet I should hardly have been able to refuse the call of that message."

"Then I am very glad," she returned, "that I am here. Can you leave me work to do?"

"I am afraid not, beyond that already laid out for to-day. Won't you rest while I am gone? This is vacation time for most people, you know."

72

She shook her head. "With only father to look after I shall have little enough to do."

"You won't—forgive me!—go up into that blistering attic and make rugs? I hope not!" She felt that he was looking keenly at her.

"Why should you hope not? I am one of the people who must be busy to be contented. How soon do you go, Mr. Jefferson?"

"On the noon train." He looked at his watch. "I have an hour to make ready. No, don't go. I will come back when I am ready, and we will put things in shape to leave, so that we shall know exactly where to take them up again."

In half an hour he was back, and together the two put the results of their joint work into such shape that at a moment's notice they might resume it. This done, they went to Mr. Warne, and the intending traveler explained briefly the situation—without, as Georgiana fully realized, explaining it at all. Then, shortly, he went away, with something in his manner which subtly told her that he was very glad to go, and that he was thinking of little besides the errand which took him from them, careful though he was in every courteous detail of leave-taking.

When he had gone Georgiana and her father looked at each other.

"Daughter," said Mr. Warne, looking intently at the vivid face, with the eyes which saw so many things, "do you know what you remind me of?"

"No, Father Davy. Of a cross child?"

"Of a young colt, penned into a very small enclosure, with only one lame and blind old horse to keep it company. And within sight, off on the hillside, is a great, green pasture, with other colts and lambs sporting gayly about, and the summer sunshine over all— except in the corral, over which a dark cloud hangs. And I am sorry—sorry!"

"Father Davy!" Georgiana choked back a lump in her throat. "But it is hot July, and the cloud makes it cooler and nicer in the corral. And besides—the lame, blind horse is such a dear—has drawn such heavy loads and would be so lonely now without company. And—and the colt has many long years to sport on hillsides."

Mr. Warne smiled, more sadly than was his wont. "But not while it is a colt." Then, after a pause, "My dear, we shall miss Mr. Jefferson."

"Shall we?"

"I shall miss him more than I should have realized till I saw him go down the path. And James Stuart, too. That is why I know that you will miss them."

"We shall live through it," prophesied his daughter cheerfully, and betook herself to the kitchen, which she found looking, in spite of its well-ordered neatness, more like a jail than ever before.

The following days went by on feet of lead. Never had Georgiana had to make such an effort to maintain ordinary, everyday cheerfulness and patience. She found herself longing, with one continuous dull ache from morning till night, for something to happen, something which would absorb her every faculty. She rose early and went for long walks, and went again in the late afternoons, with the one purpose of tiring her vigorous young body so that it would keep her restless mind in order. She worked at her rug-making many hours, spent many more in reading aloud to her father, and still there were hours left to fill. She forced herself to go to see all her acquaintances, to visit those few who were ill; there was nobody in want in the whole place, it seemed, in this summer prosperity of garden.

"There's nothing to do for any one," she said to her father one day. "I feel guilty times without number because I'm not of more use to the people about me."

Her father studied her. "Dear," he said slowly, "what you need just now is something the good Father knows you need, and I believe He will not deny it to you. In the meantime, remember that simply being cheerful and patient under enforced waiting is sometimes the greatest service that can be rendered."

"If you haven't taught me that, it isn't because you haven't illustrated it every day of your life," she cried—and fled.

In her own room she beat her strong young hands together. "Oh, dear God!" she said aloud, "if I could only, only have the thing I want, I would take anything, *anything* that might go with it and not complain!"

And then, suddenly, one early August night, Mr. Jefferson returned. He came up the path, bag in hand, and saw a solitary figure standing on the small front porch, where a latticework sheltered opposing seats. It was a white figure in the early dusk and it rose as he approached.

"The fortnight is not quite up," said Georgiana quietly. "But I put your room in order to-day, hoping you would come. My father never missed anybody so much."

"That sounds very pleasant." He set down his bag and shook hands. "It makes it the harder to say that I must be off again in the morning. And—I shall not be coming back. If it had not been that I could not leave without seeing you and Mr. Warne I should have sent on to ask you to pack and send my trunk."

"Really? How very unexpected! But I would gladly have sent on the trunk," said Georgiana. Something cold clutched at her heart.

"Would you? That sounds rather inhospitable! Do you care to hear my plans?"

"If you care to tell them, Mr. Jefferson."

"I wonder," said he, "if you would be willing to go around to the other porch and sit there. I have a fancy for being where I can get the scent from your garden. I shall miss that spicy fragrance. Is your father still up?"

"He has just gone to bed. He would be very happy if you would go in and speak to him," said Georgiana.

Mr. Jefferson ran upstairs with his bag, and made a brief call upon Mr. Warne. Then he came down, to find Georgiana standing with her arms about a white pillar, her face looking off toward the garden. The lamplight from the central hall, whose rear door opened upon the porch, gleamed rosily out upon her.

Mr. Jefferson came out and stood beside her. "I came back," he said, "just to offer you my friendship in any time of need. I couldn't go away without doing that; I couldn't be content merely to write it back to you. I have lived here in your home with your father and yourself until it has come to seem almost as if I belonged here. But my work calls me; I must go back to it. The book must wait, to be finished in spare moments as other books have been finished. I thought I could give myself this year away from my profession to accomplish this task and perhaps to lay in fresh stores of energy. But I find I can't be easy in mind to do this longer. So I am going back."

After an instant Georgiana answered, without turning her eyes away from the garden: "You are a very fortunate person."

"To have work that calls so loudly? I am sure of that. And it is work which absorbs me to the full. But I shall always have time to give to you or to your father, if in any way I can ever be of service to you. I have no family to call upon me for any attention whatever; I have no near relative except the married sister who lives abroad, as I have told you. By the way, Allison has bidden me more than once to thank you for her for taking such good care of me. You know her by her picture, if you have noticed it—the one on my bureau."

Georgiana nodded. She did not trust her lips, which were suddenly trembling, to tell him that though he had often spoken of this sister he had never mentioned the fact that the photograph on his bureau was hers. But—what did it matter now? It was far better that she had not known, that she had had this restraint upon her imagination to keep her from ever letting herself go. It was far better—— But he was speaking; she must listen.

"While I have been in this house I have felt," he was saying, "as if I had a real home. It is hard to give that up. Association with your father has become much to me. I can't tell you what he has given me out of his stores of wisdom and experience. And you—have been very good to me; I shall not forget it."

"I have done nothing," murmured Georgiana with dry lips, "except feed you and dust your room. You might have had such service anywhere."

"Might I? I doubt it. And there is something else. If I may I should like to tell you how I have admired you for your steady facing of each day's routine. There is no heroism in the world, Miss Georgiana, equal to that, to my thinking."

She shook her head. "I'm not heroic; please don't tell me I am."

"But you are, and I must tell you so. Why not? I have seen more than you may have realized. My whole life's training has been in the line of observation of other human beings. And you must know that no one could be with you and not understand that the fires of longing to live and live strongly and vitally burn in you with more than ordinary fierceness. Yet you subdue them every day for the sake of the one who needs you. That is real heroism, and the sight of it has touched me very much."

Suddenly she found herself struggling to keep back the choking in her throat. How well he had understood her—and what unsuspected depths of tenderness there were in his rich and quiet voice. She could not speak for a little, and he stood beside her in a comprehending silence.

"I can't go away," he said presently, "without telling you that your happiness has come to seem very important to me. I have—necessarily—a fairly wide knowledge of men, their characters, their motives, their ideals—or their lack of them. Miss Georgiana, when you come to choose—will you let me say it?—don't be misled by superficial attributes, even the most attractive. Don't let the desire to have your horizon apparently expanded, to go far and see much and live intensely, overbalance your appreciation of fine and lasting qualities in one who could give you little excitement but much that is real and worth having. It may be very daring in me to say this to you, but I find myself impelled to it. I want you to live, and live gloriously, and find employment for every one of your splendid energies, and there is only one being in the world who can help you do that—the man whom you can respect as well as love, and love as well as respect. Will you promise me to choose him and nobody else?"

She turned suddenly and fiercely upon him. "How can you think I——" She stopped short, her eyes blazing in the darkness.

"I can foresee," said he, very gently, "an hour for you when you will be tempted out of your senses to do the thing which promises change, any change. You are starving for it; you are desperate with longing for it——"

"Mr. Jefferson——"

"Miles Channing came into town when I did: his car raced my train for the last two miles. He has gone to the hotel. Doubtless you will see him within the hour. Miss Georgiana, I can't let you marry him without telling you that if you do you will be an unhappy woman for the rest of your life."

She was speechless for a moment with surprise. She forgot her encounter with the speaker in her astonishment at his news. Channing had come back, then, even as he had vowed, long before the rest of the party. The knowledge that he was close at hand again, bringing back with him such a wild will to accomplish that of which he had been thwarted that he had not been able to brook delay upon the other side of the water, was knowledge of the sort which stopped the breath.

"Will you forgive me?" said Mr. Jefferson's low voice in her ear.

"But—but I—don't understand," she stammered—and now at last she showed him her unhappy eyes.

"What I have to do with it? How can I fail to have something to do with it? When I let you sail in the same party with this young man without warning you, it was because I had no possible notion that he was to be along. When I learned that he had gone and that he had followed you back, I knew that he was in earnest—at least in his pursuit of you. I had thought there was no actual danger for you on account of your friend—your real friend— the young man whom you had known and trusted so long and with such reason. But now, with him away and you alone here and lonely and full of the hunger for life—yes, I know I am speaking plainly, but I feel that I must put you on your guard. And I want you to feel that though I shall be gone to-morrow night I am here to-night, and if you have any need for me—for an elder brother———"

"Oh, how can you think———"

"I do think—and I know—and I fear for you. Not because I do not believe in you, but because I know the manner of man who will approach you. You have never known his sort. Let me be a brother to you—just for to-night, if only in your thought. It may help to steady you."

There was silence between them for a little. Then steps upon the front porch, quick, ringing steps, as of one who comes with eagerness. Georgiana felt her hand taken for an instant and pressed warmly between two firm hands. Then her companion left her....

Three hours afterward Georgiana flung herself, breathing fast, upon her knees beside her open window and lifted her face toward the sky. She would have fled to her garden for this vigil she must keep, but the extraordinary truth was that she did not dare be alone there. Her hands gripped the sill, her eyes stared without seeing at the vaulted depths above her. After a long time—hours—she rose and went to her door, opened it without making a sound, and, listening till she had made sure that the house was as silent as all houses should be at two in the morning, she stole slowly along the upper hall. Presently she stood outside the closed door of the guest who was sleeping under the roof for the last time. With a fast-beating heart she noiselessly laid her hand upon the panel of that door.

"You did steady me," she whispered. "I couldn't have done it if you hadn't warned me—fortified me. Oh, what shall I do without you?"

Inside suddenly a footstep sounded, the footstep of a shod foot. Instantly the girl was off down the hall like a frightened deer. In her own room she stood with her hand upon her breast. "Up—at this hour!" her startled consciousness was repeating. "Why? There was no light in his room. Couldn't he sleep either? Why? Is *that* what it means to him to be a brother?"

In the morning Mr. Jefferson took his leave. His parting with Mr. Warne was like that between father and son. When he came to Georgiana he looked straight down into her eyes.

"Remember," he said, "that what I have told you of my wish to be of any possible use to you and your father holds good, even though I should be at the other side of the world. I shall write now and then to ask about you both. I can't tell you how I hope for your happiness—Georgiana."

When he had gone she went to her room and dropped upon her knees beside her bed, her arms outflung upon the old blue and white counterpane.

"O God," she whispered passionately, "how could You show it to me if I couldn't have it? How *could* You?"

CHAPTER XIX

REVELATIONS

Summer had gone at last, its fierce heat giving way to the cool, fresh days of an early autumn. August, September, October—the months had dragged interminably by, and now it was November, bleak and chill, with gray skies and penetrating winds and sudden deluges of rain. Georgiana, sweeping sodden leaves from a wet porch after an all-night storm, looked up to see the village telegraph messenger approaching. With her one dearest safe upon a couch within, and Stuart long since at home again, she could not fear bad news. She thought of Jeannette, who was always, in the absence of a telephone in the old manse, telegraphing her invitations and demands.

She tore open the dispatch with a hope that it was from Jeannette, for she had sadly missed her letters. Jeannette, indeed, it was who had inspired the message, but its sender was her sister. Rosalie Crofton wired that Jeannette had been taken suddenly and violently ill while on a visit in New York and was to be operated upon at once; that she had begged Georgiana to come and to bring James Stuart with her; that Rosalie herself was dreadfully frightened and prayed Georgiana not to lose a train nor to fail to bring Stuart.

Action was never slow with the receiver of this message; it had never been quicker than now. With one brief explanation to her father, she was off to find Stuart. Just at the dripping hedge she met him, his face tense with the shock it was plain he had received. At sight of her he drew a yellow paper from his pocket.

"You've heard?" he cried.

"Yes; this very minute."

"There's only an hour to catch the ten-ten. You'll go?"

"Of course. I was coming to tell you. I'll be ready."

She turned again and ran back. There was much to do in the allotted hour, but with the help of Mrs. Perkins she accomplished it. When she and Stuart were in the train, sitting side by side in the ordinary coach of the traveler who must conserve his resources, as Georgiana had decreed, Stuart spoke the first word of comment upon the situation.

"Of course, there was nothing to do but go," he said, "after that telegram."

"Of course not," agreed Georgiana simply.

"She was perfectly well—last week," said Stuart.

"Was she? You know I haven't seen her since they came back."

"She said she had tried every way to get you there."

"She has. I was going—when I could. You know father hasn't been as well since they came back in September."

"I know. But she's wanted to see you. She says she can't write half so well as she can talk."

"No. One can't."

There was silence for some time after this exchange. Stuart seemed restless, stirred often, once got up and stood for a long time at the rear of the car, staring back at the wet

77

tracks slipping away behind. When they had changed trains and were headed for New York, with their destination only a few hours away, Stuart, again in the vestibule of the car, looking out through the closed entrance door upon a dull landscape passing like a misty wraith through the November fog and twilight, found Georgiana at his elbow.

"Jimps," she was saying in her straightforward way, "what's the use of bothering to keep it covered when it shows so plainly? Do you think I don't understand? I do—and it's absolutely all right."

He turned quickly, and his gloomy eyes stared down into her uplifted face.

"O George!" he muttered. "Can you honestly say that?"

"Honestly. I know how it happened. You couldn't help it. It was meant to be. The other—wasn't. That's all there is of it."

"I've been feeling such a sneak."

"Why should you? I've told you over and over——"

"I know you have. But—that last time——"

"That was really the beginning of—this other," said she with decision. "You were not yourself and you didn't know just why. You thought it must be because you cared for me, but it was—the stirring of your first real feeling for any woman, only you didn't recognize it. That's the whole thing, Jimps, and you are not to reproach yourself, particularly now when——" She faltered suddenly, and he drew a quick breath that was as if something stabbed him.

After a little he began very slowly: "It didn't really happen till—Devonshire. Those two weeks—I can't tell you. No mortal man could have resisted her. Yet I tried; I did, George. She didn't know about you; she never has, except that we were old friends and dear ones. She thinks the trouble is that she's a rich man's daughter and I'm only a farmer."

"You're no ordinary farmer and she knows it. Her family know it. And if she wants you she'll have you; they've never refused her anything."

"I haven't asked her."

"James Stuart!" It was her old tone with him. For the moment both forgot the possible issue of this errand upon which they were going; only the vital relations at stake seemed involved.

"But—she knows," said Stuart very low.

"Of course she does."

By and by Stuart spoke again. "George, you were never quite so close to me as now."

She slipped her hand into his. "I'll stay close, dear; and I'll do all I can for you both."

This was all they said until the first lights of the great city, miles out, were flashing past them. Then it occurred to Georgiana to put a startled question:

"Jimps, have you any address to go to? There was none in my telegram."

"I know where they are staying." Stuart put his hand into his pocket and drew out a thick letter, upon which Georgiana recognized her cousin's handwriting. "This came only yesterday morning."

In spite of herself the girl felt a wild thrill of pain. Her chum—her chum! And it was the first time he had ever failed to be open with her.

As if he recognized that the sight of the letter had told even more plainly than words could have done, the degree of intercommunication between the two presumable lovers, Stuart said quickly:

"I was going to tell you, George—on my word I was. I knew you didn't care for me— that way, but I was afraid it might hurt just the same, after all our vows. Somehow the days went by so fast and—well, you see there was Channing. A while back I thought you were going to marry him, more than likely."

"You didn't really think it, Jimps."

"I don't know what I thought. George, we're getting in. Oh——" And he broke off.

She knew what had happened, for with the first glimpse of the great terminal station the things which thus far had been never really vivid in her consciousness had in the twinkling of an eye taken terrible form. This was New York, and somewhere in it they were to find Jeannette, stricken in the midst of her youth and beauty and joy of life and love. If only they might find the worst of the danger safely past!

They were rushed in a taxicab to the great uptown hotel, to find there a message saying that the whole family were at the hospital and that they were to follow at once. In the second cab Georgiana's hand again found Stuart's and stayed there. His face was set now; he spoke not a word, and even through his glove his hand was cold to the touch. Then, presently, they were at the big, grim-looking hospital with the characteristic odour, so suggestive to the senses of the tragedies which take place there night and day, meeting them at the very portal.

It was Georgiana who made the necessary inquiries, for Stuart seemed like one dazed with fear of that which was to come. He followed her with his fingers gripping his hat brim with a clutch like that of a vise, his eyes looking straight ahead. An attendant led them to a private room, and here in a moment Georgiana found herself caught in Rosalie's arms, with pale faces all about which tried to smile reassuringly but could succeed only in looking strained. It was Aunt Olivia who seemed most composed and who made the situation clear. Uncle Thomas could only grasp the newcomers' hands and press them, while his lips shook and his speech halted.

"It is a very peculiar case, and we had to wait till a certain surgeon came who was out of town—Doctor Craig. They seemed to think it safer to wait for him. He has had extraordinary success in similar cases. He—is with her now, operating. My dear, I am very glad you have come—and you, Mr. Stuart. She wanted you both, and we felt that if her mind were at rest her chances——" But here even Aunt Olivia's long training in composure under all circumstances deserted her, and she let Georgiana put her in a chair and kneel beside her, murmuring affection and hope.

It was a long wait—or so it seemed—interrupted only once by the entrance of a young hospital interne, who came to advise the family of the patient that thus far all was going well. It had proved, as was expected, a complicated case, and there was necessity of proceeding slowly. But Doctor Westfall had sent word to them to be of good cheer, for the patient's pulse was strong, and Doctor Craig's reputation, as they knew, was very great.

"It's Dr. Jefferson Craig, you know," explained young Chester Crofton softly to Georgiana. "We're mighty lucky to get him. He only came back from abroad two days ago, and he was operating out of town somewhere last night. Doctor Westfall was awfully keen to have him and nobody else."

Georgiana knew the name, as who did not? Jefferson Craig was the man whose brilliant research work along certain lines of surgery had astonished both his colleagues and an attentive general public, and his operative surgery on those lines had disproved all previous theories as to the possibilities of interference in a class of cases until recently considered hopeless after an early stage. It was indeed subject for confidence if Doctor Craig's skilful hands were those now at Jeannette's service.

But there is no beguiling such periods of suspense with assurance of former successes in similar cases. Jeannette's family had need of all their fortitude for the bearing of such suspense before Doctor Westfall, the Crofton's family physician from the home city, appeared in the doorway. He had been brought on by them when they were summoned to Jeannette's bedside. He had known the girl from her babyhood, and the signs of past tension were clearly visible in his face as he looked upon his patient's family, though his eyes were very bright and his lips were smiling.

"Safely over," was his instant greeting, and his hand fell with the touch of hearty friendship on the shoulder of Mr. Thomas Crofton. "I wouldn't come till I was sure I might bid you draw a long breath and ease up on this strain of waiting."

They came around him, Aunt Olivia's lips trembling, her hand fast in Georgiana's. Young Chester Crofton gave a subdued whoop of joy, and pretty Rosalie, scarcely out of emotional girlhood, burst into hysterical crying which she struggled vainly to keep soundless.

"Mind you," warned Doctor Westfall, wiping his own eyes though he continued to smile, "I don't say all danger is past. Doctor Craig would be the last man to countenance such a statement. We must hold steady for several days before we can speak with absolute assurance. But every sign points to safety, and certainly—certainly—well,"—he paused as if he could not readily find words for that which he wished to say,—"if it had been anybody but our Jeannette I should have congratulated myself on the chance to see such a piece of work as that. I've never seen Jefferson Craig operate, though I've been a fascinated follower of his research and have read every word he has written. And he's astonishingly young. I expected to see a man of my own age."

"We must see him, Doctor," murmured Mrs. Crofton, striving to regain her composure which, as is often the case, was more shaken by the assurance of good news than by the fear of bad. "We must thank him for ourselves. He will come in to see us?"

"As soon as he is out of his gown. I'm going back for him in a minute, for I knew you would want the words from his own lips. You will like him—you will like him immensely."

He went away again presently on this errand, an imposing figure of a man of fifty, accustomed to responsibility and able to carry it, a typical city physician of the class employed by the prosperous, but with certain clearly defined lines about his eyes and lips which proclaimed him a lover of human nature and a sympathizer with its sufferings, in whatever class he might find his patients.

"He's such a dear," declared Rosalie, wiping away her tears and smiling at James Stuart. "He's adored Jeannette ever since she was born, and I know he's been just as anxious as we were. Do cheer up, Jimmy. I'm just as sure she's going to get well now as I was sure she wasn't before."

"I don't dare to be sure," he answered in a low tone.

Georgiana looked at him and saw how shaken he still was, notwithstanding the reassuring news. In spite of her anxiety she had been observant, ever since she entered the room, of the attitude of Jeannette's family toward James McKenzie Stuart. It had not been difficult to come to the conclusion that for Jeannette's sake they would accept him, and that for his own sake they were forced, in varying degrees, to like him. How could they help it? she wondered, when they looked at his fine, frank face and observed his manly bearing. He was college bred; he was a successful worker with his brain as well as with his hands, for his farming was scientific farming, and his results established a model for the community. He was by no means poor—and yet—Georgiana realized that the change for Jeannette from a home of luxury to one of comparative austerity of living would be a tremendous one. Well, such events had occurred before in the world's history, and it was by no means unthinkable that they should occur again. As Georgiana noted the tense look on Stuart's face, and saw the hardly abated suffering in his eyes, she said to herself that if Jeannette cared as much for him as he for her, she cared quite enough to bring her family to terms at any price.

The door opened again, as quietly as hospital doors invariably open, and Doctor Westfall advanced once more into the room, followed by a younger man with a grave, clean-cut face and the unassuming, quietly assured bearing of established success. As Georgiana's eyes fell upon the distinguished surgeon whose name was Jefferson Craig she recognized her former lodger, Mr. E. C. Jefferson. That she did not for a moment wonder what Mr. Jefferson was doing here in the famous surgeon's place was due to the fact that her mind instantly bridged the chasm between the two personalities and made them one. Yet there was a subtle, but easily recognizable, difference between the personality of Mr. Jefferson and that of Doctor Craig. There could be no question that here his foot was on his native heath! The literary worker had for the time vanished, and here was the man who did things with his hands and did them better than other men. She had long understood that he had another and more active place in the world than that which he had temporarily occupied as solely a writer of books. This was the place, and nothing could have seemed less surprising than to find him in it.

At the same time, the finding occasioned a difficulty in maintaining her own composure of face and manner. She had known Mr. Jefferson; she did not know Doctor Craig. She understood instantly, without any explanation, that he had chosen to be known in the obscure village by only a part of his name, because that name was so notable that even the two village doctors, the old one and the young, would have recognized it and been at his heels, to the detriment of those months of rest from surgery which he had dedicated to the exposition of his methods upon paper. She was quick to perceive also that it would be easy enough for Doctor Craig to prove as different from Mr. Jefferson in relation to his acquaintance as he was different in his position in the world. What, indeed, had Dr. Jefferson Craig and little Georgiana Warne in common? Certainly far, far less than had had Mr. E. C. Jefferson and that same Georgiana Warne.

He did not see her at once, for the father and mother of his patient met him in the middle of the floor, and his first glance fell upon them and remained there while he spoke to them of their daughter. Even in his manner of speaking Georgiana felt a decided difference. There was a curious crispness and succinctness of speech that marked the professional man, which was decidedly different from the more expanded conversational manner of Mr. Jefferson.

"Yes, she is sleeping quietly under the last effects of the anæsthetic," he was saying when Georgiana took note of his words once more. "We will let her sleep. It will spare her some hours of consciousness."

"Will she suffer very much when she wakes, Doctor?" was the mother's anxious question.

Doctor Craig's smile was the very one Georgiana had first liked about him, for it transformed his face and gave it back the youth which his early responsibility in a serious profession had done its best to age. "We shall not let her suffer very much," he promised. "That's not necessary nor desirable."

"When may we see her?" Mrs. Crofton pursued.

"You may all see her for a moment before she wakens, if you wish. Afterward her mother and father for just a word, and—I am told she expressed a very strong wish to see a young man who was on his way. Has he come? For the sake of her contentment I have agreed to allow him a word with her by and by—just a word, if he will be very quiet."

It was Uncle Thomas who turned to beckon James Stuart forward, and then to nod at Georgiana. Immediately Stuart was presented to Doctor Craig, who, looking intently into the young man's questioning face, said straightforwardly: "Mr. Stuart and I have met before under quite different circumstances. He knew me as a writer of books and may be surprised to find me here—as I am surprised to find him."

"Let me present you to my niece, Miss Warne, Doctor Craig," said Aunt Olivia, and Georgiana was glad of the preparation the minutes had given her, for here indeed was need for all her powers of self-control. Her eyes had no sooner looked into those which met them with such a keen and searching glance than she was stirred to the depths. She had thought she had known what it would be to feel those eyes upon her again, but she had not reckoned with the effect of absence.

He made no effort to conceal the situation. "When your daughter sees me next, Mrs. Crofton," he said, without turning from Georgiana, "she will know me, as Miss Warne and Mr. Stuart do. I spent last winter in Miss Warne's home, under the name of Jefferson alone, to find time to work at a book I am writing. I gave it up sooner than I had expected, because my work here would not be denied."

"Didn't Jean know you when she saw you before the—the operation?" cried Rosalie, full of curiosity at this unexpected turn of affairs.

"She did not see me before she was anæsthetized," explained Doctor Craig; and Doctor Westfall added, patting Rosalie's hand: "It's rather like a story, isn't it, Rosy? Doctor Seaver, of the staff here, was telling me this morning how Doctor Craig tried to take a year off to rest and write, but how they got him back—and glad enough to have him, too. And yet we want that book. It's rather hard to have a reputation so big it won't give you time to rest. He needed the rest, Seaver told me."

"I had it. Six months in the country did more for me than a year in town," said Doctor Craig. He turned at the sound of a light knock upon the door. He gave the impression of a man whose senses were every one alert.

An apologetic interne came in with a message for Doctor Craig and he left them, with a final word of confidence and the request that they all retire to rooms at the nearby hotel where they were staying.

Georgiana found Rosalie at her side. "O George! is he really the man you had in your house all this year? You lucky thing! Didn't you fall in love with him instantly? Why, he's perfectly wonderful!"

"You think so now, child, because you know he's distinguished. If you had seen him quietly working at his book you probably wouldn't have looked at him a second time."

Rosalie studied her cousin's face so intently that Georgiana had some difficulty in maintaining this attitude of cool detachment. The young girl shook her head. "He couldn't have changed his face," she insisted. "He's not a bit handsome, but he's stunning just the same. Oh, how astonished Jean will be when she finds out who's saved her life! When do you suppose he'll let Jimmy Stuart see her? He'll die if he doesn't make sure she's alive pretty soon."

CHAPTER XX

FIVE MINUTES

It was not many hours before Doctor Craig himself led Georgiana and James Stuart together into the room where Jeannette lay. She had asked to see them together, he said, and they might remain for precisely five minutes. He immediately left the room again and took the nurse with him.

The five minutes were spent by Stuart with Jeannette's hand in both his own, as he knelt beside the the the bed where she lay, no pillow under her head, her face very white but her eyes glowing.

Jeannette's look met Georgiana's. "Is it all right?" she said very low.

"Of course it's all right, dear; and I'm perfectly happy over it," whispered Georgiana.

Jeannette smiled. "I couldn't be happy till I was sure," she breathed. "I thought—I might die, even yet—and I wanted it like this—first."

An inarticulate murmur from Stuart answered this, but Georgiana assured her very gently: "You're going to be happy with Jimps for years and years, Jean darling."

They were silent then, as they had been bidden, but the silence was eloquent. Doctor Craig, coming in to put an end to the little interview, saw the unmistakable tableau. As Stuart, catching sight of him, rose slowly to his feet, the surgeon's fingers closed upon his patient's pulse. He nodded.

"As a heart stimulant you have done very well, Mr. Stuart," he said. "But small doses, frequently repeated, are better than large ones."

Jeannette's hand weakly caught his. "Isn't it queer, Georgiana," she murmured, "that it should be your Mr. Jefferson who has saved my life?"

In spite of herself, Georgiana could not prevent the rich wave of colour which swept over her face. She knew, without venturing to look at him, that Doctor Craig's eyes flashed toward her with a smile in them. She stooped over Jeannette with a gay reply:

"And he began his acquaintance with you by snowballing you till you almost had need of his surgery on the spot!"

Then she and Stuart were out in the wide, bare hospital corridor, and Stuart was saying with a shiver: "Does she look all right to you, George—sure?"

"Of course she does, Jimps. You never saw her before with her hair down in braids; and any face looks pale against a white bed."

He shook his head. "I shall not stir out of this town till she looks like herself to me."

"Of course you won't. I wish I needn't, but I must go back to father to-night."

They all tried to dissuade her from this course, but she was firm. She knew well enough that all Jeannette had wanted of her was to assure herself that she possessed a clear right and title to Stuart's love. Evidently Jeannette had guessed more at Stuart's past relations with Georgiana than either of them had imagined, and she would not allow herself to be happy without the knowledge that she was not making her cousin miserable.

One brief conversation with Doctor Craig was all that was vouchsafed Georgiana before she left the city, and that took place in the presence of others, in Aunt Olivia's apartment. It was clear enough how busy a man he was in this his own world, for when he came into the room he explained to Mrs. Crofton that it had been his only chance since they arrived to make a brief social call upon the family of his patient. It was but an hour before Georgiana's departure, and when he learned this, Jefferson Craig came over to her, where she sat upon a divan at one end of the long private drawing-room of the suite. Seeing this, the others of the party began conversations of their own, after the manner of the highly intelligent, and for those five minutes Georgiana lived in a place apart from the rest of the world.

"Please tell me all about your father," he began, and the tones of his voice, low as are habitually those of his profession, could hardly have been heard by one across the room.

Georgiana told him, unconsciously letting him see that the fear of her probable loss was ever before her, though she could not put it into words. She knew as she spoke that his eyes did not leave her face. She had no possible idea how alluring was that face as the light from the sconces nearby fell upon it. She was conscious, womanlike, that the small hat she wore was made over from one of Jeannette's, and she did not think it becoming. Though it was November, she still wore her summer suit, for the reason that since her return from abroad Jeannette had not found time to pack and send off the usual "Semi-Annual," and previous boxes had not included winter suits at at all. Altogether, with many-times-mended gloves upon her hands, and shoes which to her seemed disgraceful, though preserved with all the care of which she was mistress, Georgiana felt somehow more than ordinarily shabby.

Doctor Craig asked her several questions. He spoke of the rug-making, watching her closely as she answered. He asked how often she went to walk and how far. He asked what she and her father were reading. He would have asked other questions, but she interrupted him.

"It's not fair," she said. "Please tell me about the book. Does it get on?"

"Do you care to know?"

"Very much. I'm wondering if your copyist makes those German references any clearer for the printer than I did."

"Nobody has copied a word. I have not written a word. The book is at a complete standstill. I see no hope for it until I can take another vacation—under the name of E. C. Jefferson."

"And that you will never take," she said positively.

"I never shall—in the same way. There are reasons against it. The book will have to be written as the others were—on trains, on shipboard, in my own room late at night."

"Is it right to try to put two lifetimes into one?" she asked, and now she lifted her eyes to his.

Before, she had managed to avoid a direct meeting by those many and engaging little makeshifts girls have, of glancing at a man's shoulder, his ear, his mouth—and off at the floor, the window—anywhere not to let him see clearly what she may be afraid he will see. And Georgiana was intensely afraid that if Dr. Jefferson Craig got one straight look with those keen eyes of his he would recognize that her whole aching, throbbing heart was betraying itself from between those lifted lashes. But now, somehow, with her question she ventured to give him this one look. The interview might end at any moment; she must have one straight survey of his face, bent so near hers.

He gave it back, and until her glance dropped he did not speak. Then, very low, but very clearly, he said deliberately:

"When may I come?"

The room whirled. The lights from the sconces danced together and blurred. The floor lifted and sank away again. And Chester Crofton chose this moment—as if he were not after all really of that highly intelligent class which knows when to pursue its own conversations and when to break into those of others—to call across the room:

"Oh, I beg pardon, Doctor Craig, but when did you say Jean might have something real to eat? Rosy says it's to-morrow and I say it's not yet at all."

Doctor Craig turned and answered, and turned back again. He was not of the composition of those who are balked of answers to their questions by ill-timed interruptions. But the little diversion gave Georgiana an instant's chance to make herself ready to answer like a woman and not like a startled schoolgirl. So that when he repeated, his voice again dropped:

"When, Georgiana?"

She was able to reply as quietly as she could have wished: "Do you want to come, Doctor Craig?"

84

"I want to come. I have never wanted anything so much."

"Then—please do."

"Very soon? As soon as I can get away for a few hours? Perhaps next week? It is always difficult, but if I plan ahead sometimes I can manage to make almost the train I hope for."

She nodded. "Any train—anytime."

There was an instant's silence. It seemed to her that she could hear one or two deep-drawn breaths from him. Then:

"Would you mind looking up just once more? I must go in a minute; I can't even take you to your train."

But she answered, with an odd little trembling of the lips: "Please don't ask me to. I'm—afraid!"

A low laugh replied to that. "So am I!" said Jefferson Craig.

He rose, and she rose with him. The others came around and he took leave of them. His handclasp was all that Georgiana had for farewell, for when she lifted her eyes she let them rest on his finely moulded chin. But she knew that in spite of his expressed fear it was not her round little chin he looked at, but the gleam of her dark eyes through their sheltering lashes, and that his hand gave hers a pressure which carried with it much meaning. It told her that which as yet she hardly dared believe.

Since the journey home was made up of changes of trains, no sleeper was possible, and Georgiana sat staring out of her car window while those about her slumbered. There was too much to think of for sleep, if she had wanted to sleep. She did not want to sleep, she wanted to live over and over again those five minutes with their incredible revelation. And as the wheels turned, the rhythm of their turning was set to one simple phrase, the one which had sent her world whirling upside down and made the stars leap out of their courses:

"When may I come?"

CHAPTER XXI

MESSAGES

Hope to reach Elmville at seven to-night.—E.C. Jefferson.

This was the first of them. When Georgiana received it she had been waiting eight days for this first word. She had known well enough that until Jeannette was entirely safe Doctor Craig would not leave her. Georgiana had not minded that she had had no word. She had not really expected any. A man who was too busy to come would be too busy to write, and she wanted no makeshift letters. And she had not minded the delay in his coming; rather, she had welcomed it. To have time to think, to hug her half-frightened, wholly joyous knowledge to her heart, to go to sleep with it warm at her breast, and to wake with it knocking at the door of her consciousness—this was quite happiness enough for the immediate present.

Meanwhile, what pleasure to put the house in its most shining order, to plan daily little special dishes, lest he come upon her unawares; to sit and sew upon her clothing, shifting and turning her patchwork materials until she had worked out clever combinations which conveyed small hint of being make-overs!

For the first time in her life she said nothing to her father of her expectations. What was there to tell as yet? She could not bring herself to put into words the memory of that brief interview, in which so much had been said in so few simple phrases. And if Father Davy read—as it would have been strange if he had not—the signs of his daughter's singing lightness of heart, he made no sign himself; he only waited, praying.

Georgiana received her first telegram at noon. She had flown for two wonderful hours about her kitchen, making ready, when the despatch was followed by another:

Unavoidably detained. Will plan to get away Thursday.

This was Tuesday. Georgiana put away her materials, and swept the house from attic to cellar, though it needed it no more than her glowing face needed colour. What did it matter? Let him be detained a week, a month, a year—he would come to her in the end. Now that she was sure of that, each day but enhanced the glorious hope of a meeting, that meeting the very thought of which was enough to take away her breath.

On Thursday came the message:

Cannot leave this week. Will advise by wire when possible.

No letter came to explain further these delays. Georgiana felt that she did not need one, yet admitted to herself that the ordinary course in such circumstances would be to send a letter, no matter of how few words. Toward the end of the following week a telegram again set a day and hour, and as before, another followed on its heels to negative it. The last one added, "Deep regret," and therefore bore balm.

And then, after several more days, came a message which was all but a letter:

It seems impossible to arrange for absence at present. Will you not bring your father and come to my home on Wednesday? Will meet train arriving seven-fifteen. Journey will not hurt Mr. Warne, and visit here will interest him. Please do not refuse.

E. C. Jefferson.

Well! What girl ever had a suitor of this sort? one too busy to come or write, yet who, on the strength of a few words spoken in the presence of others, ventured to send for the lady of his choice to come to him, that he might speak those other words so necessary to the conclusion of the matter. Georgiana sat re-reading the slip of yellow paper, while her heart beat hard and painfully. For with the invitation had come instantly the bitter realization—they could not afford to go! Her recent trip on the occasion of Jeannette's illness had taxed their always slender resources, and until the money should come in for the last bale of rugs sent away, there was only enough in the family treasury to keep them supplied with the necessities of life.

The time had come—undoubtedly it had—when she must confide in Father Davy. Not that he would be able to see any way out, but that she could not venture to refuse this urgent request without his approval.

Georgiana tucked away in her belt the last long telegram, and went to her father. He lay upon his couch, the blue veins on his delicate forehead showing with pitiful distinctness in the ray of November sunshine which chanced to fall upon him.

Georgiana knelt beside him. "Father Davy," she said, with her face carefully out of his sight, "I have a little story to tell you—just the outlines of one, for you to fill in. When I was in New York Mr. Jefferson—Doctor Craig, you know,"—she had told him this part of the tale when she had first come home,—"asked me when—when he might come here."

She paused. Her father turned his head upon the crimson couch pillow, but he could not see her face.

"Yes, my dear?" he said, with a little smile touching his lips. "Well, that sounds natural enough. He knows he is always welcome here. When is he coming?"

"He isn't coming. He can't get away. He has tried three different times, and cancelled it each time. He seems to be very busy, too busy even to write."

"That is not strange; he must be a very busy man. Doubtless he will come when he can make time. I shall be glad to see Mr. Jefferson."

"But—you see—he wants us to come there."

"Us?"

"You and me. Father Davy—you understand, dear; don't make me put it into words!"

Her father's arm came about her and she buried her face in his thin shoulder. "Thank God!" he said fervently, under his breath. "Thank the good God, who knows what we need and gives it to us."

After a minute's silence: "But we can't go, Father Davy."

"Can't we? I could not, of course, but you——"

"I couldn't go without you—to his house. And—we haven't any money."

"No money? Is it so bad as that?"

"And if we had—I'm not sure that I want to take a journey to a man—so that——"

"Let me see the telegram, my dear," requested Mr. Warne. When he had read it he regarded his daughter with a curious little smile. She was sitting upon the floor, close beside his couch, her brilliant eyes now raised to his face, now veiled by their heavy lashes. "It seems clear enough," he said. "Concessions must be made to a man who belongs to the people as he does. I don't think it would be a sacrifice to your dignity, daughter, if you were to go."

"But, Father, darling, don't you see? I didn't want to tell you, but there was no other way. We have quite enough to live on—without extras—till the next rug money comes. But that may not be for a month; they are always slow. And for us to go to New York— well, we could just about get there. We couldn't get clear home. Father Davy, I can't go— penniless—*to him*!"

He lay looking at her down-bent head with its splendid masses of dark hair, at the beautiful lines of her neck in her low-cut working frock of blue-and-white print, at the shapely young hands gripping each other with unconscious tenseness in her lap. His eyes were like a woman's for understanding, and his lips were very tender. Slowly he raised himself to his feet.

"Stay just where you are, daughter," he said, "till I come back."

She waited, staring at the old crimson pillow with eyes which saw again the drawing-room in Aunt Olivia's apartment and the profile of Doctor Craig's face as he turned from her at Chester Crofton's interrupting question. That was more than three weeks ago——

Father Davy was gone some little time, but he came back at length at his slow, limping pace, and sat down upon the couch. He held in his hand a little bag of dark blue silk, a little bag whose contents seemed all heavily down in one corner. Georgiana's eyes regarded it with some wonder. She had thought she knew by heart every one of her father's few belongings, but this little bag was new to her.

"I think," he said softly, "the time has come for this. It was meant, perhaps, to be given you a little later in your history, but if your mother knew—nay, I feel she does know and approve—she would be the first to say to me: '*Give it to her now, David; she'll never want it more than now.*'"

Georgiana leaned forward, her lips parted. She seemed hardly to breathe as her father went on, his slender fingers gently caressing the little blue silk bag:

"From the time you were a baby, a very little baby, she saved this money for you. It came mostly from wedding fees; I always gave her those to do with as she would. They were a country minister's fees—two-and-three-dollar fees mostly—once in a great while some affluent farmer would pay me five dollars. How your mother's eyes would shine when I could give her a five! She turned all the bills and silver into gold—a great many of these pieces are one-dollar gold pieces. There are none of them in circulation now; it may easily be that they have increased in value, being almost a curiosity in these days. I think I have heard of something like that. At any rate, dear, it is all yours. It was to have been given to you to buy your wedding outfit; but—she would have wanted you to have it when it could help you most." He held out the little bag. "She made it of a bit of her wedding dress," he said, and his hand trembled as it was extended toward his daughter. "It was not only her wedding dress, it was the best dress she had for many years."

With a low cry that was like that of a mother's for a child, Georgiana took the little blue silk bag, heavy in its corner with the weight of many small gold pieces, and crushed it against her lips. Then, with it held close to her cheek, she laid her head down on her father's knee and sobbed her heart out for the mother she had missed for ten long years.

In the little bag there proved to be almost a hundred dollars—ninety-two in all.

"She sorely wanted to get it to a hundred," said Father Davy, when he and Georgiana, their eyes still wet, had counted the tarnished gold pieces that had waited so long to be delivered to their owner. "There seemed a dearth of marriages the year before she went; the sum increased very slowly."

"She must have gone without—things she needed," Georgiana said with difficulty.

"I think she did, but she would never own it. She was very clever, as you are, at making things over and over, and she looked always trim and fine. She was a beautiful woman— and a happy one, in spite of all she was deprived of in her life with a poor country minister. 'If my little daughter can only be as happy as I have been,' she used to say, 'it is all I ask.' My dear, she would have liked—she would have loved—Mr. Jefferson. I can't get over calling him that," he added, with his whimsical smile struggling to shine through the tears which would not quite be mastered.

"O Father Davy!" was all Georgiana could say. But she lifted a flushed and lovely face with all manner of womanly qualities written in it, and kissed her father on brow and cheek and lips, as she would have kissed her mother at such words as those.

"I wonder," said Mr. Warne, sitting comfortably in the Pullman chair his daughter had insisted upon, "if I can possibly be awake, not dreaming. I never thought to take another journey."

"He said it wouldn't hurt you, and it's not. You're not too tired? I haven't seen you look so well for a long time," declared his daughter.

The eyes of other passengers, across the aisle, were irresistibly drawn to these two travelers—the frail, intellectual-looking man with his curly gray hair and his gentle blue eyes, his worn but carefully kept garments, his way of turning to his daughter at every change of scene—the daughter herself, with her face of charm under the close hat with its veil, her clothing the suit of dark summer serge with its lines of distinction, which was still doing duty as the only presentable street suit she possessed.

They were a more than commonly interesting pair, these travelers, and they were furtively watched from behind more than one newspaper.

Georgiana had no eyes for possible observers. With Father Davy she preferred to sit with her chair turned toward the window, looking out at the hills and trying to realize the thing which was happening. She was actually on her way to the home of a man whom a month ago she had thought gone out of her life forever. And, even now, he had not spoken a word of love to her, had not asked her to marry him! Yet he was to meet her at the end of this short journey; she was to look out upon the platform and see that distinguished figure standing there, waiting for her—for her, Georgiana Warne, maker of rugs for small sums of money, wearer of other people's cast-oft clothing, undistinguished by anything in the world—except by being the daughter of a real saint; and that was much after all. Fate had not left her without the best beginning in life, the being brought into it by such a father and mother—bless them!

The hours flew by, the train passed through the outlying towns and came at last to the monster city. The lights within the car and without were bright as they drew into the great station. Following the porter who carried Mr. Warne's worn black bag and his daughter's fine one—given her by Aunt Olivia that summer—her arm beneath her father's, Georgiana made her way through the car, into the vestibule, out upon the platform. No sight of Doctor Craig rewarded the hurried glance she gave about her. But before she could take alarm a fresh-faced young man in the livery of a chauffeur came up to her, saying respectfully:

"I beg pardon, is it Miss Warne?" And upon her assent he said rapidly: "Doctor Craig bid me say he was called to a case he could not refuse, but he hopes to be home soon. I am to take you up and to see to your luggage."

"We have no luggage but these bags," Georgiana told him, wondering for a moment how he had recognized her so readily, then understanding that though she herself might be a figure indistinguishable by description from many another, that of Father Davy could not fail of recognition by one who had been told what to expect.

"I have a chair here for the gentleman," the man said, and he indicated one of the station chairs attended by a red-capped porter.

Mr. Warne, being wheeled rapidly through the great station, looked about him with the eager eyes of a boy. It was twenty years—twenty long and quiet years, since he had been in New York. What had not happened since then? In spite of the myriad descriptions he had read and pictures he had studied, the effect upon him of the real city, as, having been transferred from the chair to a small but luxurious closed car, he was conveyed along the thronged, astonishingly lighted streets, was overwhelming. Suddenly he closed his eyes and laid his head back against the cushioned leather.

Georgiana bent anxiously toward him. "Are you frightfully tired, Father dear? Are you—faint?"

His eyes opened and his lips smiled reassuringly. "A little tired, my dear, and very much dazed, but not upset in any way. I shall be glad to sleep—and glad to wake in this wondrous city."

CHAPTER XXII

TOASTS

They drove downtown for many blocks, turning at last into an old and still notable square which is one of the great town's almost untouched residence districts, in the very heart of its teeming commercial life. Here, all at once, the noise of traffic was quieted. Only as a distant and not too disturbing murmur came the sounds of the warfare which raged so near. At one of the dingy but still stately old houses the car drew up, the chauffeur alighted and opened the door. He escorted the travelers up the steps and rang the bell.

The door was opened by a lad in plain livery, and he was reinforced immediately by a middle-aged housekeeper who came forward and took the guests in charge. She had a rosy face and iron-gray hair and her accent was distinctly Scotch.

"I am Mrs. MacFayden, Doctor Craig's hoose-keeper," she said. "Doctor Craig is mair than sorry not to be here to greet ye baith. He tell't me to say ye should mak' yersels quite at hame, and should hae yer dinners wi'oot waitin' for him. If Maister Warne should be tae weary tae sit up longer, he should gang awa' tae his bed. I know Doctor Craig will mak' all the haste posseeble, but 'tis seldom he can carry oot his ain plans, for the press o' sick folks aifter him day an' nicht."

"Doctor Craig is very kind," said Mr. Warne. "If it will not seem discourteous I think I shall lie down upon my bed, for I am not accustomed to travel and am a little tired."

"That wull be the best thing posseeble for ye," said the kindly housekeeper, leading the way upstairs. "Tammas, ye'll bring the luggage. I should advise, Maister Warne, havin' a small tray in your room an' then attemptin' no mair than juist tae see Doctor Craig, when he cooms tae say gude nicht."

She led her guests into a large, square, pleasant room, furnished with old mahogany. A cheery fire was burning in a fireplace. She opened a second door, and showed a connecting room, of lesser size but very attractive.

"The Doctor often has special patients stayin' in these rooms," she said, "but fortunately they were emptied three days agone, and kept for ye. The Doctor has always some puir soul he wants to mak' comfortable. I'm glad 'tis guests this time he has, an' no patients. He needs to forget his wark when he cooms hame, but 'tis seldom he has the opportunity."

She left them, saying that if the Doctor had not returned by eight she would serve dinner for Miss Warne alone.

"No, please, Mrs. MacFayden," begged Georgiana. "If my father has his tray here I will see him to his bed. I really do not care for dinner at all."

The housekeeper smiled. "The Doctor would na' be pleased wi' me, if I let ye go dinnerless," she said. "But I'm thinkin' we'll see him soon. Wull ye coom doon to the library, Miss Warne, when ye're ready? 'Tis the door at the right o' the front entrance. The door on the left is the waitin' room, an' the Doctor does na' keep office hours at nicht."

With a fast-beating heart Georgiana set about making ready for that descent to the library. The whole affair was becoming more and more a strain upon her nerves. If Doctor Craig had met them at the station it would have been far easier for her than this. But here she was, actually in his house, combing her hair in his guest-room, going down to dinner at his table—and she had not seen or heard from him, except by telegram, since the hour when he had given her hand that meaning pressure and left her with her friends. It was an extraordinary experience, to say the least.

She wondered how she should dress for dinner—the dinner that she might eat alone! She had only her traveling suit and one simple little gray silk, dyed from a white "Semi-Annual" and made very simply, with a wide collar and cuffs of white net. Anybody but Georgiana would have looked like a Quakeress in the gray silk, but with her dark hair and warm colouring she succeeded only in imitating a young nun but just removed from scenes of worldly gayety! She decided that the hour and the occasion called for this frock, and put it on with fingers which shook a little.

Eight o'clock. She dared wait no longer, so, making sure that her father, having eaten and drunk, was resting luxuriously on his bed, she opened her door. The house seemed very quiet, and she went slowly along the upper hall, and after pausing a moment at the

90

top of the fine staircase with its white spindles and mahogany rail, she began to descend. The steps were heavily padded and her footfall made no sound; therefore, as she afterward realized, a very close watch must have been kept, for the moment she came in sight of the open library door a figure appeared there.

The next moment Jefferson Craig had crossed the hall and was standing at the foot of the staircase, looking up at the descending guest. The guest, naturally enough, paused, four stairs up, looking down. The light, from a quaint lantern hood of wrought iron and crystal hanging above the newel post, shone full upon the dark head and vivid face above the demure gray frock with its nunlike broad collar and cuffs of thin white.

The man below looked for a full minute without speaking, but Georgiana could not have told what expression was upon his face or whether he smiled. She knew that at the end of that long look he stretched one arm toward her, and that obeying the gesture which was all but a command she came on down those four remaining steps. Jefferson Craig led her into the library, where a great fire sparkled and leaped and filled the room, otherwise sombre with books, full of welcoming cheer. He closed the door, then led her to the hearth.

"Where shall we begin?" he said, in that low but very distinct voice she so well remembered. "Where we left off?"

"I'm not," answered Georgiana, looking away from him into the fire, whose light flashed in her eyes less disconcertingly than that which she somehow knew leaped in his, "sure where we left off."

"Aren't you? I am. We left off where we had each seen, for just one instant, into the other's heart. And having seen there was no forgetting—no?—Georgiana?"

She shook her head.

"It was good of you to come to me," he said very gently. Her hand was still held fast in his. "I did my best to have it the other way—the usual way. There seemed a fate against it. I could have written, but somehow I didn't want to. I preferred to wait—with the memory of your face always before me, till I could see it again. And now that I see it—bent down—and turned away"—he laughed a low laugh of content—"oh, look up, Georgiana! Surely you're not afraid now. You know I've been loving you ever since I saw you first, in spite of thinking I must not, because of the one I understood you belonged to——"

She looked up then out of sheer astonishment. "Oh, no, not since you saw me first," she disputed. "It couldn't be—and I thinking all the while——" She stopped in confusion at the revelation she might be making.

But he caught her up. "You thinking all the while—what? Tell me!"

"I thought—you hadn't the least interest in me."

"Did you care whether I had or not?"

"I—tried not to care," confessed Georgiana naïvely. She smiled, a sparkling little smile. It was so clear now, that he wanted this confession.

He looked at her for a minute longer, then he said: "Don't you think enough has been said to warrant—this?"

It was then that Georgiana learned how little one may judge from outward quiet of manner and controlled speech what may happen when the heart is allowed to speak for itself.

"Forgive me," he said at last, when he had released her, all enchanting confusion under his intent gaze; "but you know the breaking up of a famine sometimes makes human beings hard to manage. If you could know the times I've watched you, when you were bent over my illegible fist of copy, and thought how I should like just to put my hand on your beautiful hair——"

A knock sounded upon the door. With an exclamation of annoyance Doctor Craig left Georgiana and opened it.

"Dinner is served, sir," announced Thomas, the boy.

His master turned back with a laughing, remorseful face. "I had forgotten all about dinner," he said, "though now I come to think of it I believe I had no luncheon. You must be famishing. Mrs. MacFayden tells me your father is resting. We will go up and see him—before dinner or after?"

"I think he will drop off to sleep for a little, he is so tired, and then wake by and by and be ready to see you."

"Good! It couldn't be better. I am eager to see Mr. Warne, but I want him to be ready for me—who have so much to ask of him. Meanwhile—shall we go?"

He offered her his arm, such graceful deference in his manner that she felt afresh the wonder of his wish to transplant her from her world to his. As they walked slowly through the dignified old hall he said in a tone of great satisfaction: "Mrs. MacFayden has ventured to hint to me more than once that this house is of the sort which needs a mistress. To-night, when she saw me come in, she said to me very respectfully: 'It's a gled day for ye, Doctor, an' now that I've seen the lassie I can congratulate ye wi' all mae hert. She'll mak' a bonny lady to be at the head o' the hoose, if ye'll permit me to say the thocht.' I assure you, Georgiana, the conquest of my good Scottish housekeeper upon sight is no small achievement."

"It must have been my gray gown and white cuffs," suggested the girl demurely.

He looked down at the hand resting on his arm. "Now that I have time to look at anything but your face," he said, "I see that you are wearing something very satisfying to the eye. I like simple things, such as I have always seen you wear."

With inward astonishment and congratulation Georgiana thought of all the dyed and reconstructed "Semi-Annuals" which had marched in a frugal procession across his vision during the past year. Suddenly she felt an affection for the very frock she wore, difficult as had been its achievement from the materials in hand. Certainly, women in beautiful and wonderful clothing, such as he saw daily, had had no chance with him against the attraction of herself in the cleverly adapted makeshifts of her own fingers. It was the girl who had made the most of herself and her home out of her restricted means who had drawn to her side this man whose judgment must approve his love or he could never love at all.

Things hadn't been so unequal after all. The wise God, who had set her life thus far in the midst of poverty, had given her with which to fight it the wit and resource which fashion weapons out of materials which more favoured mortals cast away. That greatest of gifts bestowed upon the daughters of men had been hers—the creative touch. At last she recognized it, and knew it for what it was. Using this good gift she had learned other things than the making of clothes!

A great warm surge of joy and understanding enveloped Georgiana Warne as Jefferson Craig, having led her into the dining-room and placed her ceremoniously in her chair, bent over her where she sat, saying softly:

"This place has been waiting a long time at the bachelor's board. Now that I see it filled—like this—I know how well worth while it's been to wait."

He took the place opposite her. With a nod at the boy Thomas, he dismissed him for the moment. He looked across the table, rich with the finest appointments in his house, arranged by a housekeeper who heartily approved his everyday simplicity of life, but who exulted to-night in the chance to show the lady of his choice the fine old heirlooms of silver and damask which were to come to her. Smiling, he lifted a delicately chased goblet of water which stood beside his plate.

"To my wife!" he said.

Georgiana, raising the face of a rose, took up her own glass. She looked at it a moment, her eyes like dark twin fires, her lips taking on lovely curves. Then she lifted it toward the man opposite.

"To—*you*!"

"Still afraid?" asked Jefferson Craig, watching her as one watches only that which is the delight of his eyes. "Never mind; I'll teach you by and by the word I want to hear."

Upstairs, the slender figure on the bed stirred from the brief sleep which had claimed it. Father Davy opened his eyes again upon the firelit room and the pleasant comfort which surrounded him.

"Before they come," he thought, "I must tell my Father how I feel about it. I was too tired even to pray. But I am quite rested now."

He slipped down gently to his knees and closed his eyes, folding his thin hands on the heavy white counterpane before him.

"Dear God," he said, "I have the desire of my heart—the answer to my prayers—and I am very glad to-night. Yet Thou knowest my heart is heavy, too—with longing for my Phoebe. Tell her, Father, that her child is happy in the love of the best man she could have asked for. And tell her that David loves and longs for her to-night with the love that will never die. For that love that will not die in spite of years and pain I thank Thee. If it may be, give our child the same blessed experience. And teach us to love and serve Thee, world without end, Amen."

CHAPTER XXIII

WHY NOT?

"There's just one more thing to be settled," observed Dr. Jefferson Craig. "While we are settling things, suppose we attend to that."

He stood upon the hearthrug before the fire in his library, elbow on chimney piece, looking down upon his two guests. It was eight o'clock of the evening following that upon which Mr. David Warne and Georgiana had arrived at the big New York house in the old-time, downtown square. Although they had been under the hospitable roof for more than twenty-four hours it was the first occasion on which the three had been together for more than a few minutes at a time.

On the previous evening in an upstairs room had been enacted a little scene which would live forever in the memories of them all; but Doctor Craig, perceiving with trained eyes the signs of growing fatigue in his frail friend after the unwonted strain of the day and its necessarily emotional climax, had gently but firmly insisted on withdrawing at an early hour. Georgiana had remained with her father, herself content to have the strange and wonderful day end in the old, simple, and natural way in which her days had ended for so long. She had felt, as she performed her customary daughterly offices for the beloved invalid, that she had quite enough to take with her to her own pillow to insure its being the happiest upon which she had ever laid her head.

They had seen little of Doctor Craig on the following day; but he had taken dinner with them that night, and as he had brought them back to the library fire he had given stringent directions to the boy Thomas that he be disturbed only for the most important summons. And hardly had the trio taken their places in the pleasant room before Jefferson Craig made his statement that there was something still unsettled in their affairs.

As he spoke he was looking down at Georgiana. It would have been strange if he could have kept his eyes away from her to-night. Like a flower in sunshine had she bloomed under the warm influence of the joy which had come to her when she least expected it. She was again wearing the little gray silk frock, but now its nunlike simplicity was gone—and happily gone—for a bunch of glowing pink Killarney roses at her belt, placed there by Doctor Craig's hands, lighted the plain costume into one of a charm which could no longer be called demure.

"Something still to settle?" It was Father Davy who replied, for Georgiana had no answer for that suggestion. One glance at Doctor Craig's face, as he said the words, had told her what was coming.

"The most important thing of all. Everything else is in order. You, dear sir, have agreed to come and live with us. We are convinced that it's not a sacrifice, except for the leaving of certain old friends. You have a zest still for seeing and hearing the things you have been denied; it's to be our keen pleasure to make your days go by on wings. You're going to have plenty of room here for the bookcases and the books, all the furnishings you care to keep—in short, you're to live the old life with a fine new one as well. Altogether, everything is in train for the great change, except"—he crossed the hearthrug at a stride, and laid a son's hand upon the thin shoulder of Father Davy—"except the date of it," he finished, smiling down into the uplifted face.

"But that," replied Georgiana's father without hesitation, "is not for me to settle. It is for you two."

Craig looked across at Georgiana and for a minute studied her down-bent profile as she sat gazing into the flames; then came round to her, plucking a pillow from a big leather couch by the way, to drop it at her feet and throw himself down upon it. So placed he could look straight into her face. "You'll have to take an interest in the ceiling now if you succeed in avoiding me," he said, with a low laugh.

"I don't want to avoid you," answered Georgiana, and let her eyes meet his fairly for an instant. She could not yet do this in a quite casual way.

He crossed his arms upon her knee, sitting in a boyish attitude and looking not unlike a big boy for the moment, for all the lines of care were gone from his face in the soft firelight, and happiness had laid its rosy mantle over his shoulders as over hers. He began to speak rather quickly:

"For the life of me, I can't think of a reason why you should go back and spend a winter in the same old grind, waiting till spring and—making me wait till spring. Why should anybody wait till spring? I've let you talk about all the work you were going to do this winter at home, but that was just because I didn't want to make you feel as if you were caught in a trap. I had an idea that for a few hours, anyhow, it might seem enough of a change to come down here and promise to marry a perfect stranger of a surgeon instead of the 'literary light' you knew. I thought we'd let it go at that for those few hours. But now—it doesn't seem to me possible to go back to bachelorhood again, even with such a prospect before me in the spring. Not after having tasted—this. Georgiana, why must I?"

Her face was the colour of her roses. There was no getting away from the challenge of those eyes that watched her so steadily—not even by following his suggestion and gazing persistently ceilingward. Craig glanced at Father Davy, to find that his soft blue eyes showed no sign of shock, and that his face was perfectly placid as he looked and listened.

The younger man went on, coming straight to the point: "Georgiana, marry me before you go back! You've promised to stay a week. Let's have a wedding here, next Wednesday. Then we'll leave Father Davy here comfortably with Mrs. MacFayden, and run up to see about getting things packed and shipped. I'll take that much of a vacation now. Then, in April, we'll go abroad for a real honeymoon and take Father Davy with us. I'd propose that now, but the seas are stormy in December and January and we mustn't risk it for him. But, let's not wait! Why should we? Now, honestly, why should we?"

The girl turned her face, with a strange little look of appeal, toward her father, to meet such a look of entire comprehension as stirred her to the depths. Suddenly, obeying an impulse she did not understand, she drew herself gently away from Craig, rose and went to the figure in the big chair opposite. She sat down on the arm and, bending, dropped her face upon the fatherly shoulder, hiding it there. Craig sat perfectly still, watching the pair, as Father Davy put up a thin, white hand and patted the dark head. Then the two men smiled at each other.

After a while Craig got up and quietly left the room.

By and by Father Davy whispered: "What is it, dear? You're not ready? You shall not be hurried. Or is it——"

She spoke into his ear. "I want to go back home—and earn—and earn—enough to——"

"Can you earn it, daughter? Can you ever get enough ahead to provide what you would like? And meanwhile—he wants you very much, my dear. I think I know more of his heart than you do, in way. Last winter we had certain talks that showed me a little of that. Would it be such a blow to pride to do as he asks? Unless—in other ways you are not ready. If your love for him isn't quite mature enough yet——"

"Oh, it isn't that; it's mature enough. It—it hasn't grown, in spite of me, all this year like—a—tumbleweed"—her voice was a little breathless—"not to have got its growth——"

"Its first growth," amended her father, with a meaning smile.

She nodded. "But—if you could know how I want—time to make the most of—what mother left me. I could do so much if I just had time. If I used it now I should have to use it up so fast! There'll be fifty dollars left when we get back. I could almost make that do, if—no, of course I couldn't. But I could earn more. O Father Davy, is it wrong of me to be so proud?"

"Not wrong, my girl, but very natural, I suppose. Yet to me—well, dear, I hardly know how to say what I feel. I confess I should like to see you married to this man. Life is—so short——"

They sat together in silence for a time; then Georgiana slipped back into the seat where she had been.

Presently Father Davy said that it had been a full day, and that he thought he should be fitter for the morrow if he should go to bed. Georgiana went up with him, saw him comfortably resting, listened while he whispered something in her ear as she bent above him, kissed him with her heart on her lips, and finally stole like a mouse down the stairs again.

When she came into the library once more it was to find herself in arms which held her close. "Do you think I don't understand, my dearest?" said the low voice which had such power to move her. "Do you think I don't respect and love you for your perfectly natural feeling about it all? But, Georgiana, you bring me a dowry bigger than any I could ask for—the inheritance from such a father as he is—and from the mother who gave you all he left her to give. What are towels and tablecloths—I don't know what it is brides bring!—beside such things as these? Won't you give me the real thing, and let me furnish the ones that don't count? Dear, if you could know the pleasure there is for me in the very thought of buying you—a hat!"

She could but smile, his tone put so much awe into the word. Suddenly she grew whimsical; it was so like Georgiana to do that when she was deeply stirred!

"What do you suppose that hat was made of, I wore here?" she asked him. "I'll tell you. I found the shape for twenty-five cents at the village milliner's. I cut it down and sewed it up again into another shape. Then I hunted through the old 'Semi-Annuals'; you don't know what those are, do you? I found a piece of velvet that had been a flounce. I steamed it and covered the shape. Then I had to have some trimming. It came from an old evening cloak of my Cousin Jeannette's—a bit of gilt, a silk rose, some ribbon from—I can't tell you what it came from, but it had to be dyed to match the velvet. I couldn't quite get the shade. But the hat, when it was done, wasn't so bad."

"Where is it now?"

"Upstairs in my room."

"Would you mind getting it?"

She laughed, hesitated, finally ran upstairs and down again, the hat in hand. Pausing before an old gilt mirror in the hall she put it on, then came to him, lifting her head with a proud and merry look which bade him beware how he might venture to criticise the work of her hands.

Adjusting his eyeglasses with care, he viewed it judicially. "It looks very nice to me," he said. "Suppose you keep it on and put on a coat and let me take you out in the car for a few minutes. There's a certain window uptown I should like to look at, with you."

"I have no coat," she said steadily, and now the colour ebbed a little from her warm cheek, "except the one that belongs with the suit I wore. It's short; it wouldn't do to wear with a dress like this."

"I see." Suddenly he came close again, gently lifted the hat from the dark masses of her hair, laid it carefully on a table near by, and drew her with him to a broad, high-backed couch at one side of the fire.

"I can see," he said, very quietly, "that you and I have much to do in getting to know each other. Let's lose no time in beginning. Listen, while I try to tell you what marriage means to me—and to find out what it means to you."

It was a long talk, and, by the kindness of the fates which rule over the irregular schedule of the men of Craig's profession, an uninterrupted one. Long before it was over Georgiana learned many new things concerning the man who was to be her husband, not the least of which was his power of making others see as he saw, feel as he felt, and believe, from first to last, in his absolute integrity of motive. And when he told her what he thought he could do for her father if he should have him under his eye during the coming winter, the period which was always so long and trying for the sensitive frame of the invalid, whose resisting powers were at their lowest when the winter winds were blowing, she gave way and the question was settled.

But she did not give way in everything after all, nor did he ask her to do so. When he suggested details of preparation, and she shook her head, he smiled and told her it should all be as she wished. And when he said, very gently, that he hoped she would let him provide her with the means to buy whatever she might need, because everything that he had was hers already, he took with a submission that was all grace her refusal to use a penny of his until she should bear his name. If he made certain reservations of his own as to what might happen when he should hold the right, that did not show.

96

"So that I get you, dearest," he said at the end of the evening, just before he let her go, "I am willing to take you in any sort of package you may select for yourself. Personally it seems to me that jeweller's cotton is the most appropriate background for you, if you won't have a satin-and-velvet case!"

At which Georgiana laughed, and assured him that she was no real jewel, only one of the secondary stones, and uncut at that. The answer she got to this sent her off upstairs with thrilling pulses, to lie awake for a long time, recalling his voice and look as he said the few suddenly grave words which had given her a glimpse of his bare heart.

CHAPTER XXIV

MAGIC GOLD

The days which followed were to be remembered with peculiar delight all Georgiana's life. Each morning, in Doctor Craig's own car, accompanied by her father, she went shopping. Mr. Warne could not use his strength in following her into the shops, but he could sit at ease in a corner of the luxurious, closed landau, an extra pillow tucked behind his back, an electric footwarmer at his feet, his slender form wrapped in a wonderful fur-lined coat which his son-in-law to-be had put upon him with the reasonable explanation that it had proved to be too small for himself. From this sheltered position he could watch the hurrying crowds, study the faces and find untiring interest in the happenings of the streets.

Not the smallest part of his pleasure lay in receiving his daughter again each time she came hurrying out of some great portal, the tiniest of packages under her arm. Although Duncan, Doctor Craig's chauffeur, was always watching, ready to jump from his seat and assist her, she was usually too quick for him to be of much use, though she always gave him her friendly smile and thanks for his eagerness. It may be said that Duncan himself, a young Scotsman whose devotion to his master was now augmented by his admiration of his master's choice, enjoyed those shopping expeditions with an unusual zest.

"Oh, but these shops are wonderful, Father Davy!" Georgiana was fain to cry, as she came back with her purchases. "Of course I have to shut my eyes and simply fly past the counters where I'd like to buy everything in sight. But I do find such glorious little bargains, such treasures of left-overs—you can't think how I'm making my money hold out! I'm so thankful for all my training in turning and twisting; it's such a help just now!"

If Father Davy rejoiced within himself that the days of "left-overs" for Georgiana were all but past and that there was to be no more "turning and twisting," at least with material things, he did not say so. Instead he surveyed the contents of the small packages with eyes which were nearly as bright as hers, and made her supremely content with his approval.

The climax of the shopping came on the morning of the third day. Georgiana returned to the car after a more than usually long absence, during which, for the first time, Mr. Warne had become slightly weary of using his eyes in watching the ever-moving throng, and had dropped off, in his warm corner, into a little refreshing nap. He wakened to find Georgiana beside him, the car moving uptown by a less congested route than they had taken before, and his daughter's hand firmly clasping his.

He looked round at her and saw, to his surprise and dismay, that her heavy lashes were thick with tears. But she smiled through them, and bade him wait to hear the reason until

97

they were in the Park, where each morning a drive, according to Doctor Craig's suggestion, was taken before the swift run back to the downtown square.

The moment they were well within the precincts and had entered upon the less frequented drive which she had asked for, Georgiana turned to her father. She held up something before him, and, looking at it, he discovered the little old bag of dark blue silk which her mother had fashioned from her own wedding gown, and which had contained the treasured gold pieces which had made it possible for Georgiana to have a wedding gown of her own.

"It's nearly empty now," said the girl softly. "It's bought so much, Father Davy; I've begun to think it was magic gold! Everybody—all the shopgirls and women—have helped me spend it. It was as if they knew I must make it go a long way and wanted to do it. I really think"—she gave a tremulous little laugh—"it was a good thing I wasn't dressed to match the car I came in, or they never would have taken the trouble to hunt up the things I wanted—at the prices I could pay. The fact that I looked like a shopgirl, too, was such a help!"

"A shopgirl!" repeated her father. "You, my dear? What would Jefferson say to that? No matter how you were dressed you could not possibly look anything but what you are."

"Oh, but, Father Davy, dear, you don't know what many and many of the shopgirls, especially these city girls, look like. There are such beautiful faces among them, such soft voices, such really charming manners. Of course there are plenty of the other kind, the cheap and common sort, but so many of the nice kind! I don't mind looking like some of them, indeed I don't. And the fact that I'm wearing this little old summer serge suit, now in December, with this hat, which any clever girl would know I made myself—well, it has helped me to interest their sympathies in my search. And now I've found"—her voice sank—"I've found what I couldn't have expected to find in all New York. And I'm so glad—so glad—I can't tell you. Look!"

She slowly unwrapped a long, slim, cylinderlike parcel, and brought to view what it contained. Inclosed in its pasteboard protector, to keep it unwrinkled in its soft perfection, lay a roll of dark blue silk, of a small brocaded pattern.

Georgiana silently laid the little blue-silk bag upon it, and held up the two so that her father could see how close was the resemblance. The colour was precisely the same, making allowances for the slight dimming of age; while the design of the brocade was so similar that the two might have been made in the same period, if not by the same hand.

Mr. Warne studied the two fabrics intently for a moment, then looked into his daughter's eyes. He was too moved to speak. When she herself could talk again composedly she told him what she meant to do. The blue silk, made by her own hands in the three days left her, was to be her wedding gown. She had bought a little fine lace, fit for such a use, with which to make the finishing; and no matter what Doctor Jefferson might think of such a substitute for the customary bridal attire, for herself she should be far happier than in the finest white silk or satin that could be bought.

"God bless you, my little girl!" Father Davy murmured, wiping his eyes, their clear blue depths misty.

His thin hand clasped the little blue bag again, his heart ached with the sorrow which is part joy and with the joy which is part sorrow. Nothing his Phoebe's daughter could have done would have proclaimed her so truly the child of her mother as this unexpected act. He looked again and again at the roll of blue silk in Georgiana's lap.

"How strange it seems that you could find it," he said, "now when everything is so different from the fashions of twenty-five years ago."

"It's a revival, the silk man said. He explained that the styles of the moment call for the fabrics and patterns of the past, and that it's a constant revolution, bringing back every once in so often what is old-fashioned between times. But he himself was surprised that the very newest thing on his shelves was the one that matched the old. I think he was almost as pleased as I was—without knowing anything about it, except that I was very anxious to find the silk. And now to hurry home and make it!"

Her unconscious use of the word "home" struck pleasantly upon Mr. Warne's ears. He himself was beginning to feel very much at home in the old square. Small wonder, since he had found there the son he had longed for all his married life.

Back at the house Georgiana fell to work without delay. She had told Mrs. MacFayden her intention, and had enlisted the warm interest of that motherly Scotswoman. She had offered Doctor Craig's young guest the use of her own sitting-room, with that of the sewing-machine which stood there, and here presently Georgiana unrolled her breadths of silk and laid upon them the pattern she had selected.

And now, indeed, she was glad of the long training in the dressmaker's trade, glad of the clever art she had cultivated for so many years. It was to her a simple enough matter to fashion herself a dress which should be in form and line all that could be desired. To do it out of unbroken yards of material, without necessity for piecing and patching, was a delightful novelty. To accomplish it in three days was only a matter of working at top speed, with fingers which flew at the behest of a brain which also worked like magic at its task.

During this period Doctor Craig himself was more than ordinarily busy, to judge by his infrequent appearances at his home. For those last three days before his marriage he was out of town, returning only on the evening preceding the date set. But Georgiana found no lack in him as a lover, for during the brief moments when he could be with her he made the most of his opportunity, letting her see plainly that she was always in his thoughts, and giving her every evidence that he was the happiest of expectant bridegrooms. Each day a great box of flowers was brought to her, in which she revelled as she had only dreamed of doing. While he was away he called her up each evening on the telephone, managing to send her somehow, over the wire, a sense of his nearness and his devotion. Altogether those few days brought to Georgiana an experience unique in a lifetime, and one which she would gladly have prolonged.

Then, it seemed quite suddenly, it was Wednesday morning, and the sun was shining brilliantly in at Georgiana's windows over a thousand roof-tops. The marriage was to occur at noon, because, for a bride whose bridal finery was limited to a little frock of dark blue silk and whose traveling attire was the plainest of ready-to-wear suits and simplest of small hats, without furs or furbelows of any sort, it seemed the only fitting hour.

It had been arranged that the two essential witnesses to the ceremony should be two close friends of Doctor Craig's, an elderly couple whose name, if the Warnes had known, was one of the old names of the city, standing for the bluest of blue Knickerbocker blood, though for only moderate wealth and for no ostentation whatever. Georgiana had begged that no other guests be asked, being anxious, on her father's account, to have the whole affair over with the least possible agitation for him. To this Doctor Craig had cordially agreed.

At eleven o'clock, however, a third guest arrived, a most unexpected guest, who with a ruddy, eager face, came running up the old stone steps of the house, a great florist's box under his arm. He demanded of the boy Thomas instant entrance, and waved back at a taxicab driver the summons to bring along a much larger box which was nearly filling that vehicle.

Georgiana, peeping out of her father's window, beheld, and was off and down the stairs before Thomas could fairly begin his explanation that Miss Warne was engaged and could not be intruded upon at this hour.

"O Jimps!"

"Well, well, George! You came pretty near giving me the slip, didn't you? But not quite—thanks to Doctor Craig."

Georgiana showed her surprise. "Did he let you know?"

She had led him instantly inside the library and had unconsciously closed the door all but in the face of the interested Thomas, ignoring both florist's box and big package, which that young man would have brought in to her. She had both hands on James Stuart's shoulders, and was looking him straight in the eyes, which looked as straightly back. If there had ever been the beginning of romance between these two, clearly it was far in the background now. Never did brother and sister face each other with their relationship more clearly defined.

"I should say he did—since you didn't! What did you mean by trying to steal a march on us all like this? Jeannette is furious, though of course she isn't strong enough to come, wild though she is to do it. She wanted me to tell you that she'll have revenge when she gets about, and that you won't escape her wedding presents. Meanwhile she's sent you something she had on hand, because there was no time to get anything else. She thought you would find a use for it somehow. She sent her love with it—and I can tell you that's pretty valuable."

"Of course it is! Jimps, I'm so pleased, so wonderfully pleased that you are here—I can't tell you!"

"Then, why in the name of old friendship didn't you send for me?" Stuart demanded, for plainly this still rankled. "Evidently Doctor Craig had more belief in that than you did."

"I wanted to, indeed I did, Jimps, dear, but I thought—I was sure—well——"

Stuart laughed. "Thought I wanted to save every penny for my own wedding, eh? I rather guess I can squander a few on yours. I wouldn't have missed it for worlds, though I'd give a good deal if *my* sweetheart could have been here, too—and so would she, bless her! She's coming on splendidly, George—looks almost herself again. In a month more her doctor will let up on restrictions."

They talked fast, with an eye on the library clock, and when its deep, slow chime proclaimed the half-hour Georgiana rose.

"I must go now. Come and stay with father till the hour arrives, will you? It will steady him to see you. Not but that he seems as serene as ever, but I know inside it's a pretty big strain for him."

"All right, I'd like nothing better, since I can't see you any longer. Where's the principal man for this occasion, anyhow? Can he take the time to be married, or is he liable to send up word he's detained? You can't put your finger on these popular surgeons till they're here."

"I had a telephone message from him an hour ago," Georgiana assured him, with a conscious little smile. "I really think he'll be here, though not till the last minute, probably."

"If he isn't I'll go after him with a gun. If he doesn't show up I'd marry you myself if it wasn't for a previous engagement," dared Stuart, with a happy laugh.

"Never! If I couldn't have my man I'd never marry anybody," she whispered, as she turned to look back at him for an instant, her hand on the library door.

Stuart caught the hand, and whispered back: "George, is it like that with you, too?" She nodded. His face flamed. "It's wonderful, isn't it? Unbelievable!"

She nodded again. They looked into each other's faces, smiling through a mist of happiness, then Georgiana flung open the door and ran out into the hall.

100

Stuart followed, caught up the big box and ran after her up the stairs. "Here," he said under his breath, as they reached the top, "be sure to open this before you go. Jean wanted you to wear it away with you; she said you'd be sure to need it, traveling. It's a beauty; it just came home for her."

He gave her the big box at the door of her room, while she pointed him down the hall to her father's door. He patted her arm with a brotherly gesture, and hurried along.

Inside her room, with a glance at the clock, she opened the box. Under the tissue lay a soft, luxurious-feeling mass, all dark blue cloth of a velvety texture, with glimpses of dark fur. She opened it, with a sigh of pleasure, for it meant that now she might look fit to be Dr. Jefferson Craig's traveling companion, with this cloak, fur-lined, all-enveloping, to slip on over the plain little suit which was not half warm enough for severe winter weather.

"It's the last of my 'Semi-Annuals,'" she said to herself, "and the best. How dear of her! And oh, how good it is that Jimps is here! Now I have a family, a real family to see me married—a father and a brother!"

The clock again—warning her to fly. She had ever been rapid at dressing—she had never been quicker. A cold plunge—the second that morning, bringing the blood leaping—the donning of fair garments lying ready to her hand—the arrangement of hair in the old way, simplicity itself—then the slipping over her white shoulders of the blue silk gown. When it was fastened Georgiana went to stand by her window, looking out with eyes which did not see.

CHAPTER XXV

GREAT MUSIC

"Wull ye be comin' soon, Miss Warne?" said the voice of Mrs. MacFayden at her door. Georgiana opened it quickly, and the housekeeper entered, quietly resplendent in black silk with fine lace collar and cuffs, her hair in shining order, an expression of great solemnity on her face.

"Mr. and Mrs. Peter Brandt are here," she announced with impressiveness. "Doctor Craig is doonstairs with them; he cam' ten minutes ago. He bade me say he wad coom for ye himself when ye were ready. It's a gled day for him, Miss Warne, an' for us a'."

Georgiana advanced, her heart very warm toward this good woman, who, as she well knew, was quite as much the friend of Jefferson Craig as his housekeeper, and well esteemed, even beloved by him. The girl came close.

"Mrs. MacFayden," she said, very low, "I have—no mother to kiss me before I go down. May I——"

The sentence was left unfinished, for with one step forward Mary MacFayden opened wide her arms, and for a long minute the two enfolded each other, while both hearts beat strongly.

Then Georgiana, suddenly mindful that she must not let go for an instant of her self-control, pressed a kiss upon the fair, smooth cheek of the Scotswoman, received one equally warm upon her own, and drew away smiling. "Thank you," she murmured uncertainly. "I couldn't go without it."

"Thet ye could na', lassie," responded Mrs. MacFayden heartily. "Noo—wull I send the doctor up?"

"Just in a minute—when I have seen my father——"

Georgiana ran into his room from her own. A deep embrace, a lingering kiss—while James Stuart looked out of the window, a lump suddenly appearing from nowhere in his sturdy throat.

Then Georgiana said softly at the young man's elbow: "Thank you again for coming, Jimps. It's such a comfort to have my brother here."

Before he could reply she was gone again.

He led Mr. Warne downstairs, where Doctor Craig presented them both to the Brandts—delightful people Stuart thought them, too—so simple and unaffected—almost like village people.

As he stood waiting with them, in the same dignified big room which he had been in before he went upstairs, he was conscious that in his brief absence its character had changed. Library though it still was, with its massive bookcases filled with rows upon rows of finely bound books, it had taken on a festal air. Great bowls of roses, deep crimson, glowing pink, rich amber, had been brought in; they stood on table, chimney-piece, and floor; hundreds of them it seemed to him there must be. He realized that Georgiana herself could not have seen them; they would be a surprise to her. Evidently the simple little wedding was to have a character all its own.

With the quiet departure of Jefferson Craig from the room James Stuart was all eyes for an appearance at the door. How would Georgiana come to her marriage? In shimmering white, he supposed, for that was the traditional garb of all the brides he had ever seen—mostly village girls they were. Once, while at college, he had attended a city wedding, that of a classmate who had not been willing to wait till his college course was finished. Stuart remembered how pale the bride had been; she, had looked as if she were going to faint. He hoped Georgiana would not look like that: he could not conceive it.

The next moment he saw her, entering the wide door, on Doctor Craig's arm—the same Georgiana he had always known, as simply dressed, even more simply, he thought, though he had little time for looking at her dress, so held was his gaze by her face. Never could he have conceived so radiant a bride. And then he thought—Jefferson Craig had gone up alone to bring her down. Stuart wondered if he himself could make Jeannette look like that, at such a moment. He thought he could!

Georgiana looked into Father Davy's eyes as she stood before him. He was not tall; his face was almost on a level with her own. It seemed to her she had never seen eyes so clear, so blue, so comprehending. Her own never left them for a moment while the service lasted, until the closing prayer.

Father Davy's voice, at first very slightly tremulous, gathered force as he went on with the words he had spoken so many times, but never as he was speaking them now—to his child, to Phoebe's child, and to the man of her choice. A little flush crept into his thin cheeks. More than once his eyes rested on the dark-blue silk which covered his daughter's shoulders; the sight of it seemed to give him strength.

When the service ended, and his voice sank into the words of prayer, the hand of Mr. Peter Brandt went for a moment to his eyes; Mrs. MacFayden felt suddenly for her handkerchief; James Stuart softly cleared his throat, winking once or twice rather rapidly. Never had any of them heard just such a prayer as that. It was as if he who made it were very near the invisible Presence whom he so tenderly and trustingly addressed.

Stuart never forgot the moment when he looked for the first time into the eyes of Jefferson Craig's newly made wife. For one instant he suffered a pang of jealousy—a queer, irrational feeling. It was as if he had lost his friend, as if this star-eyed creature before him could never find room for him again in her full heart. But he knew better in the next breath, for she lifted her face, ever so little, and with a sense of deep relief he gave her the brotherly kiss she thus permitted. When he looked at Jefferson Craig he found that the keen, fine eyes were regarding him with a very friendly intentness, and he wrung the hand offered him as he would have wrung the hand of a brother.

"You're the luckiest man in this whole big town," declared Stuart. His lips had been dumb before Georgiana, but now he turned to her again. "George, there's no use trying to tell you how I feel about this. All I can say is that nothing's too good for you—or for him. That's pretty lame, but—whatever eloquence I'm capable of is tied up somewhere; I can't get it out."

"It's out, Jimps, dear," she assured him. "Isn't it—Jefferson?"

"It certainly is—Jimps," Craig answered heartily. "It was for just that genuine feeling that I sent for you. I knew we couldn't spare it."

Stuart watched the pair eagerly during the next hour—the hour during which the little party sat at the wedding breakfast which followed. The table was a round one, and his place was next the bride, so he missed nothing. He had never been present on such an occasion, nor could have guessed the beauty and charm of the setting wealth and art can give. It was perfection itself, arranged by whose hand he had no notion, but he understood well enough by whose order had been created all the simple elegance which so well suited the house and the people. And as he looked at Georgiana he said to himself:

"She fits into this as if she had been born to it. She *was* born to it, for it's just the kind of thing she'd have made for herself if she'd had the means. No show, no fuss, just niceness! And it's the sort of thing my wife shall have, somehow, even in the country, before long. We'll *bring* this there; she'll know how. There's no patent on it. Bless her—how George deserves this! If only Jean could have been here. But I'll tell her; I'll get it over to her. And she'll understand!"

At the end of the hour the car was at the door, and Georgiana was coming down the stairs in her traveling clothes, her bridal bouquet on her arm. How those splendid roses had lighted up the little dark-blue frock!

"I've no bridesmaid to throw it to," she said, extending it toward Stuart. "Will you take it to Jeannette?"

"I should say I will. I'll be with her this evening; she made me promise." And Stuart received the offering with a glad hand.

A long, silent clinging to her father was the only parting embrace for this girl. If James Stuart longed for one of his own, after these years of friendship, he was obliged to be content with the lustrous look he had from eyes lifted for a moment to his as Georgiana took her place in the car, and with the lingering pressure her hand gave his, which spoke of love and loyalty.

Then she was gone, with Jefferson Craig sending back at Stuart a special brilliant smile of gratitude for the office he had performed, that of taking the place of the whole group of young people usually present on such occasions, saying good-bye with bared head and face of ardent devotion, with the first light snowflakes of winter falling on his fair hair.

"I can't believe I'm quite awake," said Georgiana, by and by. She sat in one of the drawing-rooms of a fast train, the door closed, the curtains drawn between herself and the rest of the carful of passengers, and only the flying landscape beyond the window to tell of the world outside.

Craig sat watching her; he seemed able to do nothing else. In his face was the most joyous content; there seemed almost a light behind it. "Not awake?" was his amused comment. "I wonder why. Now I feel tremendously awake—after a long, uneasy sleep, in which I dreamed of losing what I most wanted."

"But it's not all strange to you as it is to me. I can't quite believe that there's nothing on my shoulders—no care, no anxiety, just—well, *your* shoulders! Oh, but," she went on hastily, "don't think that means I want you to carry everything for me; indeed I don't. I want to carry—half!"

"Ah, but that's it," he answered. "My shoulders for your burdens, yours for mine. That way neither of us will feel half the weight of either. I'm not pretending that I shall give you a life of wholly sheltered ease; it won't be that, and you don't want it, not in this burden-bearing world. But—you shall have some things that you have been denied, my brave girl! Georgiana, I can't tell you how it touched me—the dress you made to be married in."

Her eyes went down now before the look in his.

"I'll tell you fairly that I longed with all my heart to take you to some place worthy of your beauty and find a wedding gown for you—not necessarily a very costly one, but one that should bring out all you are capable of showing. But when I saw you, looking just yourself, in the silk that was like your mother's,"—he leaned forward, taking both her hands in his and looking straight into her face, compelling her gaze to lift to his lest she should miss what she knew was there,—"I felt something inside my heart break wide open—with worship for you, little, strong, splendid spirit that you are!"

He pressed the hands against his lips. Then he touched two rings upon her left hand: exquisite and rare jewels were set in both engagement and wedding rings, after the modern fashion. But there was a third ring there, guarding the others, a slender band of gold, worn thin by many years of hard, self-forgetting work—the ring which David Warne had placed twenty-seven years ago upon the hand of his bride. Jefferson Craig studied all three, turning them round and round upon the rosy finger they encircled.

Presently he spoke again, very gently: "My rings on your hand mean to me love and beauty, loyalty and truth. But her ring stands for all that and—service. We need it there, to remind us what we owe the world we live in. She paid her debt; we'll pay ours, in memory of her. Bless her for giving me her daughter!"

For a minute Georgiana could not speak. Then, with her dark eyes sparkling through the mist of tears which had taken her unawares, she seized his hand and lifted it to press her glowing cheek against it, saying passionately: "Oh, *how* you understand!"

They were silent for a long time after that, while the train flew on, through the gathering darkness of the late December afternoon, into the night....

Georgiana had supposed that they were to go at once to the old home, for she knew that Craig could not be long away at this time, and there was much to do there. But she found that instead of changing trains in the great city, sixty miles beyond which lay the home village, they were leaving the station to be conveyed in a waiting car to a hotel.

"If you had been spending all these years in cities," was Craig's explanation, "I should have felt like plunging at once with you into the solitude. But as it is—well, I wondered if we shouldn't like to hear some great music to-night. Do you feel as I do—that there are times when nothing but music can speak for you?"

"But you," she said, "who live in the rush all the time——"

"There's no rush here for me," he answered. "Nobody is likely to know me here; I can forget the whole world in the midst of the crowd with you to-night. As for the music— I've been on short rations a good while myself. I think we can feast together, don't you?"

It was all a fairy tale to Georgiana, that evening in the city. Her college days had been spent in a small college town which, though it had lain not many miles away from this same great metropolis, had seldom seen her leave it for the privileges which richer girls enjoyed at every week-end.

As for the superb hotel to which Craig took her, although she had seen its impressive front, she had never so much as stood within its stately lobby. Now she experienced all sorts of queer little thrills, as she watched the accustomed ease with which her husband led her through the brief details of arrival and noted with what deference he was received. Evidently he had been expected, for there was no delay in the smooth service which took them to an apartment reserved by wire, as Georgiana gathered from a word she overheard.

He was quite right; a touch of this was what she needed, as a bird long confined needs a chance to stretch its wings. To this girl, with vivid life stirring in her pulses, the unaccustomed experience could but be a delight, with such a companion to show her the way. Every detail had its own fascination, such as might never come again when she should be more wonted to such scenes. The dinner served in their own small drawing-room, the flowers which crowned the table, the blithe talk Craig made during the little feast, with all its pretty, ceremonious detail of service; finally the short drive to the place where the great music, as Craig had called it, was to be heard—it all made a richly enchanting picture in Georgiana's mind.

When at length she sat beside her husband in the immense, silent audience, listening to such splendid harmonies as only once or twice in her lifetime she had heard before, her heart was far too full for words. He did not ask them of her, understanding something of what was passing in her mind, though not even his more than ordinary powers of sympathy could have guessed at all that held her breathless through those hours of supreme delight.

Certain words of a Psalm, which she had often heard her father quote, came into her mind and repeated themselves over and over. She had smiled with a bitter irony sometimes when she had heard him speak them in a tone of utter thankfulness, while she had been quite unable to imagine how he could use them of himself. But now—now—surely they applied to her!

Along with the sweep of the conductor's baton, with the rise and surge of one of the greatest of the symphonies, ran the triumphant words of the singer of old time: "*Thou hast set my feet in a large room.*"

Surely it was a large room into which, from a cramped and restricted one, she had emerged. She would do small honour to the devout life which had so long been lived beside her if she should fail to give the praise to the Maker of all life, who, according to her father's firm belief, had known from the beginning all for which He had been so wisely fitting her.

CHAPTER XXVI

SALT WATER

It was the tenth day of April. A great ship was making ready to sail; she lay like some inert monster at her pier, while all about her, within and without, was apparent commotion yet really ordered haste, the customary scene of bustling activity.

Few passengers had yet arrived, for the time of sailing was still some hours away. One party of three, however, had just driven down to the very gangway, allowed by some special privilege a closer approach than most at this hour. The reason was apparent when the party alighted, for one of its number was clearly an invalid, a frail-looking man with curly gray hair, who leaned upon the arm of a much younger man with a keen, distinguished face. The third person was a young woman, the sort of young woman who looks as if no buffeting wind could blow her away, because she would be sure to face it with delight, her eager face only glowing the brighter for the conflict.

"This is the advantage of coming early, isn't it?" said Mrs. Jefferson Craig, with a look of congratulation at her husband. "It's not much as it was when we saw Mr. and Mrs. Brandt off last week. You can walk on board as slowly as you please, Father Davy; there's no one to push."

Mr. David Warne was drawing deep breaths of the salty air, with its peculiar mixture of odours. He was also gazing about him with delighted eyes, seeming in no haste to cross the gangway.

"When I was a boy," he said to his daughter, who remained close at his side, "I lived, as you know, in a seaport town. Ever since I came away, it seems to me, I have been longing to smell that salty, marshy, briny smell again. It takes me back—how it takes me back!"

"The voyage is going to do you worlds of good," exulted Georgiana, her eyes bright with hope. "Jefferson was quite right: the winter at home, to help the poor spine; now the sea air, and the complete change, to make you strong. We'll have you marching back and forth with the other learned men, under the lindens at Trinity, while we are in Oxford—hands clasped behind your back, impressive nose in air—the very picture of a gentleman and a scholar."

"As if there were anything of the scholar about me," murmured Mr. Warne, smiling at this picture of his undistinguished self. "Well, my children, I suppose you are ready to go on, and I imagine we are not wanted in the way here. Let us proceed across that little bridge, and then we can look back at all this interesting activity."

Half an hour later, having taken possession of their staterooms, the party returned to the deck, where Georgiana and her husband established Mr. Warne in his chair, well tucked up in rugs—for the April air though balmy was treacherous. They then fell to pacing up and down, according to the irresistible tendency of the human foot the moment that it treads the deck.

"He seems deliciously happy, doesn't he?" said Georgiana's voice in her husband's ear. "If he were twenty-six instead of fifty-six he couldn't enter into it all with more zest. How pleased he was with Mrs. Brandt's flowers, and how dear it was of her to send them to him!"

"However happy he may be," declared Jefferson Craig, "it's not within the bounds of possibility that he is so happy as we!"

"Oh, of course not!" agreed Georgiana to this decidedly boyish speech. She realized suddenly how quickly the sense of relaxation from care was beginning to show in her husband. Her hand within his arm gave it a warm little squeeze. "That couldn't be expected. To be torn apart, at any and all hours, and kept apart day after day, just when we most want to be together—and then to come down to a big ship and know that no telephone bell can ring, nobody can make a single demand upon us that can prevent our being by ourselves—well, words simply can't express how wonderful it seems!"

"It *is* wonderful, and we'll make the most of it. There's just one thing I want to get out of this vacation in the way of work, and then all the rest of it shall be at your service."

"The book?"

"The book. How did you guess? I haven't spoken of it."

"No, but I've seen you looking wistfully at your notebook time and again, and guessed what you were thinking of. Well, we can make it fly. I'm ready for you."

Georgiana plunged her hand into a small bag she carried on her arm, and brought forth a notebook—of her own. She produced a pencil. "You may as well begin to dictate now," she said demurely. "What's the use of losing time? Just don't go too fast, that's all."

He stared at her. "What do you mean, dear? You don't know shorthand."

"Don't I? Well, perhaps I can write fast enough in long hand. Try me."

"My idea is," he said, "that we might spend a couple of hours every morning, and another couple in the afternoon, if you don't mind, and really get ahead quite a bit while we are at sea—provided you prove a good sailor, which I have an idea you will if—— See here, what are you doing? You're not taking that down in signs!" He looked over her shoulder at the notebook, where a series of dashes, angles, hooks and dots was forming with great rapidity. "You don't mean to say——"

"No, I mean to write, and let you do the saying. Go ahead, sir—only be sure you say something worth while."

"But—you didn't have that accomplishment when we worked together last summer."

"How I did wish I had, though! You kept insisting that I was doing all I could for you by copying endlessly, but I knew perfectly well that if I were a stenographer you could accomplish just three times as much in a given time as you did. You know perfectly well you only took that course to give a poor girl the chance to earn. If it hadn't been for helping me you would have had a secretary at your elbow, after you got to the point of needing him."

"I took that course, as you well know, because I wanted you at my elbow. If you had been able to write only a word a minute, I should have wanted you there just the same."

She gave him a merry, understanding look, then read him the words he had just spoken from her book.

"Where in the world did you learn, and how?" he demanded. "And how have you become so proficient in so short a time?"

"I'm afraid it's rather blundering work yet, but it will grow better all the time. Why, I've been taking lessons all winter, dear sir, at the best shorthand school in the city. I made up my mind that it was the thing I could do that would be of most use to you. It's a shame that a man who is doing the original work that you are shouldn't have time to give other people more benefit of it. It seemed to me you could write an important monograph in an hour, if you just had me at hand to take down the words of wisdom as they fell from your learned lips. Why you haven't used a secretary before for this purpose I don't know, but I certainly am glad you haven't. It insures me the position."

If she had wanted a reward for long and severe labours she had it in his look. "Other men dictate such papers," he said, "but somehow it has never seemed to me I could. I tried it once or twice and didn't get on at all as I did when I had the pen in my fingers. But with you, it may be different."

"It will be different," she told him confidently. "You're going to become used to my being so much a part of you that you can think as if you were using my brains—or I were using yours, which would be more to the purpose, I admit. Oh, we're going to accomplish all sorts of things together."

He looked down into her eager face, glowing with colour, the dark eyes apparently seeing visions which gave them keen delight. "You are a partner worth having," he said, much moved. "I knew you would be, and it's seemed to me all winter that no wife could be more of one. But if you're going to add this to your other activities you will make yourself even more indispensable than you already are, which is saying much."

She could hardly wait until she had made a trial of this new form of partnership. The ship had barely turned her face out to sea, parting company with her pilot, before the work began.

Doctor Craig had secured a small suite of staterooms opening upon a central sitting-room, and here he and Georgiana could be sure of much time to themselves. While the pair were engaged Mr. Warne was supremely content to lie in a sheltered corner of the deck, book in hand, reading or watching the ever new glory of sea and sky, or talking with some fellow passenger who possessed intelligence enough to discover what manner of man was here.

When Georgiana, ardent as a child in her joy over what was to be revealed, unpacked a small, portable typewriter and set it upon the table of the sitting-room, Jefferson Craig suddenly caught her in his arms.

"My blessed girl," he cried, "this, too? What haven't you done with your winter, when I thought you were spending your time getting acquainted with New York, as I meant you to do? You and Mrs. Brandt were supposed to be seeing everything worth seeing, on those morning drives. Were you shut up in your room all that time learning machines?"

"No, indeed. Do you imagine I made up all the stories I told you of those expeditions? We did all that, and this, too. I spent only an hour each morning at the school; the rest of the study I put in at all hours. Many of them were when I was waiting for you, Doctor Craig, to take me to a dinner or the opera. My notebook lived with me as if it had been a treasure I couldn't have out of my sight. It was just that. I never was so proud of anything I learned at college as I was when the gruff man who had my special training in charge told me I would make a stenographer. Not all of them did, he said. Some never could get hold of it, or acquire any speed or accuracy. Just give me a year, and I'll put down your thoughts before you think them!"

"I haven't a doubt of it," he agreed, with a laugh of amusement and delight.

Thus the work began, and thus it proceeded, with only one day's interruption when, in mid-ocean, came twenty-four hours of moderately bad weather.

To Georgiana's joy she proved herself the sailor her husband had prophesied, but her father was not so fortunate, and she promptly tucked him in his berth, where she kept him fairly comfortable until the rough seas quieted. When he was recovered he lay for one morning on the couch in the sitting-room, while the two workers resumed their task. Here he seemed to slumber much of the time, but in reality he kept rather a close watch on the absorbed pair, whom he had never before seen thus engaged, much as he had heard of their labours.

Looking up suddenly Georgiana discovered the blue eyes upon her, and when her flying fingers next stopped she put a question: "A penny for your thoughts, Father Davy. Don't we work together rather well, in spite of my being such a novice?"

"You two pull excellently well in double harness, it seems to me," he responded. "I can't see that either is taking all the load while the other soldiers and lets the traces slack."

Doctor Craig looked around at him. "She's always ahead by a pair of ears at least," he declared with a laugh.

"But I hear his steady pound—pound—at my side, and I'm afraid he's going to get a shoulder ahead," his wife explained.

The interest the pair excited on shipboard was greater than Georgiana guessed, though Doctor Craig was quite aware of it. Somehow or other the word had gone around, as words do go in a ship's company, as to the literary labours they were engaged in, and as Jefferson Craig's name was one known to more people than Georgiana had the slightest notion of, there was cause enough for the attention given them. Craig's noteworthy personality—one which marked him anywhere as a man of intellect and action—Georgiana's fresh young beauty, her spontaneous low laughter as she paced the deck at her husband's side, her readiness to make friends with those whose looks and bearing attracted her—these attributes made the Craigs the target for all eyes.

"I never saw people who looked so absolutely content," fretfully murmured one swathed mummy in a deck chair to another, as the pair passed them, on the tenth round of a long tramp, one gray morning when the wind was more than ordinarily chill. The speaker's black eyes, heavily lidded in a pale, discontented face, followed the Craigs out of sight as she spoke.

"Oh, they're on their honeymoon—that accounts for it," replied the other, languidly. Her glance also had followed the walkers.

"No, they're not—I've told you that before. They were married last December—plenty of time for the glamour to wear off. They act as if they never expected it to wear off. Sue Burlison must hate to look at them—she certainly had her mind made up to marry Jefferson Craig, if it could be done."

"So did Ursula Brandywine," contributed the languid one.

"You could say that of a dozen—twenty. I presume there are at least four disappointed mothers on board, besides Jane Burlison. Not that any of them ever had much encouragement from him—I'll say that for him. They'd about given him up as hopeless when he went off and married this country girl. One thing is certain—in spite of her fine clothes she hasn't the air his wife ought to have—she's not his equal."

"What's that you say?" The questioner was a sallow-faced youth upon the black-eyed lady's other side. Sunk deep in a fur-lined coat, his cap pulled low over his eyes—which were precisely like hers, even to the expression of discontent—he had seemed for the last hour to be slumbering. But at the moment he looked quite wide awake, as he turned his head toward his mother and challenged her latest statement. "What's that you say?" he repeated, in her own acrimonious tone.

"Oh, have you come to at last?" she inquired. "It is quite impossible to remember that though you sleep for hours you are liable to wake in time to contradict me on any point whatever. In this case it is of no consequence what I may have said."

"You were handing us the hot dope about Mrs. Craig's not being in the same class with Dr. Jeff. It certainly does take a woman to stick her claws into another woman's fur. There's one thing I can tell you—there isn't a man on board who'd agree with you. If she's a country girl—you can say good-bye for me to the little old town. I'm going to take to rural life till I find another. Talk about peaches and cream!"

"I believe I did not mention her complexion," his mother observed coldly.

"Neither did your little son—though it would bear mentioning. I should say yes! You said she hadn't any air. Jupiter—there she comes now. No air!"

He subsided into his high-turned fur collar but his eyes watched intently as the Craigs, still walking briskly after at least an hour's exercise, came up the deck from the stern. His mother, on the contrary, let her drooping lids fall indifferently. The moment they were out of possible hearing the young man sat up.

"By Jove, if you call that no air, tell the grande dames to get a move on. She walks like a young goddess—that's what."

"Silly boy! Nobody is talking of her face or her gait. If you don't know what I mean, no one can tell you."

"Oh, I know what you mean," her son assured her. "I get you. What I say is—you don't get her! Jefferson Craig's the one who gets her—lucky chap! Maybe he doesn't know it—oh, no! Maybe not!" And turning his back he once more appeared to slumber.

It was fortunate for Georgiana that she never even imagined such comments, though she passed these rows of critical eyes a hundred times a day, sat at table with people who were keenly observant of her every act and word, and spent some reluctant hours in the society of those who strove to cultivate her for their own blasé enjoyment. She only knew that among the company she met a number of interesting men and women, with whom she and her husband were thoroughly congenial, and that it did not matter in the least about the rest. If those whom she liked so much, and with whom she could talk with the greatest zest, turned out to be the men and women of scientific or literary achievement, this seemed only natural to the college-bred girl, and she cared not at all that she did not get on so easily with those whose distinction lay in purely social or financial lines.

During the winter just past her experience had been much the same, in a larger way. Her husband's acquaintance was naturally a large one, but the circle of his real friends was bound almost wholly by these same congenialities of mind and tastes. Georgiana had met and been entertained by many people whose names stood high on the list of the distinguished, though their personal fortunes were small, and their social activities were ignored in the society columns of the Sunday press. A college president, several famous surgeons, not a few noted authors of scientific books, as well as certain social workers, and two or three clergymen—these, with their wives and families, were the sort of people who gave to Georgiana Craig a hearty and sincere welcome, recognizing her at once as one who belonged to them. It was small wonder that the young wife, trained in a school of life in which nothing counted except worth and ability, found no lack, nor thought of sighing for the privilege her husband could easily have given her, had he cared for it himself, of mingling with a quite different class, that of the rich and gay who cared for little except that which could give them the most powerfully emotional reactions in the way of diversion, acquisition, or notoriety.

So they continued to work and walk their joyously contented way across the wide Atlantic during the six days between port and port. Georgiana enjoyed every hour, from that early morning one in which she first came on deck, running up with her husband to breathe deeply of the stimulating sea breeze before breakfasting, to the latest one, when, furry coat drawn hurriedly on over her pretty evening frock, her dark hair lightly confined under a gauzy scarf, she with Craig and a merry half-dozen of the evening's group came up again upon a deserted deck, to "blow the society fog out of their lungs," as one young biologist of coming reputation put it, in the silvery April moonlight, with only a few similarly inclined spirits to share with them the big empty spaces.

"I shall really be sorry to land to-morrow," sighed Georgiana, leaning upon the rail on the last night of the voyage, and staring ahead toward the quarter where her husband had just indicated they would be seeing land when they came up in the morning. "It has been so perfect, this being off between the sea and the sky together. When shall I ever forget this first voyage? It's a dream come true."

"You will enjoy the second one just as much, for you're a born sailor, and there'll be a long succession of voyages for you to look back upon by and by. Not just my annual pilgrimages to foreign clinics, but journeys to the ends of the earth if you like. Will that suit you, eager-eyed one?"

"Suit me? Oh, wonderful to think of! Am I eager-eyed really? I try so hard to cultivate that beautiful calm of manner I admire so much in other people. Haven't I acquired a bit of it yet?"

"A beautiful calm of manner—all that could be desired. But your eyes still suggest that you're standing on tiptoe, with your face lighted by the dawn," Craig answered contentedly. "Heaven forbid you ever lose that look! It's what gives the zest to my life."

CHAPTER XXVII

"CAKES AND ICES"

Jefferson Craig found plenty of the zest which he had told Georgiana—that last evening on shipboard—her eager-eyed look added to his life, when, the next day, in a compartment reserved for the three travelers, he watched her as she fairly hung out of the windows. All through Devonshire and on to the northeast. She was drinking in the fair and ordered beauty of the English countryside in April, exclaiming over apple orchards rosy as sea-shells with bloom, over vine-clad cottages and hedge-bordered lanes, masses of wall flowers at each trim station, and such green fields as she had never seen in her life. Father Davy was not far behind her in his quiet enjoyment of the unaccustomed scenes.

A night at Bath, picturesque and interesting, and then before the eldest of the three travelers could be really weary they were in famous Oxford. Professor Pembroke and his wife, Allison Craig, met them at the station, to convoy them to the comfortable quarters in the dignified stone house near Magdalen College, which Craig had more than once described to Georgiana.

Here the young American had her first taste of a manner of life which enchanted her. From the moment that she set eyes on Jefferson Craig's sister, the original of the photograph she had so often studied with a constriction of the heart, not knowing whose it was, she was drawn to her as she had never been drawn to any other woman.

Sitting with her in the pleasant, chintz-hung living-room, walking with her in the garden which was like no garden she had ever imagined, she was conscious of a stronger sense of wonder than ever that a man whose family was represented by a sister like this could ever have chosen the crude young person she still considered herself. From Mrs. Pembroke, however, she received only heart-warming assurance of her welcome and her fitness.

"My dear," Allison said, as the two stood at an ivy-framed window one morning, looking out at Mr. Warne and his son-in-law as they slowly paced up and down beneath a row of copper beeches between house and garden, "I never saw my brother so happy in his life. Jeff always was hard to please as a boy. I used to think it was merely a critical disposition, but later I discovered that it was his extreme distaste for all artifice, acting, intrigue—all absence of genuineness. Only those boys and men interested him whom he had absolute faith in.

"I don't mean that he himself was a goody-goody—far from it; he was a terrible prank maker, and more than once narrowly missed suffering serious consequences. But when he really grew up and it came to an acquaintance with women, very few have even attracted him. I began to fear that he was becoming hardened and would never find just what his fastidious taste could approve—not to mention what his heart might soften to. But now— well, I think I am almost as happy as he is, that he has found you. He seems like a different being to me, and evidently it is you who have wrought the miracle."

"I surely have made no change in him," Georgiana protested. "He has been just as he is now from the beginning—except, of course, that I know him better. I can't imagine him hardened to anything."

Allison Pembroke looked at her, smiling. She was herself an unusually beautiful woman, more mature than Georgiana, but still with a touch of girlishness in her personality which made her very appealing to her young guest.

"Evidently the softening process began the moment he met you," she said. "He frankly admits that himself. I am going to tell you what he wrote to me last winter, after you had begun your work with him. 'I feel like a footsore traveler,' he said, 'who has been walking for many miles along a hot and crowded highway, with the dust heavy on his shoulders and thick in his throat, who suddenly finds his course turned aside through a deep and quiet wood, with flowers springing on all sides, and a clear stream running beside him, where he may bathe his flushed face and cool his parched throat.' I have never forgotten the words, because they struck me as so unlike him. I knew then that something had happened to him there in the old manse. And when I saw you, dear, I didn't wonder that he chose just those words."

"I should never have thought," murmured Georgiana, incredulously, "that I could ever have reminded anybody of a quiet wood—I with my hot rebellion at having to spend my days in the country, which I could never quite cover up."

"I know. Just the same, Georgiana, after having known so many artificial women, posing, as women do pose for a man in Jefferson's place, it refreshed his very soul to find a girl like you, who dared to be herself from head to foot, whether she pleased him or not. And oh, I am so thankful you could care for him, since he needed you so much!"

Such talks brought these two very close together.

It was a happy week which Georgiana spent in the fine, classic old town, walking or driving with Allison, exploring quaint, winding streets, ancient halls, and flowery closes; or meeting interesting people of all ranks, from the chancellor of the University himself to the young undergraduates who offered her in their old and dingy but distinguished rooms tea and toasted scones, along with their fresh-cheeked admiration.

Not the least of her pleasure was in watching Father Davy's keen enjoyment of everything that came his way, and in noting how many of these English people seemed to find him one of them in his appreciation of all they had to offer and in his intimate knowledge of their time-honoured history. He apparently grew a little stronger with each succeeding day; certainly he grew younger, for happiness is a tonic which has special power upon those who carry the burden of years; and Father Davy's years, while not so many, had been heavy of weight upon his slender shoulders and had bowed them before their time.

After Oxford came London—a fortnight of it, and a very different experience. Living at a luxurious hotel with Allison Pembroke, who had come up with them, to show her all the ways of which she felt herself ignorant; with Craig coming and going from hospital and lecture room, suggesting each day new wonders; with hours spent daily in the dear delight of exploration in all sorts of out-of-the-way, famous places; Georgiana felt as if it were all too miraculous to be true.

That she, "Georgie Warne," as the village people had called her all her life, should, for instance, be walking with charming Mrs. Pembroke along Piccadilly in the May sunshine—real London sunshine and no watery imitation such as she had heard of—dressed in the most modish of spring costumes, violets in her belt purchased on a street corner from a young girl with the eyes of a Mrs. Patrick Campbell and the accent of Battersea Park—well, it simply did not seem real!

Much less did the hours seem real when she went with her husband to take tea on the Terrace at the Houses of Parliament, or with all three of her party to dine with some friendly Londoner who appeared eager to offer hospitality to the whole party. Best of all, perhaps, were the late evening walks upon which Craig took her alone, to stroll along the Victoria Embankment, a place of which she never tired, to watch the myriad lights upon the black river, and to talk endlessly of all the pair could see before them of purpose and achievement.

112

"Do you know what you remind me of these days?" Craig asked one night, when the two had returned to the hotel after one of these long, slow walks, during which they had been unusually silent.

He threw himself into a deep armchair as he spoke and sat looking up at his wife, who stood at the open balcony window, gazing down at the street below, with the interest in everything human which seemed never to abate.

She turned, smiling. She was particularly lovely to look at to-night, wearing a little pale-gray, silk-and-chiffon frock (lately purchased at a French shop in London), which, in spite of its Parisian lines and graces, was distinctly reminiscent of a certain other gray-silk frock worn on a never-to-be-forgotten occasion.

"Of a child at her first party?" she asked. "That's what I feel like. Only there's no end to the cakes and ices, the bonbons and surprises. And I never have to worry because before long I must go home!"

"No, not like that; your similes are always too self-deprecatory. You seem to me more and more like a young queen who has just come to the throne, but who is shy about picking up her sceptre. She prefers long-stemmed roses, and every now and then she catches up her train and runs down from her dais and out-of-doors, until some shocked courtier rushes after her and brings her back!"

"Now you *are* laughing at me!" Georgiana wheeled to confront her husband, who, stretched lazily in his chair, after a long day at the side of a great biologist in his laboratory, was relaxing muscles and nerves at the same time.

He put out one arm toward her, and she came slowly to his side. "Not a bit. It just delights me to see you your natural self in spite of all that London can do to you. Allison tells me that it is the most interesting thing in the world to watch you decide whether you will buy a new hat or a new book. She declares that milliners admire you and seem anxious to please you, but that when you get into a bookshop you have every old bookseller climbing about his ladders to bring down his choicest treasures for you."

Georgiana laughed. "I can't get used to buying hats at all—not to mention silk stockings—and as for buying hats and books and silk stockings on the same day, it's simply past belief that I can do it. Why do you fill my purse so full? I'm afraid I'm losing all the benefit of my long training in frugality."

"I hope so. I can never forget last winter watching you dissemble your good healthy appetite and pretend you didn't want beefsteak, while you fed your father and me on a juicy tenderloin. Brave little housekeeper on nothing a month!"

She looked at him quickly. "I never dreamed you noticed. And besides, I really didn't want——"

"Take care! The table was the only place where I ever caught you playing a part. I forgave you, only—how I did long to divide with you! Now all the rest of my life I can divide, equal shares, with you—my Georgiana!"

The weeks flew by, bringing never-ending interest. After London came Edinburgh, city of stately beauty, where among Scottish friends of the Craigs Georgiana learned whence her husband's family had sprung, and their noble origin and history.

Then the vacation was at an end "for this time," as Craig said, and the little party turned their faces homeward.

A letter from James Stuart, in the same mail with one twice its length from Jeannette Crofton, caused them to hasten their date of sailing by a week in order to be in time for a great event. Stuart wrote characteristically:

You simply have to come home, George, and help me through it. Of course I knew from the first I'd have to face a big city wedding, but the actual fact rather daunts me. Of course it's all right, for we know Jean's mother would never be satisfied to let me have her at all except by way of the white-glove route. The white gloves don't scare me so much as the orchids, and I suppose my new tailor will turn me out a creditable figure. But if I can't have you and Dr. Jeff Craig there I don't believe I can stand the strain.

The worst of it is that after all that show I can only take her back to the old farm. Not that she minds; in fact, she seems to be crazy about that farm. But it certainly does sound to me like a play called "From Orchids to Dandelions."

So, for heaven's sake, come home in time! The date's had to be shoved up on account of some great-aunt who intends to leave Jean her fortune some day if she isn't offended now, and the nice old lady wants to start for the Far East the day after the date she sets for our affair.

"Of course we must go," Craig agreed. "We'll stand by the dear fellow till the last orchid has withered—if they use orchids at June weddings, which I doubt. As for the dandelions, I think there's small fear that Jean won't like them. I fully believe in her sincerity, and I'm prepared to see her astonish her family by her devotion to country life. Stuart's able to keep her in real luxury, from the rural point of view, as I understand it, and she will bring him a lot of fresh enthusiasm that will do him a world of good."

"I'm trying to imagine Jimps's June-tanned face above a white shirt front," mused Georgiana. "He'll be a perfect Indian shade by that time."

"Not more so than any young tennis or golf enthusiast, will he?"

"Oh, much more. Jimps is out in the sun from dawn till sundown; his very eyebrows get a russet shade. But of course that doesn't matter, and his splendid shoulders certainly do fill out a dress coat to great advantage. You don't mind being considered one of his best friends by a young farmer, do you? That's the way he feels about you."

"I consider it a great honour. I never was better pleased than when Stuart first made friends with me, even after I discovered that he was, as I thought, my successful rival. It was impossible to help liking him. In fact, I've often wondered why—he didn't continue to be my rival."

"Oh, no, Jefferson Craig, you couldn't possibly wonder that!" contradicted Georgiana, in such a tone of finality that her husband laughed and told her that flattery could go no farther.

The voyage home was nearly a duplicate of the one outward bound, except that the two workers put in much extra time on the book and pushed it well toward completion.

Father Davy acquired the strength to take short walks on an even deck and boasted hugely of his acquisition, a twinkle in his eye and a tinge of real colour in his cheek.

"Imagine my coming home from abroad with trunks full of clothes and books and pictures," murmured Georgiana, as the three stood together watching the big ship make her port. "I feel like a regular millionairess."

"A regular one would smile at your modest showing," was Craig's comment. "I'm quite certain no man ever found it more difficult to persuade his wife to buy frocks, even when he went with her and expressed his anxiety to see her in particular colours."

"Confess," demanded Georgiana with spirit, "that you would be disappointed if I suddenly became a devotee of clothes and wanted all those gorgeous things we saw, and which that black-eyed Frenchwoman tried so hard to make me take."

"Those wouldn't have suited you, of course. I don't want to make an actress of you, or even a society woman who gets her gowns described in the Sunday papers. But when you refuse simple white frocks with blue ribbons——"

"Costing three figures! And I could copy every one of those myself for a fraction of the money."

"What would you do with the money saved?"

"Buy books."

Georgiana and Father Davy exchanged a smiling, tender glance which spoke of past years of longings now satisfied.

Craig laughed heartily. "Incorrigible little book-lover! Well, it's a worthy taste. I happened to overhear a comment on your reading the other day which amused me very much. When you left your steamer chair to walk with me you left also a copy of *Traditions of the Covenanters*. A little later, coming up behind that young Edmeston, who spends most of his time lounging in the chair next yours, I heard him say to a girl: 'She doesn't look such an awful highbrow, but believe *me*, the things she reads on shipboard when the rest of us are yawning over summer novels would help weight the anchor if we got on the rocks!' Then with awe he mentioned the name of that book, and the girl said:' How frightful! But I'm crazy about her just the same. I do think she wears the darlingest clothes.' So there you are! The men impressed, the girls envious, and your husband— worshipful. What more could a young wife ask?"

"Absolutely nothing," acknowledged Georgiana with much amusement.

CHAPTER XXVIII

A TANNED HERCULES

In spite of the fact that the holiday was over it was good to get back to the old house on the Square, to hear Mrs. MacFayden's warm "It's a gled day"; to smile at Thomas and Duncan and the maids; to hug dear Mrs. Brandt; and to receive a hearty welcome from the other friends, who were mostly still in town in the middle of June.

Then came eager summonses from Jeannette, who, with Aunt Olivia and Rosalie, was staying at an uptown hotel for the finishing of the trousseau. Georgiana found herself involved in a round of final shopping and hurried luncheons, while Rosalie talked incessantly, Mrs. Crofton argued maternally, and the bride-elect herself turned to Georgiana as the one person—with the exception of her father—who understood her.

"I can't convince mother and Rosy that I'm not really to spend the summer in the country with Jimps, and most of the rest of the year at home doing the usual round," sighed Jeannette, unburdening herself to her cousin during a half-hour's needed relaxation between luncheon and a visit to a famous jeweller's.

"I know; you'll just have to be patient, let them equip you for what they expect of you, and then—live your own life as you and Jimps have planned it. After a while they will see that you really do mean to live in the country, not the city, and that décolleté evening gowns don't suit the fireside, nor afternoon calling costumes the five-mile tramp. Meanwhile, don't let the poor boy ever guess at the size or quality of your outfit. I think he'd run away and hang himself!"

"He never shall know. And, Georgiana, I really have managed to have some quite simple little frocks made—by a young woman whom Madame Trennet recommended when I whispered in her ear. And I've bought the jolliest dark green corduroy suit, with a short skirt and pockets, and a little green corduroy soft hat to match, for the tramps. Oh, I'm going to be a real farmer's wife, I promise you!"

"Of course," mused Georgiana gently, lifting quizzical eyebrows, "I've never happened to see any farmer's wife thus equipped, but there's no reason why you shouldn't set the fashion. I suppose you will wear green silk stockings and bronze pumps with this picturesque tramping costume, with a bronze buckle in your hat to complete the ensemble. All you will then need will be a beautiful painted drop of the Forest of Arden——"

"You unkind thing! If *you* begin to scoff——"

"But I won't. I know there's heaps of sense in your pretty head, and you'll make Jimps the most satisfying sort of a wife even though you don't carry the eggs to market or milk the cows. There's no reason why you should, with your own private income. Jimps is too wise to forbid your spending it to decorate both your lives, for he knows you couldn't stand real wear and tear, while a reasonable amount of country life will make you stronger. Go ahead, dear; hang English chintzes at the farmhouse windows, set up your baby grand piano in that nice, old living-room, and hang jolly hunting prints in the dining-room. Wear the corduroys—only, instead of bronze pumps, I should advise——"

"You needn't. I've got them. The heaviest kind of tanned buckskin boots. And you all may laugh, but you just wait!"

"I'm not laughing; you know I'm not. I wish I could help you by convincing Aunt Olivia that you don't need some of the things she insists on including. But, since I can't, I'll comfort you by assuring you that Jefferson says he's counting on your being one of the sort who will prove the great contention—that beauty and poetry *can* be brought into the farmhouse."

Thus spoke Georgiana, though in her heart of hearts, as she watched Jeannette in all her costly elegance, at counter after counter, selecting supplies of one sort or another, she couldn't help having her doubts whether a lifelong training in luxury could be turned into a fitness for living, in spite of many mitigations, the truly simple life. These doubts, however, she suppressed, only dropping a word of caution here and there, which Jeannette took kindly, being eager to prove herself practical, and undoubtedly sincere in her longing to bring to James Stuart the helpmate he needed.

So came on the great day; and when it had arrived, and the Craigs were guests of Aunt Olivia, making ready for the ceremony, Georgiana had her chance to return to Stuart the support he had given her in the hour of her own marriage. She had just completed her dressing, and was about to descend with her husband to the waiting bridal party below, when Stuart came to their door.

Craig admitted him, and he entered, the dreaded white gloves in his hands, visible agitation on his brow.

"You young Hercules!" Georgiana cried. "Aren't you splendid!"

"I feel anything but splendid," he returned nervously. "I look like a boiled lobster on a white platter!"

"Nonsense, man," denied Dr. Jefferson Craig, his hand on Stuart's shoulder, "you're the picture of a healthy young bridegroom. I've seen plenty of tallow candles standing up to be married; you're a refreshing contrast."

After a minute of heartening talk, Craig slipped out of the room, leaving the two old friends together.

"Cheer up, Jimps," Georgiana bade Stuart, as she gave a straightening little touch to his white cravat, woman fashion. "This part won't last long. And don't be frightened when you catch sight of Jean in all her glory. She would much rather have been married as I was, you know, and she's really precisely the same girl in spite of her veil. She worships you, and everything's all right. Stop looking as if you wanted to run away!"

116

"But I do—if I could just take her with me," he answered, in such a melancholy tone that Georgiana laughed in his ruddy face.

"You can't; this is the only way you can get her; so stand up straight and look everybody in the eye. You're perfectly stunning in those clothes, and lots nicer to look at than most men. And Chester will take you serenely through all the forms, so you've nothing to worry about. That's right—give me a ghost of a smile. One would think you were about to be hung!"

"I came to you to be braced up, so it's all right; but call off the dogs of war now. I did pretty well till I saw the total effect, and then I thought maybe Jean would wish she had a man who could turn pale instead of crimson. But I'm going through with it, and I don't intend to look knockkneed, anyhow."

"Good for you. Just remember that Jean would swim through a flood of water to reach you, wedding gown and all, if the aisle should happen to be inundated, so you certainly can stand at the altar while she walks up that aisle."

"I sure can." And James McKenzie Stuart shook his broad shoulders, lifted his head, and held out both hands to Georgiana Craig. "Much obliged for the tonic. And, George— just remember, will you, that I'm precisely the same brother to you I've always been! Nothing can ever change that!"

"Of course you are," she agreed, with a rush of vivid recollections which brought a curious little smile to her lips. "Now go, my dear boy, and heaven bless you!"

Half an hour later, standing beside her husband in the flower-fragrant church, Georgiana watched with a beating heart to see Stuart bear himself like the man she knew him to be, in spite of all the pomp and ceremony to which he was such a stranger. She had been half angry, all the way through the preparations, that Aunt Olivia had insisted on every last detail of formality and ostentation—or so it had seemed to her, as unaccustomed as Stuart himself to the great church wedding with its long processional, its show of bridesmaids and flower girls, its ranks of ushers, its elaborate music, its pair of distinguished clergymen in full canonicals. But now, somehow, as the age-old words sounded upon her ears, it seemed to matter less under what circumstances they were spoken, so that the answers to the solemn questions came from the hearts of those who spoke them. And of this she could have no possible doubt.

By and by, when in her turn, back in the festally decorated house, she came to give the newly married pair her felicitations, she was well pleased to see Stuart quite himself again, smiling at her with the proud look of the bridegroom from whom no human being can wrest the prize he has just secured. And as she noted Jeannette's equally evident happy content with the man she had married, Georgiana took courage for their future. Surely—surely—they could go from these scenes of luxury to the plainer life that awaited them, and miss nothing, so that they took with them, as they were doing, the one thing needful.

"It's all right, I'm sure it's all right, dears," she said to them, and she said it again to her husband when they were rushing back to New York by the first train after the bridal pair had gone.

"Yes, I think it is," he agreed. "It's an interesting experiment, but not more hazardous than many another in the matrimonial line. If it succeeds Jeannette will come out a finer woman than she could ever have been by any other process. It's amusing, though, to see her family. Evidently they regard her as one lost to the world quite as much as if she had gone into a convent to take the vows perpetual."

"All but Uncle Thomas. He knows; he understands, little as he says. He grew up on a farm himself; he told me once that he could never smother the longing to get back to one. Poor Uncle Thomas, chained to a mahogany desk, with a Persian rug under his feet! That one little trip across the water, when the family went last year, was the only vacation he had taken in five years. And he came back on the next ship!"

"Jean and Stuart will have him often with them, see if they don't."

"I hope so. Change is what he needs very badly. Change! Oh, if everybody could have that when they need it! How it does make lives over! I know—how I do know! It's the deadly monotony that kills. Jean will bloom under the old farmhouse roof, away from all the fuss and frivolity she's so tired of."

"You've done some blooming yourself," observed her husband, "though I'll venture to say you work harder than you ever did before, even at the old loom."

She gave him a quick glance. "Oh, it wasn't play I needed—just work—the sort of work I love. I have that now. I love the visits to the hospital, the looking after the patients you bring home, the taking notes of your lectures, the teaching of my evening class of Italians—every bit of it is a delight. And then, when we do run away for a few hours, like this——"

"We enjoy it all the more for the contrast. Yes, I think we do. It's a pretty fine partnership, and it grows more satisfying all the time. Here's hoping the two we've just seen start follow in our contented footsteps. A year from now we'll know!"

CHAPTER XXIX

MILESTONES

Georgiana would not have believed that it would be a full year before she should have a chance to see for herself what sort of life Jeannette and Stuart were making for themselves under the conditions which seemed such doubtful ones. But so it turned out.

It had been before Jeannette's marriage that Georgiana found a change coming in her own life, and the months of the summer and autumn which followed were busy with the happy preparations for the new experience. In January her first son was born, and she learned that even a full and joyous partnership between two human beings is not the most complete thing that can happen to them. When she saw her husband take the round, little pink-blanketed bundle in his arms for the first time, and watched his face as he explored the tiny features for signs of the future, her heart beat high with such rich content as she had not dreamed of.

"Strange, isn't it, dear!" Craig said, when he had laid the pink bundle back in the arms of the nurse, who bore it away to the pretty nursery close at hand. "It's an old miracle always new, and never so wonderful as when it comes to us for the first time—how that little life can be neither you nor I, yet both of us in one. Big possibilities are wrapped up in that bit of flesh and blood; it's going to be a great interest, the watching them begin to show."

"Oh, yes!" she murmured, lying quietly with her hand beneath her cheek, too weary and too happy for speech.

"I wonder if I dare to tell you how soon it was after I knew you that I began to think of you as playing this part in my life," he said very softly.

"Did you? I'm so glad." It was hardly more than a whisper.

"Are you glad? I often think a girl little dreams of how often that vision comes to a man long before she has thought of it at all. I was only a very young man when I began to think of it. Even when there was no woman in my mind I used to plan what I would do for my own son when I should have him. And when I saw you I thought—with the greatest reverence, darling: 'If *she* might be my son's mother!'"

He did not need the look her eyes gave him to tell him how this touched her. When he went quietly away to leave her for the long sleep she needed it was with the consciousness that the bond between them was more absolute than it had ever been.

It was in the following June, on the anniversary of the marriage of the James McKenzie Stuarts, that the Jefferson Craigs had their first opportunity to see with their own eyes how that marriage was prospering. Letters from Jeannette had come to Georgiana from time to time, with an occasional postscript from Stuart, and these letters always breathed of happiness.

"But one can't be perfectly sure from letters," Georgiana argued. "After all the opposition and skepticism they would never own to anybody that life didn't flow like a rose-bordered stream. But one glimpse of their faces will tell the story. If Jeannette has a certain look I've often seen on the faces of girls who have been married about a year I shall guess what causes it. As for Jimps—he will be as easily read as an open book. Jeff, you won't let anything prevent our being there for the fête they ask us for?"

"Nothing that I can foresee and provide for," Craig promised. "I'm quite as eager as you to discover how the transplanting of the hothouse plant into the hardy outdoor soil of the country has worked out. There are two results about equally probable in such cases— hardly equally probable, either. The natural result, I should fear, would be the dwindling and stunting of the growth, unless protected by expedients not common to the country, and fertilized until it should be really not growing in country soil at all."

"But the possible result?" urged Georgiana.

"The one we're hoping for in this case—though I'm not sure how close an analogy I can draw, being no gardener—is the gradual process of adaptation to environment, so that the plant takes on a hardier quality, at an unavoidable sacrifice in size of bloom but with a corresponding gain in sturdiness and ability to bear the chilling winds and the beating sunlight of outdoors. Great size in a flower never appealed to me anyhow. I like a blossom that stands straight and firm upon its stem, that gives forth a clean, spicy fragrance and doesn't wilt when it has been an hour in my buttonhole."

"That's the sort Jimps wants, I'm sure. He used to be always tucking one of his scarlet geranium blossoms into his coat when he came over to see me. We all think of Jeannette as the frailest sort of an orchid, beautiful to look at but ready to wither at a touch. This letter of invitation doesn't sound like that at all. You really think the long drive won't hurt little son?"

"Not a bit, if you keep from getting tired or overheated yourself. We can manage that very nicely, with Duncan to drive, Lydia to look after the boy, and a long stop on the one night we must spend on the way. The change will do you good, faithful young mother."

This proved quite true, and the two days' journey in the great car was indeed an easy one for all concerned. Little Jefferson Junior, six months' old, slept away many hours of the trip, and spent the rest happily in his nurse's or his mother's lap, watching with big, dark eyes the spots of colour or life on the summer landscape as it slipped smoothly past. Georgiana had wanted to bring Father Davy, but though he had grown considerably stronger during the past year, it had not seemed worth while to put his endurance to so severe a test. He had not been left forlorn, however, for the Peter Brandts had taken him to their home, a welcome and a delighted guest. No doubt but there was a place for David Warne in the great city, as there had been in the country village.

On the afternoon of the second day, as they neared the old home village, to which Georgiana had returned only once since her marriage, she found herself noting with quickening pulse every familiar landmark.

"It seems so strange to think of my going away from such scenes for good and all, and Jean's coming to them," she said to herself more than once. "How little either of us would have believed it, just two short years ago!"

When they passed the old manse she gazed at it with affectionate eyes. "Oh, how shabby and poor it looks!" she said under her breath to Craig. "Did it look like that when you first saw it?"

He nodded, smiling. "Just like that. But the moment the door opened the first time I knew its shabbiness was just a blind to mislead the traveler, who might otherwise stop and try to steal the treasure that it held."

Her eyes were searching next for the chimney tops that should mark the other home for which they were bound. How often had she looked at those chimney tops, because they told her where was her best friend during those solitary days that were already so far past. A moment more and Georgiana's first exclamation of surprise broke from her lips. There were to be many before the day was done.

"Look! All those ugly little buildings at the back are gone, and the house stands all by itself at the top of the slope. Isn't that an improvement? It's freshly painted, too; how that clear white brings out the beauty of the old house! It used to be such a dingy slate! I always knew it was a pleasant place, but I didn't fully appreciate it. The lawn is as trim as can be, and there's a border of shrubs and flowers all along the drive. How little real change to make so much! That's Jean, I know. Oh, and there's Jean herself, running down the steps! She sees us!"

"Is that really Jeannette Crofton?" Craig doubted. "Yes—for a fact! Well, well!"

They might easily doubt the evidence of their eyes, for the slim figure they had known so well had rounded until it showed softly blooming curves, and colouring which put to blush the cosmetics which the society girl had not altogether eschewed, though it had been long before the less sophisticated cousin had found this out. No need for rouge or powder now, for nature had laid on the lovely face her own unrivalled tints of rose overlying the soft browns of summer tan.

"Oh, you darlings, to come and bring the baby! Do let me look at him—the blessed thing! Isn't he a beauty?—but, of course, how could he help it? Jimps! O Jimps! Here they are!"

Thus cried Jeannette out of sheer exuberance, though the fact of the arrival was obvious enough, and James Stuart was already dashing across the lawn from the opposite direction.

As she looked at her cousin, Georgiana's first impression was the one she had hardly dared hope for, that of Jeannette's entire content and well-being. Not only was the physical improvement noteworthy but a certain worn and worldly look had vanished— one which had not affected her beauty and had been discernible only to the closely observing eye, but which had been there none the less and was gone now.

This change grew more and more apparent as Georgiana continued to regard her young hostess. From the moment the party first entered the wide-thrown front door, it was easy to discover that both Stuart and his wife were eager as two children for the approval of their guests. Such approval was not long in appearing.

"How pleasant—how charming!" cried Georgiana, as her quick eye took in attractive effect after effect. "Oh, you clever things, to do it like this! How absolutely in keeping it all is, and how quiet, yet how beautiful!"

"She's done it," vowed James Stuart proudly. "I was a duffer at it till she showed me what she was after. I wanted to buy brocaded silk furniture, like that in her home—while my money held out. But she would have nothing but this sort of thing. Homelike, isn't it?"

It was the word which described it, if one qualified the term by making it apply only to homes built on foundations of good taste and suitability to environment. As she looked about her Georgiana saw everywhere evidences of the use of abundant means, and she realized that Jeannette had been clever indeed to supply so much without impressing Stuart with the undoubted fact that she had contributed more than he to the final result.

The whole effect of the house's interior was one of well-chosen but unostentatious comfort, and the materials and furnishings used were all so nicely adapted to their setting that only to more discerning eyes than those of the Stuarts' neighbours would they have expressed unusual resources of supply.

"It's an achievement!" Craig declared.

His enlightened gaze traveled from one point to another of the long, low-ceilinged living-room, sunny with new windows, and with walls and hangings of soft browns and golden yellows. He noted that Jeannette had had the good sense to make use of the old furniture the house possessed wherever it was fit for preservation, and that she had dignified the walls by retaining certain dim old portraits, done in fading oils, of Stuart's ancestors. Everywhere could be seen similar interesting blending of the new and the old, though it was often difficult to tell which was which.

The elder Stuarts were living in a wing of the house, that being the portion where they had spent their lives, making little use of the upright and the corresponding wing, which were now turned over to the son and his wife. Since the elder people wisely preferred this semi-independence, the younger were able to be much by themselves, Stuart explained, though always near and ready to lend a hand at any hour. Since the stalwart son could not be entirely spared by the somewhat feeble old couple, the arrangement seemed an admirable one, and thus far it had worked very well.

"Jean's such a dear with them," Stuart said covertly to Georgiana, leading her aside for a moment to look at a curious old buffet which had been long in the family. "They adore her, and she really seems very fond of them. Of course they have old Eliza to look after them, as they have had for so long; but we ask them in to dinner every few days, and often have them sitting by the fire with us here on cool evenings. The funny part, though, is when Mother Crofton comes. She can't get over it, or get used to it; she sits and looks at Jean as if she were an actress in a play, and by and by would take off her make-up and be herself again."

"I wonder how far that is from the real truth," thought Georgiana to herself, as she watched the young mistress of the place with fascinated eyes.

Certainly if Jeannette were acting it was very skilfully done. As she led her guests about the house, and then established them on the lawn, beneath the great elms which furnished a grateful shade at this afternoon hour over nearly the whole expanse, she seemed the embodiment of health and happiness.

By and by, when the Crofton car arrived, bearing Uncle Thomas and Aunt Olivia, with Rosalie and Chester following a few moments later in Chester's roadster, Jeannette grew fairly radiant. .

121

CHAPTER XXX

QUESTIONS AND ANSWERS

It was not until late that evening that Georgiana had a chance really to learn the whole state of the case.

During the intervening hours had occurred the event for which they had all been invited—the entertaining of at least two hundred people from the surrounding country and the village. For this event, which Stuart naïvely called a "party," Jeannette a "lawn fête," and the guests themselves, for the most part, a "picnic," porches, lawn and trees had been hung with gay lanterns, bonfires had been built, the small village band engaged, a light but delectable supper provided, and as much jollity planned as could be crowded into the hours between five o'clock and eleven.

From the standpoint of those entertaining, at least, the affair had been a success, for Stuart, long accustomed to the ways of his fellow countrymen, considered himself fully able to tell from their manner, if not from their expressions of pleasure, whether they had really found enjoyment in the efforts of their hosts.

"They had a mighty good time, no doubt about it!" he declared, when the last reluctant guest had departed in the last small car which had waited at the edge of the roadway. (Not the least of young Chester Crofton's enjoyment had been occasioned by the sight of the long row of vehicles, from two-seated wagons to smart and even expensive motors, which had lined the road for many rods.) "And a lot of them are well worth knowing," Stuart added.

His eye chanced to fall on his father-in-law, Mr. Thomas Crofton, as he made this assertion. The party were sitting in a group upon the lantern-lighted porch and its steps, and the senior Crofton's face was plainly visible.

That gentleman nodded. "You're quite right, Jim," he said. "I don't know when I've had a more interesting conversation with any man than I did with one of your neighbours, nor found a more intelligent set of opinions on every subject we touched on. He wasn't the only one, either. As a rule I found the people who came here to-night possessed of rather more than the average amount of brains. I should like to try living among them—for a change, at least."

"I struck a tongue-tied dolt or two," remarked his son Chester, "but dolts aren't uncommon anywhere, even when not tongue-tied. And I did run up against some chaps I liked jolly well. One of them invited me up for a week-end; I nearly fell over when he did it. I didn't know country people ever talked about week-ends. I thought they called it 'staying over Sunday.'"

"You mean Wells Lawson," Stuart informed him. "If you could see the list of newspapers and magazines, not to mention books, that the Lawsons take, you'd open your eyes. He and his family have traveled a lot more than I have, and their home is one of the finest model farms in the county. There's no hayseed in their hair."

"I didn't discover much hayseed in anybody's hair," observed Dr. Jefferson Craig. "I think it's gone out of fashion."

"There were some of the prettiest girls here to-night I ever saw," was Rosalie's contribution to the list of comments. A figure of exquisite modishness, she perched upon the porch rail near Chester. "I did want to tell them not to let any one young man stick by them every minute the way they did, but I could hardly blame the young men for wanting to stick, the girls were so sweet, and some of them were quite stunning."

"You certainly gave them an example of how to make eyes at fifteen or twenty fellows, one after another," laughed her brother, at her side. "You'd have had them all coming, Rosy, if they hadn't been tied up to their respective girls. A lesson or two from you, and those girls would begin to play 'round in proper shape."

"Rosy's going to stay and take a few lessons herself," insinuated Jeannette, who sat with her shapely young arm resting upon her father's knee, as she occupied the step below him. "I'll promise to put some flesh on her little bones if she's here a month. She's too thin, after only her second season."

"Oh, I'll stay," promised Rosalie promptly. "I simply love it here; I'm crazy to stay!"

"It's all very well now," came Aunt Olivia's low murmur in Georgiana's ear—there had been many of such murmurs in the same ear during the afternoon and evening, though why, Georgiana herself could not guess, since the elder woman knew the younger to be unreservedly committed to upholding Jeannette's whole course—"very well now, in June, with flowers blooming and friends about, but how the poor child is going to face a second winter I can't imagine."

"She faced the first one very happily," Georgiana reminded her.

"The first one was a novelty and of course she was determined not to acknowledge how lonely she must often have been. I do not say that James Stuart is not a very attractive and trustworthy young man; I am fond of him myself—very. But I shall always feel that Jeannette has made a terrible mistake. Brought up as she has been, it is not conceivable that she should continue to find this sort of life possible."

It was with this moan in her ears that, a few minutes later, Georgiana listened to James Stuart. He had drawn her away from the group and was strolling with her across the lawn.

"Well, George, tell me your honest opinion. Is my wife happy?"

It was a blunt question, but Georgiana understood. He asked it not to be reassured but because he was confident of the answer.

She spoke guardedly: "I never saw her seem more so, Jimps. You are sure of it yourself?"

"I want you to ask her point-blank. Will you?"

"It's not the sort of question to ask anybody point-blank, is it?"

"It is in this case. Do you think I don't know the doubt in all your minds?—yes, even yours, for you've become another person since you married Craig."

"Oh, no!"

"Oh, yes! You've been thinking ever since you came that you're dead thankful you don't have to come back to it—now, haven't you?"

"Jimps, dear, I lived all my life in the hardest, narrowest economy. If I had had all this beautiful experience Jean is having——"

"I know. But you wouldn't come back, even to this place of ours——"

"That's begging the question. For Jean it's a wonderful change, and any one can see what it's done for her."

"Physically, yes. But I want you to find out whether she's actually happy or not."

"I will," promised his friend with a nod; for she knew James Stuart much too well to imagine she could put him off without complying with his expressed desire.

It looked as if Jeannette herself were anxious to assure her cousin's mind, for Stuart had no sooner brought Georgiana back to the porch than his wife took possession of her.

"Georgiana, dear, I want you to tell me one thing," began Jeannette, as the two moved slowly a little away from the rest. "Do you think we are making a success of it?"

"A wonderful success, Jean. I couldn't have believed it, even what I see on the surface. How about it—inside? That's a pretty searching question, and you needn't answer it if you don't want to. Everything about you seems to answer it."

Jeannette stopped short and turned to face her cousin. "Haven't I written you the answer, over and over?"

"Yes. That's why I want to hear it from your own lips."

"You shall. First, though—Georgiana, you knew Antoinette Burwell married Miles Channing last December?"

"I heard of it. How do they come on?"

"Separated; she's gone back to her father. She was the most wildly happy bride I ever saw. Think of it, George—in six months! What do you suppose would have happened if you——"

"Don't! I didn't." And Georgiana's grateful thoughts went back to one of the crises in her life, the one from which Jefferson Craig had rescued her.

"Do you know the Ralph Hendersons? Married two years now—I'm sure you've heard me speak of them. Everybody knows they quarrel like cats and dogs; they're hardly civil to each other in public. And I know several more of our old set who are none too happy, if one may judge by their looks. Yet they all married 'in their own class,' as mother is so fond of saying, as if I didn't!—I married *above* it! And I am supposed to have cast away all my chances for this life, not to mention the next, by marrying my farmer! Georgiana, I'm getting to hate that word *farmer*! Why isn't there a new word made for the man who reads and studies and uses the latest modern methods on his farm? There are such a lot of them now. College graduates, like Jimps, and men who have taken agricultural courses and are putting their brains into their work. Why isn't there a new word?"

"The old word must be made to acquire a new dignity," Georgiana suggested. "Never mind the word; you're glad you married your farmer?"

"Glad! I thank God every night and morning; I thank Him every time I go running down the lane to meet my husband coming up from the meadow! Of course I know, Georgiana, that the life I'm living isn't the typical life of the farmer's wife at all—thanks to Jimps' success and my own little pocket-book! But it has all outdoors in it and lots of lovely indoors; and I'm growing so well and strong—you can see that by just looking at me. And I'm getting to know my neighbours, and like them—some of them—oh, so much! Life never was so full. Mother talks about how hard I'll find it to get through my second winter. It doesn't worry me. We'll order books and books, and we'll go for splendid tramps, and every now and then we'll run into town—for concerts and plays. And best of all, Georgiana,"—her voice sank—"I'm sure—sure—Jimps isn't disappointed in me."

"Disappointed! I should say not—the lucky boy!" Georgiana agreed, all her fears gone to the winds.

When they returned to the porch it was to hear an outcry from Jeannette's mother: "Chester Crofton! Have you gone absolutely crazy?"

"I think so, mother. Positively dippy. Got it in its worst form. It's been coming on me for some time, but it's taken me now, for better or for worse. I'm going to buy that small farm across the road and try what I can do."

"I'll back you," came in Mr. Thomas Crofton's deepest chest tones.

"Hear, hear!" Dr. Jefferson Craig's shout drowned out Mrs. Crofton's groan.

"O Ches—I'll come and keep house for you—part of the year, anyhow!" This was dainty Rosalie, her silk-stockinged ankles swinging wildly, as she sat upon the porch rail.

Georgiana was laughing, as her eyes met her husband's in a glance of understanding, but her heart was very warm behind the laughter.

Beyond the gleam of the lanterns she caught the golden glow of a summer moon rising, to illumine the depths of the country sky—the immense, star-spangled arch of the heavens. Beneath lay many homes, big and little, all filled with human lives, each with its chance somehow to grow; each with its chance, small or great, as a beloved writer has said inspiringly, "*to love and to work and to play and to look up at the stars.*"

THE END